Deadly Crescendo

By Paul Myers

PAUL MYERS

Deadly Crescendo

A CRIME CLUB BOOK
DOUBLEDAY
New York   London   Toronto   Sydney   Auckland

A CRIME CLUB BOOK
PUBLISHED BY DOUBLEDAY
a division of Bantam Doubleday Dell Publishing Group, Inc.
666 Fifth Avenue, New York, New York 10103

DOUBLEDAY and the portrayal of a man
with a gun are trademarks of Doubleday,
a division of Bantam Doubleday Dell
Publishing Group, Inc.

Library of Congress Cataloging-in-Publication Data

Myers, Paul.
   Deadly crescendo / Paul Myers. — 1st ed. in the U.S. of America.
      p.   cm.
   "A Crime Club book."
   I. Title.
PR6063.Y47D384   1990
823'.914—dc20   89-49471
CIP

ISBN 0-385-26365-1
Copyright © 1989 by Paul Myers
All Rights Reserved
Printed in the United States of America
August 1990
First Edition in the United States of America

London

ONE

THE ROOM, although large and high-ceilinged, was gloomy and claustro-phobic. It contained too much heavy furniture: a huge desk and behind it an oversized chair, a candlelit table laid for supper, an ornate couch uphol-stered with silk, a massive stone fireplace running half the length of one wall, and a dusty bookcase covering another. The thick curtains had been drawn for the night, damping all exterior sounds. The candlelight gave a soft glow, but the uncertain tremor of the flames threw grotesque shadows, and the light from the embers in the fireplace was almost blood red.

The woman stood, immobile, looking down at the man she had stabbed. He was already dead, and without taking her eyes off the body, she backed away towards the supper table. There was blood on her hands, and she took a napkin and dipped it in the water jug, then carefully wiped her fingers clean. She paused for a moment in front of an ornate gilded mirror on the wall, peering at her reflection in the dim light to tidy her hair. Then she moved quickly to the desk and began ruffling through its papers, searching for the document she needed. It was not there.

She remembered where it must be and, kneeling by the body, she un-clenched the fingers of the man's right hand and extracted a small sheet of paper, which she folded and hid in her dress. She stood slowly, looking down at the corpse.

"And all Rome trembled before him." Her voice seemed to express wonder at the thought.

The woman turned to leave the room, but a moment of remorse made her hesitate. Taking two candles from the table, she placed one on either side of the dead man. There was a small wooden crucifix on the desk, and she placed it on the man's chest. She stared at the arrangement, and crossed herself, as though seeking absolution. After a moment, she turned and walked swiftly from the room, closing the door quietly.

The applause was thunderous as the curtain fell. The man sitting next to Mark nodded approvingly.

"She's not the greatest Tosca in the world, but I've seen a lot worse. Her *'Vissi d'arte'* wasn't bad. The trouble is that she really doesn't have the stature for the part. I couldn't avoid the feeling that I was watching a suburban hausfrau who'd got herself into the middle of a nasty scene at the supermarket."

Mark smiled. He had the suspicion that Joshua Levin had been preparing his condemnation for the last ten minutes of the act. Record producers had a tendency to be blasé. Perhaps they spent too much time in the opera house. "I thought she was rather good."

Levin shrugged. "I suppose so, but if you're going to sing Tosca, you've got to be nothing less than great. I have the theory that it's one of those roles that nobody can sing, until somebody comes along and disproves me. Did you ever see Callas?"

"Only the old film clips."

Levin stared at the curtains of the Royal Opera House, not bothering to join in the applause as the soloists—Tosca, Scarpia, Cavaradossi—came out to take their individual bows. "She was incredible! The film doesn't do her justice. It can't reproduce her hypnotic presence. I saw her half a dozen times."

"You don't look old enough to have."

Levin looked pleased. "I'm older than you think. God, she was amazing! I suppose I should count myself blessed to have lived through her era. It's only later, when you watch her successors, that you realize what's missing."

"Wait until you see Bianca Morini."

"I'm really looking forward to it. She's the only one since Callas in that class. I wish I could have heard her at the Met last year, but I was stuck in Milan with that Bulgarian cow who wobbled her way through *Bohème*. She was a nightmare!"

"Why did you record her?"

The producer sighed. "New York makes the decisions. She had a big success there in *Fidelio*, so they automatically assumed she could sing Mimì. Thank God they didn't want a film. The mind boggles at the thought of Olga wasting away to her last two hundred pounds!"

The young woman sitting next to Joshua leaned across, her arm resting on his knee. "Shall we make a quick escape? Wiesman's waiting for us upstairs in the Crush Bar."

Levin stood. "By all means. Film producers don't like to be left alone for more than five minutes, otherwise they start thinking about money. Did you meet my assistant Diana, by the way? She crept in as the lights were going down." He turned to her. "This is Mark Holland. He manages both Bianca Morini and Maestro Cavalcanti, so you'd better give him the VIP treatment."

She was an attractive young woman, her face framed by ringlets of brown hair which seemed to cascade to her shoulders. When she smiled, she was beautiful. "I'll say hello properly when we get upstairs. How was the first act?" Without waiting for a reply, she patted the producer's shoulder. "Come on, Josh. If you hang around now, you'll be trampled to death by the chinless wonders." Behind her, the aisle was already crowded with elegantly clad women in evening dress, who greeted one another elaborately, their voices shrill, causing endless bottlenecks in the flow of human traffic. Their escorts, uniform in black tie, waited obediently, smiling vaguely.

Levin grunted. "No wonder they have such long bloody intervals. God help us all if there's ever a fire!"

Mark stood. "I wouldn't worry. Most of the men look as though they served in the Guards. They'd run an evacuation with all the precision of a military exercise."

"Probably. It's not a pretty sight, the Establishment in full battle dress." He bore down on a bulky dowager who had stopped at the end of the row to talk to some friends, and tapped her on the shoulder. The woman's apologies were extravagant, but she scowled at him.

Mark followed close behind Levin, working his way past crushed knees. Diana was already progressing towards the rear end of the stalls, moving gracefully between the slower pedestrians with the ease of a centre forward evading the defence.

"They're not so bad. At least the lady apologized for holding you up."

"I didn't note a great deal of sincerity in her voice. They don't have to behave as though they own the place. Come to think of it, they probably do. They're the only ones who can afford the outrageous prices. The rest of us have to depend on expense allowances." He gazed up at Mark. "It's at times like this that I envy tall men like you. At least you can see where you're going."

"Diana seems to manage quite well." Her diminutive figure had already disappeared down the staircase leading to the foyer.

"True. In her case, small is beautiful, but I'll bet she's glad she's not sitting behind you."

Wolfgang Wiesman, executive producer of OpFilm AG of Frankfurt, was waiting for them in the rapidly filling Crush Bar. He had commandeered one of the few available tables, and was filling glasses with white wine. As a film producer, he did not portray the traditional image of an obese little man with shifty eyes and a receding hairline. He was, as always, impeccably dressed in a three-piece grey suit that bore no wrinkles, the silver-grey tie perfectly knotted. It was hard to tell his age—Mark guessed he was in his middle forties—and his face had the clean-shaven pink flush of a man accustomed to hot towels and a professional barber. His finger-nails were carefully manicured. At first glance, he had the fashion-plate handsomeness of men who model executives in the glossier magazine ad-vertisements. His only concession to his occupation was the large Havana cigar clenched between his teeth. As Mark steered Joshua and Diana through the crowded upstairs foyer, with its glittering chandelier and cream-and-red decor, Wiesman rose to greet them.

"Come and have a glass of wine. I remembered to order it during the last interval. Tremendous opera, isn't it?" His English was perfect and unac-cented, and his after-shave was healthily pleasant but slightly overpowering. "Simon Vincent promised to join us if he could. He's been in the cutting room all day, but I asked him to be here in time to say hello to everyone." He handed a glass to Diana, his eyes still scanning the crowd.

Joshua helped himself to one of the glasses on the table and swallowed half its contents. He pursed his lips appreciatively. "Nice! This is the Gar-den's expensive plonk. That's one of the things I like about working with film people: they don't cut corners on life's little luxuries. Do you know Vincent?"

Mark shook his head. "I don't think so."

"He's one of the newer directors. Did his homework at the BBC, shoot-ing their operas, before he moved on to bigger game. He's good."

Wiesman refilled Levin's glass. "My dear fellow, he's a genius! I've never seen such extraordinary work in the context of a live performance. Some of his sequences look as though they had been set up with a week of rehearsal in a studio. I couldn't think of anyone more suitable for our project. I do hope he's able to join us."

As Wiesman turned to speak to Diana, Levin drank again. He leaned towards Mark and, almost under his breath, added, "He's also a screaming little faggot with an excess of thyroid and a genius for stirring up trouble. Thank God my job finishes before his starts."

"How do you mean?"

"I'll be producing the soundtrack at the recording sessions in Geneva—two soundtracks, if you want to be accurate—after which he'll take over the actual shooting in Rome."

"Why two?"

"We'll make our standard recording on one set of machines, but we'll run a multitrack machine at the same time, with the voices more isolated, so that Vincent can change the perspectives according to the picture, as well as add his sound effects."

"Then the cast will mime to a playback tape when they film?"

"It's the best way to do it, otherwise you can waste hours while they do retakes for their singing. With an expensive camera crew standing around, that can break the bank."

"I always think lip sync looks artificial. You can see they're not really singing."

"Not these days. Some of them are pretty good at it. The trick is to persuade them really to sing along while you're filming. Anyway, that's not my problem. I've promised Wolfgang a finished master tape by the beginning of September, which is going to be tough enough. By the time they start filming in Rome, I'll be doing sessions in Vienna."

"You must do a lot of travelling."

Levin nodded. "Never off the buses, as they say, but I'm not complaining. It's a way of life more than a job. Frankly, I don't know what I'd do with myself if I was stuck in the same place for months on end. I've been on the road for nearly thirty years, and the expense account makes up for a hell of a lot of deficiencies in my salary." He smiled. "You know you've been around for a long time when the reviews start describing you as a 'veteran' record producer!" He drained his glass. "This wine's delicious."

"Let me give you a refill." Wiesman was solicitous. "I can't think what's happened to Simon. He promised to meet me during this interval." Film producers were not accustomed to disobedience. Still holding the bottle, he turned to Diana. "But you haven't drunk anything."

"If you wouldn't mind, I think I'd prefer Perrier." She looked apologetic. "I don't drink."

"But of course." For a moment, Wiesman looked uncertain, torn between hospitality and anticipation of his director's arrival. The crowd waiting at the bar was large, and one couldn't play host while fighting to be served.

"I'll look after it." Mark turned away.

Diana placed a hand on his arm. "Please don't bother. I'll get something when the first rush is over."

"No problem." Mark strolled over to the bar, where expensively clad gentlemen politely tried to elbow each other out of the way. There was an open space a few places down, and he stepped into it, waiting while harassed bartenders worked their way down the line of customers, serving each in turn in an effort to maintain a British sense of fair play. It was a more elegant way of forming a queue.

"You're Mark Holland, aren't you?" The man standing to his right must have taken up his position within moments of Mark's arrival. He spoke quietly.

"Yes." The face was vaguely familiar, but Mark could not place him. In contrast to most of the other patrons, the man was dressed in a dark tweed jacket and grey slacks. His blue shirt was open-necked.

"I thought I recognized you." The man stared straight ahead, examining the row of bottles at the back of the bar. His grey hair was rather long and untidy, and it was apparent that he had not shaved for a day or two. He turned to face Mark. "You probably don't remember me."

"I'm sorry, no." Mark was about to continue, but the man interrupted.

"Tony Rossiter. We met once, many years ago. I didn't expect you to remember."

Mark hesitated, feeling a sudden caution. Anything that had happened many years earlier had a special significance for him: a period of his life that he preferred to forget. He glanced towards the bartender, who was still several customers away. "I'm sorry, but I don't—"

"I thought I would find you here." The man spoke calmly, but there was a nervous edge to his voice. "You see, I wanted to get in touch with you." He faced towards the bar again, and Mark could see a muscle playing on his jaw.

"I'm going to be rather busy. I'm only in London for a couple of days."

"It's very important. May I phone you?"

"I suppose so. I'm staying at the Westbury." The bartender had reached the man to Mark's left.

"It's vital that we talk." Rossiter had not raised his voice, but Mark could sense the urgency.

"Oh?"

"It concerns the conductor Emilio Cavalcanti. You do represent him, don't you?"

Mark was surprised. "Yes, but I really can't imagine—"

"I'll explain it all when we talk." Mark was about to reply, when the man nodded towards the bartender. "I think he's waiting to take your order."

Mark turned to order the mineral water, and the bartender's hands moved rapidly, gathering ice, lemon and a small bottle. As Mark reached into a pocket for a coin, he turned back to Rossiter, but the man was no longer there. In his place, an elderly woman in a faded black silk dress stared at him irritably before addressing the man behind the bar.

"Young man, I have been waiting ten minutes to be served!"

"Yes, madam." The bartender, who was in his fifties and balding, was suitably humble. There were beads of sweat on his forehead.

"Kindly give me a glass of water."

Mark looked past her, but there was no sign of Rossiter, who had disappeared into the crowd. Frowning, he carried the drink back to Diana.

"Thank you very much. I'm sorry to have been such a nuisance." She eyed him curiously. "You look as though you've just seen a ghost."

"Not really." He forced a smile. "Somebody I didn't recognize. It's always embarrassing when you don't remember."

"The shabby character with the designer stubble? It's funny, but I thought I recognized him too. I can't think where from. We haven't said hello properly, have we?" She smiled, and Mark was again conscious of her radiance. "I'm Diana Nightingale, and I work for Joshua at Magnum Records. I'm his assistant, but to be honest, that makes me a kind of senior secretary. Record producers are a one-man operation."

"Hello. I think I've received letters from you in the past."

"More than likely. Josh is much too busy to commit himself to paper, and a major part of my job is to pick up all the pieces." She took his arm. "I'd better take you back to Herr Wiesman. The great man has arrived, so we can all relax." When Mark looked puzzled, she explained, "Simon Vincent, together with his boyfriend—I mean, assistant—Cliff, the Australian muscleman." She laughed. "I'd better not make too many jokes about assistants, or you might get the wrong idea. Thank you again for the drink. I'm sorry I landed you with it."

Wiesman and Levin had been joined by two ill-assorted characters whose presence caused several well-groomed heads to turn and stare. The shorter of the two, whom Mark guessed to be the director, was resplendent in a maroon velvet jacket and black trousers, with a pink shirt and a brilliant scarlet silk scarf draped casually about his throat. His hair, cut fashionably short, had been bleached to a pale blond, and his slightly bulging eyes confirmed Levin's diagnosis of a thyroid condition. Standing slightly behind him was a tall young man with a badly pockmarked face, wearing a black tee shirt and leather trousers which displayed an inordinate number of zip fasteners. The tee shirt bore the slogan "Opera Sucks" in silver letters. Presumably, this was Simon Vincent's Australian assistant, Cliff.

In a low voice, Diana said, "My God, look at them!" She giggled. "I wonder what all those zips are for."

Wiesman, visibly relieved, made the introductions, and handed a glass to Vincent, who examined it and made a moue. "You haven't got any red, have you? It's the only stuff they serve here that's drinkable." Wiesman looked crestfallen, and the director turned to his assistant. "Never mind. Cliff, be a love and get me a glass of red, would you?" Then he turned to Mark with a dazzling smile, revealing perfectly capped teeth. "You manage the legendary Morini, don't you?" Mark nodded. "I do hope you can persuade her to behave. I'm told she screws anything that moves." His smile remained, but his eyes had narrowed.

At his side, Mark was conscious that Diana had stiffened. "Hardly." He eyed Vincent coolly. "I think she's a little more discriminating than that."

"Well, I hope so. We have a very tight shooting schedule, and it's such a bore having to ring round every hotel to find out whose bed she's camping out in."

Mark remained calm. "I don't think you'll find camping is one of her pastimes."

Vincent laughed. "Touché, Mr. Holland." He did not look pleased. He turned his attention on the film producer, who was looking uncertain. "Listen, Wolfgang, I know this isn't exactly the right moment, but do we really have to have Alessandro as Cavaradossi? He's such a fat slob!"

Wiesman looked astonished. Mark had the impression that he exaggerated his surprise. "But certainly! Antonio Alessandro is one of the greatest tenors in the world. I thought that was agreed between us at our first discussions."

"I know, but he's so ungainly. He needs to lose half a ton if I'm going to make him look halfway presentable. We're supposed to be making a film, after all. I need singers who are photogenic, or the whole thing's going to be a travesty."

For a moment, Wiesman did not speak. Then he gave a tight-lipped smile. "You're quite right, Simon. This is hardly the time or place to discuss casting. It's also much too late to start making changes. I signed a contract with Alessandro six months ago, in addition to which I cannot imagine finding a suitable substitute between now and September."

Vincent sighed. "I wish I'd been consulted."

"You were. At the meeting in Frankfurt—"

"I know, but we were kicking around all sorts of names at the time. I didn't realize Alessandro was a fait accompli."

The German's face became harder. "There was never any doubt."

The beatific smile returned. "In that case, there's no point in discussing it any further, is there?"

"No."

"We'll have to see what we can manage. You're not making life easy for me, Wolfgang." He stared at the surroundings contemptuously. "God, this place looks tatty these days, doesn't it? All those women in their best Marks and Spencers!"

There was an uneasy silence. Mark and Diana exchanged glances, and Wiesman sipped his wine. A moment later, the tension was relieved by the arrival of a smartly dressed man in a dark suit. His face was lined and weather-beaten, and his jet-black hair was combed upwards to give it a youthful look. Mark wondered whether it had been dyed.

Wiesman looked pleased. "This is Craig Layton, my director of public relations. You won't have met him before. He only arrived this morning from New York." He introduced the American, who offered a firm handshake and repeated each name as he was presented. It was an old public relations trick, to establish each name in Layton's memory. Mark always envied people who remembered.

Layton was carrying a small briefcase. "I've brought a whole bunch of material with me, Wolfgang, including a number of advance squibs for the trade press."

"Excellent!" Wiesman was clearly relieved to have a change of subject. "We can go through them tomorrow morning."

"Sure, but if it's all the same to you, there's a couple I'd like to show you now, if you'll give me the time. If you approve them, I can call New York immediately. They're waiting for your okay."

Simon Vincent's voice was slightly too friendly. "Goodness, aren't you going to watch the third act?"

Layton grinned. "Work comes first. I'll leave the artistic bit to you people."

"Well, I'm glad somebody will." Cliff arrived with a glass of red wine. "Thank you, sweetie." Vincent raised his glass. "Here's to success."

The film producer nodded curtly, and moved away with Layton, who was already selecting papers from his case.

Vincent put his glass on the table. "That's much better." He beamed at Diana. "And what do you do, dear?" His voice was patronizing.

"I'm Josh Levin's assistant."

"Ah." He looked at Levin. "You're the sound man."

"Not exactly." Josh was pouring himself another glass of wine. "That's the engineer's job. I'm a producer."

"Oh yes." Vincent affected a bewildered look. "I've never quite worked out what record producers do."

Levin swallowed some wine. The alcohol had added a little colour to his cheeks. "We produce."

"What does that actually involve?"

Josh smiled. "Funnily enough, I suppose you could say that, once the record's made, it involves being invisible. All you should be conscious of is the result. How we got it out of the singers, the conductor and the orchestra shouldn't be apparent."

Vincent giggled. "The invisible man. How exotic! But what do you actually do?" He was atoning for his earlier outburst by being charming.

Levin shrugged. "Make sure that it all goes down on tape the way it should: not only the right notes but the right interpretation. You'd be surprised how easy it is to lose track of a performance in a studio, especially when you're putting it together piecemeal, like a film. I've been working on the score for quite a long time, breaking it down into performable sequences. Apart from anything else, it saves having to keep the entire cast sitting around when they're not needed. We should be able to get rid of Alessandro first."

"What a good idea!" Vincent's smile broadened, and Cliff sniggered.

The comment irritated Levin. "There's not much point in using a second-class singer, is there? There are few tenors in Alessandro's class."

"If you say so. You don't have the job of making him look vaguely attractive. Tosca's supposed to be the toast of Rome. She'd have to be pretty kinky to fall for an elephant like that!"

"Anyway, all I meant was that I can record all his first-act stuff and the third act. After that, he's got a spit and a cough in Act Two, so we don't have to keep the Scarpia in Geneva until the last day of Alessandro's recording."

"I see. Are we using Belasco as Scarpia?"

"Yes." From Levin's expression, it was clear that he knew the director was already aware of every member of the cast. Diana caught Mark's glance, and raised her eyes to the ceiling in frustrated silence.

"Well, thank heavens for small mercies! Belasco's excellent."

Diana smiled sweetly. "What a shame you only just arrived this evening. He's already dead."

The director eyed her coldly. "I've seen him before, love, and I do know the story." He returned to Levin. "I still don't see why we can't record the whole thing here in London. It's so much more convenient than traipsing over to Switzerland for two weeks. Half the cast is already here, and the orchestra's properly rehearsed. Why move?"

Joshua lit a cigarette. "Musicians' union. The rates in London are too high for soundtracks. We can make a better deal in Switzerland for the record and the film. We went through this with Wiesman at the Frankfurt meeting."

"I know, but Switzerland's expensive for the rest of us. By the time it's all set up, you could find it just as costly."

"Not really. It's a bit of a schlepp, but it's worth it. Wiesman's compared the figures, and we've already made a deal with the orchestra."

"Then I suppose that's that." Vincent shared an expression of martyrdom with Cliff.

"I'm afraid so." Josh finished his wine, and winked at Mark.

"I must confess, I'm a little concerned about your involvement with the interpretation of the opera." Vincent was preparing to mount a new attack. "We haven't really had an opportunity to discuss an overview of the piece. By the time your tracks reach me, the whole thing will be cast in stone, so to speak."

Levin smiled. "I'll be happy to discuss anything you like. Basically, I thought we were agreed that this would be, for want of a better word, a traditional performance, which means no drastic changes from the standard interpretations. My job is to make sure that happens, especially if Magnum is going to release it as a straight record set. You'll have your own soundtrack to play with."

"But I'll be locked into whatever you give me."

"Yes, I suppose so."

Vincent's smile was patently insincere. "Then I'll certainly have to attend all your sessions."

"You'll be welcome." The record producer was equally insincere. He looked up to find that Wiesman and Layton had rejoined the group. "We were just going through the schedule of the recording." To lighten the mood, he added, "You can always check anything with Diana. She knows exactly what I'm supposed to be doing long before I do."

"Excellent!" Wiesman smiled encouragingly at Diana. "I suggest that you arrange for Maestro Cavalcanti to meet Simon and Joshua for a planning meeting quite soon, to avoid any crossed wires."

"Of course."

"There's a reception tonight. Is everyone coming?" When nobody replied, he continued. "In that case, you can arrange it all later. I know Cavalcanti is eager to help, and he may have a few useful suggestions of his own. I must say he's doing a magnificent job tonight. I haven't heard the orchestra play so well for a long time." He looked at Mark. "Your young conductor is quite a find."

"His career's developing very well."

Wiesman turned down the corners of his mouth. "That must be why he's so expensive!"

Layton grunted. "Those Italian musicians are all the same. I'm told he was a member of the CP when he was younger."

Vincent looked up. "What's a CP?"

"Communist Party. Half of Italy belongs to it at one time or another. They only quit when they can afford to be capitalists!"

Wiesman raised his hand in the gesture of a peacemaker. "Oh, please let's not involve politics. We'll have enough other problems to resolve before this production is finished. Anyway, political persuasions are little more than names."

Levin nodded. "Especially in Italy. They have more parties than candidates."

"Exactly. It's just a name. One learns to live with it." He smiled at his guests. "You won't believe my middle name. Can you imagine living up to Wolfgang Amadeus Wiesman?"

Craig Layton laughed. "It gives you the best reason in the world to make opera movies. My folks were called Lipschitz four generations back, when they arrived at Ellis Island. Try living with that!"

Vincent gave an exaggerated sigh. "I feel like a psychiatrist running a group therapy session. Wasn't that the warning bell? We'd better tiptoe our way in and have a look. Incidentally, Wolfgang, are you absolutely sold on shooting this epic in Rome?"

Wiesman was astonished. "Of course. It was all arranged months ago. Why do you ask?"

Vincent shrugged carelessly. "Oh, I don't know. I still think we could do something more imaginative with sets of our own. I was checking on the availability of Shepperton Studios, and was surprised to find that they're actually free around the same period. Just shows how dead the movie industry is, don't you think?"

Wiesman's mouth was set in a firm line. "It's out of the question. I've made my arrangements with Cinecittà, and we've spent months clearing permissions for the use of all the authentic sites."

Vincent was petulant. "But they're all the same boring old locations that Unitel used years ago with Plácido and that Russian soprano. They're terribly dreary, and you can't light them properly. I was hoping you'd let me do something more interesting."

Wiesman's face had coloured with suppressed anger, but he smiled charmingly. "No, Simon, we went through this when you signed your contract. I'm afraid that is final."

"Well, I just thought I'd ask. I was hoping to avoid six weeks of pasta and men with body odour. Where are we sitting, Cliff?" The young man unzipped one of the pockets in his trousers to produce two tickets, and muttered in Vincent's ear. "We're up here. That's good. The distance will help to lend a little enchantment to Signor Alessandro. See you afterwards." He waved a limp hand, and sauntered towards the entry under the double staircase that formed an elegant archway along the wall of the Crush Bar.

Wiesman watched his departure and smiled ruefully. "I suppose we have to make allowances for talent." He looked at Levin. "Is everything under control?"

The record producer nodded. "I've handled much worse. I hope you'll help to keep him out of my hair at the sessions. We're working on a very tight schedule, and I won't be able to waste time on endless discussions about motivation. It's all in the music and the libretto."

"Of course. Nevertheless, we can probably prevent wasteful discussion if you sit down with him and Cavalcanti before we leave London." He turned to Mark. "Don't you agree?"

"Yes. I'll make sure he's available in the next couple of days. You'll also find that Bianca has some very clear ideas of her own."

"Good." Wiesman looked at his watch. "I'll give the third act a miss and go back to the Savoy now. I have too many papers to go through before tomorrow, much as I would enjoy the music. Do you want to join me, Craig? You can make your calls from my suite."

"Sure."

"Good. We can use the time now, and meet later. Do you know where it is?"

Diana said, "Yes, I have it written down. You probably have more time than you realize. It will take the cast at least an hour to change and get rid of all the backstage visitors. I doubt whether anyone will arrive before eleven-thirty."

"That suits us very well. We'll see you at the house in Eaton Square sometime before midnight." Wiesman placed a hand on Layton's shoulder and steered him towards the exit. He looked worried.

Levin held up a wine bottle. "Any more? There's still some left." Mark shook his head. "I may as well finish it, then. It's a shame to let it go to waste. You two go ahead, and I'll catch up."

Diana walked at Mark's side. "Poor old Josh. Despite that calm exterior, he's churning up inside. That little shit Vincent was deliberately needling him."

"He was having a go at anyone within scratching distance. It's all part of the act."

"I know. Fortunately, he really is a good director. Otherwise, it wouldn't be worth putting up with all his nonsense. He knows every detail of the cast, and he's already been to Rome to look at all the locations." She hesitated at the head of the stairs. "Oh Christ!"

"What's wrong?"

She lowered her voice. "The dragon lady heading this way is Katya Philips. Do you know her?"

"I don't think so."

"She's a very successful music journalist, so called. She writes exclusives for half a dozen glossy magazines and has a regular column in one of the Sunday supplements."

"And?"

"She's a muckraker: writes a gossip column and dresses it up to look like serious music journalism. A very dangerous lady. Wolfgang went and invited her to come to the sessions in Geneva and Rome before we could warn him." As the woman in question approached, Diana raised her voice and smiled charmingly. "Hi, Katya. Are you enjoying it?"

Katya Philips gave the impression of a very pretty woman trying to disguise her good looks but making sure they were still apparent. Her black hair was drawn severely back, and the upper half of her heart-shaped face was masked by a pair of oversize glasses. She was tall and slim, and her dark silk dress, elegantly simple, bore no jewellery. Mark estimated that she was in her middle thirties.

Katya drew level with them. "It's the same old Garden production. I don't think much of that American girl, but Alessandro's wonderful. Cavalcanti's good, too. I haven't heard him before."

Diana beamed. "You said just the right thing. This is Mark Holland. He's Maestro Cavalcanti's manager."

"Really?" Katya took Mark's hand and stared at him earnestly. It was slightly unsettling. "Don't you also manage Bianca Morini?"

"When she's in Europe, yes."

"Then I'm very glad we've had a chance to meet. I was going to contact you anyway. You see, I'm supposed to do a profile of her for the *Sunday Times,* so I'll need to come and talk to you before I meet her."

"I see. Bianca doesn't always give interviews."

"That's all right. One of our people already cleared it with her in New

York this week. I just wanted to have a little background information. She is still married to that banker, isn't she?"

"Ettore? Yes, of course. They're devoted to each other."

Katya looked sceptical. "That's not exactly what I've been told. That woman has become a legend in more than one field. You're not suggesting that she's a reformed character, are you? Her memoirs are going to outrank Casanova's!"

It was true. Bianca's amorous exploits had filled the gossip columns of three continents for more than a decade. In addition to being the greatest living soprano, whose performance of certain roles had already reached legendary status, she revelled in a lifestyle that made her a columnist's dream and the darling of the paparazzi. Mark sighed inwardly. Bianca was always finding herself in the headlines, and the roster of famous men with whom she had enjoyed close if brief relationships was embarrassingly full. There was an even longer list of anonymous lovers who had enjoyed her favours, but they made less interesting reading in the tabloid press. Despite her passionate associations, she always returned at the end of each romantic escapade to her gentle, loving little banker, whom she adored and who forgave each marital peccadillo with long-suffering affection. It was an ideal relationship. Sooner or later, Bianca came home, and Ettore spent his time converting her enormous fortune into a complicated empire of corporations and tax-free enterprises that made her as secure as the solid-gold ingots resting in the vaults of his banks. He was immensely proud of her extraordinary talents, slightly awed by her lush beauty, and vaguely amused by her insatiable sexual appetite.

Katya was watching him carefully. "Do you think she'll give me a frank interview?"

"I don't see why not. Bianca always tells the truth, even when it proves to be uncomfortable."

"How does she feel about working again with Antonio Alessandro?"

"I'm sure she's pleased." Diana was following the conversation intently. "They've often sung together before."

"I heard they've done quite a lot of things together before. Didn't they have an enormous fight a few years ago in Bologna? I heard it was a lovers' quarrel for the record books."

"No, as a matter of fact, I think it was an artistic disagreement." Alessandro had tried to upstage Bianca, and she had made him pay for it mercilessly with a dozen different subterfuges, including pacing restlessly throughout his solo arias. When, in revenge, he had clasped her so tightly during the duet that she could barely breathe, she had suddenly embraced him in mid-song, throwing herself at him with apparent abandon. It had been a very moving dramatic gesture. What the audience had not noticed was the careful placement of her knee in Alessandro's crotch, after which the tenor had doubled over, all the while trying to suggest that he was overcome by emotion. Backstage, a few minutes later, they had thrown things at each other. The press had a field day.

"Then everything is resolved between them?"

"Of course. She has the greatest respect for him." When Mark had told Bianca that Alessandro had been invited to sing Cavaradossi, she had been philosophical. "It is a good choice, *caro*. Antonio is the best. Tell him to lose a little weight." She had chuckled wickedly. "You'd better tell him also to wear one of those protectors that boxers put in their shorts. If he tries nonsense like last time, I will make him the world's greatest countertenor!"

Katya walked with them down the broad red-carpeted staircase. The foyer was emptying rapidly back into the auditorium for the final act. "And how does Alessandro feel about working with Morini again?"

"You'll have to ask him. I'm sure Miss Nightingale can arrange an interview."

Behind Katya's back, Diana pulled a face at him. She said, "I'll be pleased to. Are you coming to the last-night party afterwards?"

Katya smiled. "Of course. My pencil's already nice and sharp."

Diana chose to ignore the comment. "I'll see if I can put you together with Alessandro."

Katya took Mark's hand and held it for a moment. "I'll look forward to seeing you again." Then she made her way swiftly into the auditorium.

Diana's eyes were mocking. "My, my, Mr. Holland, you seem to have made a hit with the press."

"Thank you, Miss Nightingale."

"Please call me Diana. Nightingale isn't my real name, anyway. I was going to tell you about it when Wiesman and Layton were doing their double number, but Simple Simon wouldn't let me get a word in. My grandfather's name was Sänger, but he had a sense of humour when he settled in England."

"When was that?"

"About 1937. Jews weren't too popular along Unter den Linden in those days. He thought Nightingale sounded like a good old English name. You'd be surprised how many people ask me if I'm related to Florence. I sometimes tell them she was a distant relative on my mother's side, but I don't mention how distant."

"I have the feeling your adopted ancestor may come in handy before the end of this production, unless Simon Vincent was ridding himself of his aggressions at an early stage."

"Oh, Josh will manage him. He usually ends up with the cast eating out of his hand. A lot of the time, he does it quite deliberately. Says it's a record producer's stock-in-trade. I have the suspicion that you're pretty good in a crisis, too. I like calm men."

"I'll do my best." Her smile was very endearing. Her body was fuller and richer than Katya's, but she appeared to use no artifice either to display or to conceal it. He was pleased when she took his arm.

"Come on. We'd better hurry if we're going to see Alessandro do his star bit." Her head barely reached Mark's shoulder, but he was conscious of a delicate perfume when she stood close to him. "Let's hope little Mr. Vincent is suitably impressed."

"Yes." They climbed the stairs leading into the back of the stalls. It seemed to Mark that the production was heading towards an uneasy beginning.

TWO

EVER SINCE they had rebuilt and redecorated the backstage accommodation at Covent Garden, Mark had been left with the feeling that he had wandered into a recently constructed modern secondary school with tidy corridors and glass-panelled fire doors. It was not as ascetically austere as the undecorated grey plaster walls at the back of the Grosses Festspielhaus in Salzburg, and it was obviously cleaner and more efficient than before, but he missed the cosy, run-down atmosphere of the old building. Perhaps, with time, the pristine surroundings would acquire the dusty, faded grandeur of the Paris Opéra or the Musikverein in Vienna. He doubted it. There was something ruthlessly impersonal about the place, and it was hard to imagine that such hallowed passages had once been home to a Caruso, a Melba or a Flagstad. Fortunately, the dirty, brick-lined stairway down to the backstage bar had not changed, and he was tempted to follow Joshua Levin's proposal.

"Why don't we go down for a quiet drink until the worst of the crowd disappears. They'll be milling around up there for the next half hour or more."

Diana took his arm firmly. "Not now. The sooner we persuade them to change, the quicker we can get this reception over and done with." She eyed him critically. "You were polishing off most of Wolfgang's wine during the last interval. Haven't you had enough?"

The producer shrugged. "It helped to pass the time."

"I'm relying on you to go upstairs and charm that American girl. She's more than a little pissed off not to be included in the *Tosca* film."

"Instead of Bianca Morini? You must be joking!"

She exaggerated her patience. "I know, and you know, but that doesn't help her. Have a heart, Josh. She's just come off the stage, and she's still on a high. In a few minutes, she's going to come down to earth with a bang." Looking at Mark, Diana added, "She wasn't bad."

"She was very good." Mark could not bring himself to be more enthusiastic. The girl was a poor shadow of Bianca Morini. Most sopranos were.

Levin waved his arms. "What's that got to do with it?"

"It would be kind to go and tell her she was good, and that you enjoyed her performance. You never know, you might want to use her one of these days."

"That's highly unlikely. At best, she was passable, and her Italian was awful."

"Well, at least tell her you enjoyed her singing, and look as though you're interested in recording her at some future date. It doesn't cost you anything, and she probably needs reassuring, now that it's all over."

Joshua scowled. "That's what her manager's for!"

"It doesn't hurt to be nice."

"All right." The producer sighed, and led the way past the backstage desk and up the new staircase. "Relief is on the way!" He increased his pace, leaving Mark and Diana behind.

"Did you really mean that?"

Diana shook her head. "I wanted to distract him from heading towards the bar. He's been drinking too much lately. Don't worry, he'll enjoy himself once he gets there. Josh loves chatting the artists up. It makes them both feel important."

"You're fond of him."

She paused. "No, I don't think I am, really, but he's a talented man, and I hate to see him drink all the time. I suspect most producers are frustrated performers at heart."

"He's lucky to have you looking after him."

"I'm his assistant. It's part of the job. Anyway, I don't look after him more than necessary. He's just more complicated than you think. It's not easy working for New York. Their only concern is the lousy bottom line, as they keep reminding us. Josh belongs to the old school. He remembers when record companies were uncompromising about quality. Now, all they talk about is selling."

"I think they always did. It's easy to become nostalgic about the good old days."

"I suppose so, but when Josh talks about them, he makes it sound as though it was much more fun. He's not very practical, except when he's producing records." She led the way. "We'll let him charm poor old Tosca while we see what we can do with the great Alessandro. Have you met him before?"

"No. I couldn't attend the Bologna performances Katya Philips was talking about."

"You may very well be underwhelmed by his personality."

"As bad as that?"

"Worse, if anything. He may be one of the world's greatest tenors, but he's a little lacking in the charm department. Simon Vincent wasn't exaggerating. The man's gross!"

"Do you think Wiesman should have signed someone else?"

"It's hard to say. Alessandro's the best, vocally. I would have thought that was the first priority for an opera, but we're talking about a film. The camera doesn't allow for the same suspension of disbelief as the theatre. If we're going into a video era, it could have a much stronger influence on casting, even to the detriment of musical standards."

"And some of those fat old monsters we accepted in the opera house would no longer make the grade?"

"Something like that. Bianca Morini is an exception, thank God, but the days of the heavyweights are numbered."

"You've obviously given this quite a lot of thought."

She smiled suddenly, leaning closer. It was a charmingly intimate gesture. "No. I'm repeating what Josh has to say on the subject. He's the expert. I'm just a quick learner."

Swathed in a silk dressing gown that more closely resembled a multicoloured tent, Antonio Alessandro dominated the centre of his dressing room. He was an enormous man, several inches taller than Mark, and his bald head, shorn of the dark wig he had worn as Cavaradossi, gleamed with sweat. A discoloured and soggy towel, wrapped round his throat, captured the free-flowing moisture from his face, but the silk gown was darkened by damp patches, and an offensive odour permeated the room, undiluted by the aroma of expensive cologne. The combination of the two was, if anything, more unpleasant.

The walls were lined with admirers, mostly female, who stood at a slight distance from the great man, listening anxiously. In a corner, sitting tensely on the edge of a couch, his current lady friend, a tall ash blonde wrapped in a full-length mink, watched nervously.

As Mark and Diana entered the room, the tenor was bearing down angrily on Simon Vincent, his stubby index finger poking the director's chest repeatedly. His voice was raised.

"Listen, you turn the cameras and I sing. That's it! I don't want to know about ideas! You want to discuss interpretation? Go talk to Cavalcanti or my manager! I don't give a shit about your impressions!" In his irritation, Alessandro's Italian accent had become more pronounced.

Vincent flinched, stepping back to avoid the jabbing finger. He stammered. "No, of course not. I mean, I quite understand. I simply said I hoped we could meet before the recording sessions, so that I could have a better understanding of your interpretation of the role."

"What's to understand? You hear me sing; you know what it's about."

"Yes, I suppose so. I just thought—"

"You don't think!" Alessandro leaned over the director. "You just point the camera at me and tell La Morini to stand still when I am singing! Is all!" He glowered. "What do you mean about losing weight?" Several spectators eyed each other uneasily, awaiting the next outburst.

"Well"—Vincent stared up at the glowing eyes, like a rabbit hypnotized by a snake—"I thought it might be more appropriate if—"

"You don't worry about it!" The jabbing finger returned. "The public comes to see Antonio Alessandro—the real Antonio Alessandro." He slapped his chest, and the room echoed. "They don't expect some skinny little bastard in tight pants! I am a *tenore!*" He slapped his chest again, and Vincent jumped visibly. "I need support for my voice. You think I make sounds like these if I look like some pretty boy from the Via Garibaldi?"

"Well, perhaps not—"

"Then you don't talk to me about losing weight!"

Before Vincent could comment, Mark stepped out of the doorway, his hand on Diana's elbow. The air in the corridor felt refreshingly clean. "Signor Alessandro appears to be rather preoccupied at the moment." He was smiling broadly. "Why don't we wait to meet him at the reception?"

Diana nodded. "You see what I mean? The man's all heart! God, he's arrogant!" She suppressed a conspiratorial giggle. "I must admit I was enjoying myself. Our Simon's going to have to shape up if he wants to survive this production. He had it coming to him!" She looked at her watch. "I'll give him a couple more minutes to calm down. We've got a hectic day in the office tomorrow, and I'd like to go to bed before dawn."

At that moment, Alessandro's voice was raised. "Diana, was that you?"

She pulled a face and called, "Coming, Maestro. I'll be with you in a moment." In a lower voice, she asked, "Do you want to meet him?"

"No. Wait until the reception. Maybe he'll simmer down a little. I'll go and see Cavalcanti while you sort him out."

She grinned. "Chicken! I'll see you later." She reentered the dressing room, and he heard the tenor greet her effusively. Mark left quickly, before the wounded Simon Vincent emerged. He was sure Cliff would provide a more sympathetic shoulder for the director to weep on.

By contrast, the conductor's room was peaceful. A small queue of well-wishers and autograph hunters waited patiently while Cavalcanti quietly greeted each visitor. In a corner of the room, his wife, Maria, was seated at the dressing table repairing her makeup. She was a small, attractive woman in her early thirties. Her sensual lips had a slightly pouting expression, and her ample body was beginning to stretch the contours of an elegant Milanese gown. She concentrated her attention on her reflection in the mirror, ignoring the slow line of admirers. Emilio Cavalcanti, standing very straight, his arms behind his back, was listening attentively to a man in a tweed suit with an old raincoat slung over his shoulders. The conductor's face was youthful, but there were traces of grey at his temples. His smile was polite but fixed.

"I heard your *Cenerentola* at La Fenice last year. It was magnificent."

"Thank you." Cavalcanti bowed slightly. He was a broad-shouldered, stocky man, and his movements, like his conducting, were compact and efficient. He ran a surprisingly delicate hand through his dark hair.

"Will you be coming back?"

"I hope so." Cavalcanti's English was good, and he spoke quickly. "I will conduct a number of concerts at the Festival Hall, but I have no opera plans for the moment. I have enjoyed this visit very much." He extended his hand to the visitor, to indicate that the brief interview was over, and transferred his gaze to the next in line. Mark had the impression that strong self-discipline had trained him to concentrate his attention.

When it was Mark's turn, the conductor smiled. "But you should not have to wait like that! I did not know you were coming tonight. I am pleased!" He turned to the woman at the dressing table. "Maria, Mr. Holland is here."

She looked up from the mirror, and waved languidly. *"Ciao!"*

"I thought it went very well. The American girl was better than I expected."

"Thank you." Cavalcanti drew Mark away from the queue, so that he would not be overheard. His narrow, rather pointed face was sombre. "I am glad that you are in London. It will give us an opportunity to discuss this film."

"Is there a problem?"

"I hope not. It is just that I am a little nervous of the confrontation between Morini and Alessandro. The last time they worked together, it was a disaster." He avoided Mark's eyes. "I worry about the clash of temperaments."

"I wouldn't be too concerned. Singers are forever fighting and making up. They prefer things to be larger than life, like their operas."

"Perhaps."

"Recordings are very different from stage performances. They only have the microphones to worry about. They're professionals. What happened in Bologna is past history. It may even make them both extra polite when they meet again. By the time they get to Rome, they'll be the best of friends."

Cavalcanti was thoughtful. "You are probably right, but I am concerned. Signor Alessandro has been . . . difficult . . . ever since the first rehearsal. I hope he does not present new problems when we arrive in Geneva. We have very little time to make changes." He seemed ill at ease, glancing frequently towards his wife, who appeared to ignore him.

Mark smiled. "As long as they monitor his voice good and loud during the playbacks, he'll be happy. Don't worry about Bianca. She's the most professional recording artist I've ever met."

"Very well, if you say so. I trust your opinion. Will you go to the reception tonight?"

"Yes, I was hoping to beg a lift over in your car."

"Of course. We will be delighted." Mark had the impression that the request pleased Cavalcanti. "Perhaps we can discuss the recording a little more."

"Certainly. I sat with Joshua Levin, who'll be in charge of the sessions. He's very experienced. I think you'll like him."

"Good. I met him briefly a few weeks ago, when I first arrived, and he telephoned me at the hotel two days ago, to tell me that the contracts will be signed. I had expected to spend more time with him."

"He was probably waiting for the go-ahead from New York. They've only just concluded their negotiations with Herr Wiesman."

"I see." Cavalcanti turned briskly towards the few stragglers at the door, still waiting to be greeted. "Perhaps I should attend to the rest of my visitors. Will you excuse me?" He returned to the entrance to the dressing room, assuming his previous pose, and Mark had the impression that the conductor's nerves were tightly stretched. Perhaps he was still tense from the complicated drama of the score. He was a man who took his work very seriously.

When the last guest had departed, Cavalcanti busied himself with packing his clothes into a plastic-covered suit hanger and an expensive-looking leather holdall. His wife watched his neat, practised movements without offering to help.

"Have you enjoyed being in London?"

She shrugged. "It is pleasant, but a little boring. I miss Rome. Emilio is busy all the time. I never see him." There was a slight edge to her voice, and Mark had the impression that the conductor, still packing, was listening intently.

"At least the weather has been good. I sometimes think May is the best month of the year."

She pouted. "Yes, very nice, but it is no fun to spend my time looking in shop windows and reading magazines."

Cavalcanti glared at her. "I have to work!" He snapped the bag together angrily. "We should leave." Without waiting to see whether his wife was ready, he strode out of the room. They followed him in silence.

There were still a number of loyal fans waiting by the stage door for a last glimpse of Alessandro before his limousine took him away. The size of the crowd was a tribute to the tenor's performance, and it occurred to Mark that the unfortunate American soprano might have inspired a few to wait. He wondered whether Diana had been successful in persuading Alessandro to prepare for the reception. She could be very charming.

Waiting for the Cavalcantis' car to arrive, he scanned the faces in the crowd. Several had recognized the young Italian conductor, and smiled encouragingly. Mark looked across the street, and was surprised to see Rossiter, standing slightly apart from the rest, watching intently. Their eyes met for an instant, and the man nodded to Mark, holding an imaginary telephone to his ear with his left hand, and pretending to dial a number with his right. Mark inclined his head slightly, to acknowledge the message. But how was Cavalcanti involved?

Their car arrived, and as they settled into their seats, Maria smiled at Mark. "You seem to have a fan, Mr. Holland."

Cavalcanti looked up with a frown. "What do you mean?"

"I was nodding to an old acquaintance in the crowd. We spent a few minutes together during the interval, and I promised to call him sometime."

Maria looked at him. "I'm surprised he didn't come over to say hello to you."

"He probably didn't want to disturb you. The English are inclined to be diffident when confronted by famous people. I wish the Americans were the same!" Mark decided not to mention Rossiter's name for the moment. The man obviously planned to call him, and it might be wiser to hear what he had to say.

The house on Eaton Square was discreetly opulent, with a broad staircase, which almost matched Covent Garden's, leading to several connecting reception rooms on the first floor. It was hard to imagine living in such empty splendour. Perhaps they stored the furniture elsewhere when they were entertaining. Silent dinner-jacketed waiters collected coats and served champagne, and Mark followed the Cavalcantis up the stairs, wondering whether their hostess would introduce herself during the evening. At such gatherings, he seldom learned who was giving the party, and there never seemed to be a visible host. Presumably the man of the house either locked himself away somewhere or spent the night at his club. Mark had been to many similar post-concert celebrations and, after a while, they all merged in his memory. He might well have visited the same house before.

The rooms were already crowded with guests, most of whom had been at the *Tosca* performance. Their conversation was animated and, for a moment, it seemed that the Crush Bar had shifted quarters to this new location, with the addition of black-uniformed waitresses to dispense unappetizing pastries from silver trays. He searched past dinner jackets and evening dresses for members of the cast, but none had yet arrived. That was the advantage of being a conductor: Cavalcanti had no makeup to remove.

Sitting in a corner by a window and looking glum, Wolfgang Wiesman, his head bowed, was listening to a dramatic monologue by Simon Vincent. The director was gesticulating wildly, and Mark assumed he was giving a blow-by-blow report of his encounter with Alessandro. Cliff hovered behind Vincent, glowering at the assembly and nursing a pint glass of beer. Mark moved to another room before the producer could catch his eye.

"Hello again." Katya Philips greeted him, and he was once more aware of her unblinking gaze. Her eyes were slightly magnified by the lenses in her glasses, and it occurred to him that the penetrating stare was partly myopic. "I was hoping I would catch you alone, away from all those record and film people."

"Oh?"

"They're so nervous." She smiled to herself. "Anyone would think I was trying to extract national secrets from them. Every time they close ranks on me, I suspect that they're trying to hide something. Diana was watching you like a hawk when we were talking. I don't know what she thought you were going to say."

"Neither do I. Perhaps your reputation precedes you, Miss Philips."

"Katya. I write the truth, if that's what you mean. If people have nothing to hide, why should they worry? How about you, Mark? Do you have any deep, dark secrets?"

"None that come readily to mind."

"I'm curious to know why you live in Switzerland. Isn't it a little off the beaten path?"

"Not really." Mark smiled easily, but he could feel a slight tenseness.

"It's hardly the centre of the music world."

"No, but it's very convenient for just about anywhere in Europe, and I like the sort of tax returns I fill in."

"How long have you lived there?"

"About ten years."

"I thought it must be quite a long time. When I was researching Bianca Morini, your name appeared, and I couldn't find any reference to your agency in London."

"That's because I didn't start it until I settled in Geneva."

"I see. What did you do when you lived here?"

"Believe it or not, I was a civil servant." It was the answer Mark always gave. Taken at face value, it was just about true.

"Really? You don't look like the sort of man who'd work for the government."

"It was a rather obscure branch of the Arts Council." London Arts had been the Department's cover address. It afforded agents a vague enough occupation and allowed them to travel frequently. "When I learned the ropes, I decided to go into business for myself." The slight feeling of anxiety passed. It irritated Mark that memories of his previous employment still troubled him.

"I see. You were lucky to land the great Bianca Morini as a client." She lowered her voice. "Is there a story in that?"

"No. It came about through my American partner, Abe Sincoff. He helped set me up with a number of his top musicians. I look after them in Europe, and he handles their American affairs."

Katya gave a wry smile. "In Bianca Morini's case, that must be quite a handful!"

"Bianca's not as bad as she's sometimes made out to be. Besides, if she led a totally uneventful, domesticated life, you journalists would have nothing to write about."

"True. She certainly provides good copy." Katya smiled briefly, relaxing, and Mark was again aware of her beauty. "I'm curious to know a little more about you. Wife? Children?"

"No."

Her narrow eyebrows were raised. "Boyfriend?"

"Not even that. I'm not a very newsworthy subject, I'm afraid. I'm usually much too busy looking after all sorts of musicians to do anything that would interest you."

Her voice softened. "Perhaps. We must talk about that some more." Her gaze did not falter.

"You haven't asked me about Emilio Cavalcanti. He's one of my newer artists. Would you like to meet him?"

"Oh, I interviewed him last time, when he was over here for the Verdi *Requiem* at the Festival Hall. He's very bright."

Mark smiled. "No interesting copy?"

She shrugged. "Not bad. A bit too musicological for the Sunday supplements. Musicians aren't always very informative when they stop talking shop."

"Neither are architects or sportsmen, or artists' managers, for that matter."

"I suppose not. Too much specialization." Katya's attention was drawn to the doorway. Antonio Alessandro filled its frame, a broad smile on his face. He was stuffed into a slightly old-fashioned dinner jacket, which was tightly stretched across his broad chest. His blond companion stood slightly behind him. She had shed her mink coat to reveal a topless gown that displayed a flawless and ample upper torso. Several paces farther back, Diana and Joshua Levin waited for the tenor to complete his grand entrance.

Mark smiled. "Now, that looks like good copy. Who's the dazzling girl?"

Katya was contemptuous. "Some sort of model. Who cares? Alessandro always goes for the obvious. By tomorrow, there'll be another one."

"I thought that was the sort of thing your readers like to know about."

For a moment, the journalist looked angry. "Thank you very much! It may come as a surprise to you, Mark, but I am a serious music reporter. The fact that I write about people means that I write about their private as well as their public lives. My readers like to know what makes them tick, and I try to tell them. If it's of any interest to you, I've also written a biography of Anton Webern, and what is known as a "slim volume" on the subject of symphonic structures in twentieth-century music. I am not a gossip columnist."

"I'm sorry. That was rude of me."

She stared at Mark for a moment, then suddenly smiled. "That's all right. I was overdoing the personal angle earlier. You're forgiven, but you were being just a teensy bit patronizing. Besides, I like a man that's not too proud to apologize. After all, if it wasn't for musicians, we'd both be out of work." She ran a fingertip gently across Mark's cheek. "I'll catch up with you later." Then she headed in the direction of the crowd of admirers surrounding Alessandro.

Diana joined Mark. "I see you and Katya are getting on like a house on fire." Her eyes twinkled. "Shall we go and relieve Maestro Cavalcanti?" The conductor was hemmed in by several ladies whose ample bosoms were covered with enough pearls to empty an oyster bed.

"I'd rather talk to you. Where's Joshua?"

She grimaced. "Heading for the bar. What was Katya after?"

"I'm not sure. I think I was getting the softening-up treatment before she starts in earnest on Bianca. She was checking my own background."

"Good idea, but I'm sure you can look after yourself. Be careful."

"I intend to."

"We'd better save Emilio. Where's his wife?"

"I don't know. I haven't seen her since we arrived."

"What do you make of her?"

"Hard to say. I don't really know her. We're still on topics like London shops and English weather. How about you?"

Diana smiled. "I stay clear. She's one of those ladies who doesn't like another female near her husband. I got very bad vibes the first time we met. Honestly, from the reception I got you'd think I'd arrived to seduce the poor man. I was only being polite on behalf of Magnum."

"Maybe she has her reasons. Emilio is an Italian. It's almost expected of him."

"Not by me. Anyway, he's a bit too dark and swarthy for my taste. I prefer blond men." She looked at Mark and blushed. "I didn't mean . . ."

He laughed gently. "In that case, I'm not sure whether to be flattered or offended."

Before Diana could reply, Wolfgang Wiesman appeared, looking ruffled. "Ah, Diana, I am glad I found you. Would you be an angel and talk to Simon Vincent for a few minutes? Apparently, Alessandro insulted him backstage."

"We heard it. He was extremely unpleasant, in front of everybody."

"So it seems. Now, Simon is threatening to walk out if I don't do something about it. I assured him it was just theatrical nerves, but the man's furious. I would be grateful if you'd help to calm him down."

"I'll see what I can do. Shall I take Mark along for moral support?"

"Yes, if you wouldn't mind." Wiesman hesitated. "On second thoughts, no. It will only remind him that he still has Bianca Morini to contend with. Find him some red wine, and see if you can settle him down, will you? Cliff's no help at all." Diana left, and Wiesman shook his head slowly. "He's really being impossible!"

"Give it a few days. Alessandro didn't behave well, but I'm sure they'll all relax and get used to each other. Once they start working, it's very different."

"Yes, of course." Wiesman stared into space. "This is going to be a very expensive production, Mr. Holland. I've had to stretch my finances to cover it, and I'm already beginning to wonder what I've let myself in for."

"They are spoiled children, opera singers!" Giuseppe Belasco, the Scarpia of the production, had been listening to the conversation. He was an elderly man, balding, with white hair trimmed close to his head. According to his biography, he was fifty-five, but Mark suspected that he was at least sixty. Even so, Belasco's voice remained as youthful and powerful as ever. He jerked his head in the direction of Alessandro. "I have been listening to that peacock telling everybody what a splendid fellow he is, and how lucky we are to hear him. Singers! God, I can remember when he was grateful to be hired. Now he wants a fortune and he still isn't satisfied. Half these superstars travel around with more lawyers and accountants and tax experts than the president of a multinational corporation!"

Wiesman looked relieved. "I'm glad to hear that coming from you, Giuseppe. What makes you so different?"

"Me?" The old singer raised shaggy eyebrows. "I came up the hard way. You know, I once sang for Toscanini, when I was a kid. It was the first act of *Tosca*, come to think of it. That was in Milan in . . ." He smiled. "Maybe I'd better not tell you when it was. I started in the Scala chorus as a child, so I can remember when it was an honour to be invited to take part. One day, all this—the operas, the singers, the orchestras—will be finished: too expensive to keep. I may be dead and buried by then, I expect, but it will happen nevertheless." He glanced across at Alessandro. "It's those new ones that finished it for the rest of us, with their huge salaries and their recording contracts and their limousines and their fancy ladies. They've lost all sense of proportion, and the more you give them, the more they demand."

"But not you?"

He shook his head angrily. "No. I sing because I sing. That's all I want to do. I have enough to retire, if I want to. Giovanna keeps telling me to stop now, and take things easy: maybe hold a few master classes and teach the next generation." He scowled. "What for? The next generation won't have any opera houses to sing in if the present generation doesn't learn to behave itself. Spoiled children!" He started towards the stairs, and Wiesman followed him.

"Where are you going?"

"Home! To bed!" He thumped his chest fiercely. "I work for a living. *Buona notte, Herr Dottore.* I'll see you in Geneva."

Wiesman turned to Mark. "He makes a point."

"Perhaps. Opera singers were always a pampered breed. They earn very little if you compare them with today's pop stars." He smiled. "The problem is that baritones never earned the same fees as tenors!"

"But he's right about the costs."

"Yes. It's the medium itself. It just involves too many people to be profitable. The houses are too small, and the seats are already horrendously expensive. Even when it's full every night, it runs at a loss. There are too many people to be paid. It can only survive on subsidy."

Wiesman nodded sombrely. "Nobody subsidizes me!"

When many of the guests had departed, to the relief of the uniformed chauffeurs who had double-parked their cars in the street outside, Mark found Joshua Levin standing alone by the makeshift bar in one of the rooms. The record producer was surveying the scene vaguely, a glass of wine clasped in his hand, and was smiling benignly. He was swaying a little unsteadily.

"Greetings! It turned out to be a nice do after all." His glass was raised in a salute.

"Yes. I missed you earlier."

"Oh, I was talking to Nancy most of the evening. She's not such a bad singer, you know."

"I thought she acquitted herself very well."

"The trouble is that she's not really ready for Tosca yet, but she couldn't turn down the offer. She's got all the equipment to sing it. Actually, she wanted my advice on future roles to study."

"What did you suggest?"

"Well, it turned out that the part she really fancies is Magda Sorel in *The Consul.* It's one of my favourite operas. I've never understood why it isn't revived more regularly. Snobbery, probably. Menotti's scores are much too openly melodic to please the critics. I'd love to persuade Wolfgang to take it on. It would make an ideal film, and she'd be terrific." He drank some wine. "Christ, if she can sing Tosca, she'd be sensational as Magda!"

"Are you going to propose it to New York?"

Joshua looked glum. "No, they'd never buy it. I doubt whether they've ever heard of it. In fact, I'll be lucky if they've even heard of Menotti. It might be worth a try. I'd give my right arm to do a new production. The only existing records were made back in the 1950s."

Mark smiled. "You sound as though you care."

"Of course I care! Caring's what it's all about." Joshua staggered slightly, slopping wine, and steadied himself with one hand on the bar. "Producing records isn't a job. It's a way of life. We sure as hell don't do it for the money! You know, there are moments in a session when your whole being seems to hang, for an instant, on the placing of a single semiquaver or a horn note that doesn't bubble. You live through it, second by second. That's what caring involves. Do you know what I mean?"

"Not exactly."

"I'll give you an example. At the very end of the Mahler Tenth Symphony, about fifteen bars from the last note, there's a sudden upward sweep in the strings—a kind of anguished cry—that makes your heart stand still. I can't really describe it. You'd have to hear it for yourself." He stared into space. "I'll tell you what that moment means to me. Mahler wrote that symphony when he was dying. He never finished it, in fact, but he left enough of a short score for Deryck Cooke to fill in the gaps. I won't go into all the pros and cons of that. There are enough pompous musicologists giving patronizing opinions to kill the work stone dead!" His expression became passionate. "When I hear that sound in the strings, I visualize Mahler standing in an open field at night under a sky full of stars. He stares up at them and, because he knows his time is running out, he calls out in a kind of enraged frustration, "Why now? Why me? Why, when there's so much more to be said? Why?" And those silent pinpoints of light glimmer back at him, distant and insensible, offering no answers to the mystery of human existence, no suggestion that there may really be a divine spirit controlling his destiny: just an awful silence and the cruel inevitability of his death." He paused dramatically. "It's all there in those few bars of music. When we recorded it, there was a kind of stillness in the control room. The engineers and I could hardly breathe, for fear of disturbing the atmosphere. On that particular occasion, we knew that we were witnessing something rare and special. Time stood still." Joshua smiled at the memory. "A few moments later, it was all over, and we went back to normal. I called a break, we listened to a playback, found little mistakes that needed correcting. But, I tell you, for a few magic seconds, everything seemed to stop." He shook his head in wonder. "What other job gives you a moment like that?"

"You make it sound like a religious experience."

"I suppose so." Joshua smiled wryly. "And like most religious phenomena, it's what you bring to it rather than what actually happens." He became self-conscious. "Anyway, you asked me whether I care. Have I answered you?" He emptied his glass with a swallow.

Before Mark could reply, Diana appeared. She looked at Joshua severely. "I think it's time you were going home. We have meetings all day tomorrow."

"Don't be so bloody practical!" The record producer looked hopefully towards the bar. "I was just telling Mark about the Mahler sessions."

"I know." For a moment, her expression softened. "Come on, Josh, it's getting late. You can tell him more about it when we see him tomorrow. I'll drive you home. God, look at the time!" She glanced at Mark. "I think the Cavalcantis have already left. We're heading west of here, towards Chelsea, but I can drop you off afterwards if you like."

"Don't worry. I'll drive Mr. Holland home. It's on my way." Katya Philips was standing next to him, and had taken possession of his arm.

"Fine." Diana smiled with an effort. "We'll see you again soon."

Katya said little in the car. She drove quickly through the empty streets. At one point, she glanced at Mark and smiled.

"I hope you're not angry with me for ticking you off this evening."

"Not at all. I think I deserved it."

"I'm a bit touchy about my work. There are times when I write more than I should, but newspaper editors worry about circulation, even in the quality press. To be honest, I'm a little nervous about Bianca Morini and her interview. I was hoping you'd make it easier for me."

"I'll do what I can. You may be surprised when you meet her. She's not as frightening as you may think."

"I'm glad. We're all a little insecure, no matter what we write. It's easy to be brave from behind a typewriter."

At the door of the hotel, she raised her face for Mark to kiss. Her fingers on his hand tightened slightly as their cheeks brushed. "Can I take you to lunch tomorrow? You'll be the guest of my paper."

"Thank you."

"I want to know more about Bianca. The interview is important, and I don't want to put my foot in my mouth in the first five minutes." She hesitated, then spoke quickly. "I'd like to get to know you better, too. One o'clock here?"

A sleepy doorman had opened Mark's door, and he stepped out. "I'll look forward to it."

The hotel foyer was deserted, and Mark collected a handful of messages from the concierge's desk. Most of them were unimportant, and could wait until the morning. There was a telex from Abe Sincoff, confirming that he and Myra would come to Geneva for the recording sessions. Would Mark also remember to call Bianca in New York? No problem, but she was feeling neglected. He had not spoken to her for three days. Rossiter had called twice, leaving no messages. Rudi, his ever-efficient Swiss assistant, had phoned from the Geneva office, with nothing to report. Mark looked at his watch. It was after two o'clock.

He was drifting into sleep when the phone rang. Slightly disoriented in the unfamiliar bedroom, he fumbled for the receiver in the dark.

"Hello."

There was a slight pause before the caller spoke. "Mark Holland?"

"Yes."

"It's Tony Rossiter. Sorry to call you so late. I did try earlier."

"The hotel gave me your message."

"I know it's an imposition, but do you think we could meet?"

"Now?"

"Well, hopefully."

For a moment, Mark's curiosity was aroused, but he was tired. "I'm sorry, but I'm already in bed."

"It's very urgent, otherwise I wouldn't ask."

"It will have to wait until tomorrow."

"All right. Look, I'm sorry to have to disturb you like this. When can you see me?"

Mark paused, collecting his thoughts. "I have several meetings. Can I call you?"

"I can't be reached." Rossiter offered no explanation.

"Can you at least tell me what it's about? You mentioned Cavalcanti."

"I can't discuss it on the phone. The only thing I will say is that it's vital that we talk, and that it concerns Cavalcanti, or possibly Antonio Alessandro."

"How?"

"I can't discuss that now. Will you meet me?"

"All right. Why don't you come to the hotel at—"

"I'd prefer not to. I'll explain when we meet."

Mark felt growing irritation. "What do you suggest?"

Rossiter spoke rapidly, giving the impression that he had rehearsed the words. "There's a little coffee shop on Upper Regent Street, on the right-hand side, across the road from Boosey and Hawkes. Do you know roughly where I mean?"

"Yes."

"It's open for breakfast from eight o'clock. Could you meet me there?"

"Yes, I suppose so. What time?"

"Just after eight?"

"That's rather early. It's after two now."

Rossiter's voice was brisk. "I'd be very grateful if you'd make it as early as possible. It's extremely important."

"All right. I'll be there as close to eight as I can."

"Thank you. I'll explain everything. If you'll just go in and order a coffee or whatever, I'll find you inside."

It was a curious comment. Obviously, Rossiter intended to wait until Mark had arrived before entering. "Very well."

"You'll understand, once we've spoken." He laughed uneasily. "Sorry to sound so mysterious." Before Mark could reply, he continued. "I'll have to ring off now. I'm out of coins and the last one's running out. I'll see you tomorrow." The line went dead.

Mark replaced the receiver slowly. Apparently, Rossiter was calling from a public phone in the middle of the night. What the hell did he want, and how could it affect Emilio Cavalcanti or Alessandro? He lay back, closing his eyes. He did not remember Rossiter, and the man claimed they had met long ago. More than ten years? He frowned. That would have been before he left the Department. How could that affect the tenor or the conductor? Both men would have been in their early to mid-twenties. How could they—

The phone rang again. He held the receiver to his ear without speaking, expecting to hear Rossiter's voice again.

"Mark? It's Diana. Oh Lord! Have I woken you?"

"No." He smiled in the darkness. "Anyway, I had to get up to answer the phone."

"What?" She paused. "Oh dear, I did wake you."

"No. I was making a bad joke."

"I took the chance that you hadn't gone to sleep yet. I thought it might be better than waking you too early in the morning. We were supposed to meet at eleven, but Wolfgang has asked me to change it to nine. He wants to take an earlier plane to Frankfurt."

"I can probably make nine-thirty." How long would Rossiter need?

"That's good enough. I'm sorry. I didn't mean to disturb you." She hesitated slightly. "I thought Katya would probably keep you a little longer."

"No, she drove me straight here and left."

"In that case, I feel worse."

"I really was still awake. How's Josh feeling?" There was an intimacy to their conversation that made it difficult to realize that they had only met that evening.

"Sleeping it off, I hope. He shouldn't drink so much."

"He seems to hold it well enough."

"I know, but it's still foolish. Once he starts working, he never touches it." She hesitated again. "I'd better go, and let you sleep. I get so involved in this job that I forget other people live normal lives and sleep normal hours. I'm sorry."

"You're forgiven. Tell me, does your office have a bio of Antonio Alessandro?"

"Yes. I did one myself. Why?"

"I'd like to have a look at it. It occurred to me that I don't really know very much about his background."

She chuckled. "Where it all went wrong, you mean? I'll keep one out for you."

"Thank you." He pictured her smile. Her grey-blue eyes seemed to widen when she did. He wondered whether it was deliberate. "I'd better let you go, too. I seem to remember you talking about going to bed before dawn."

"Oh, this is my normal bedtime. Thank you for being so nice about my calling you this late. I'll see you later today."

"Yes."

"Sleep well." The words were almost whispered.

Mark replaced the receiver and lay back, recalling the image of her face. As he fell asleep, he vaguely remembered wondering what perfume she used.

THREE

BRILLIANT PATCHES of sunlight illuminated Regent Street as Mark walked towards Oxford Circus. There was something appealing about a city preparing for a new day. He remembered meeting a conductor very early one morning in Paris. They had arranged the playback of a recording at the Église de Liban on the Rue d'Ulm, and the conductor had asked to start at seven o'clock. While waiting for a sleepy engineer to appear, they had breakfasted at a corner bistro on jet-black coffee and croissants still warm from the bakery. Parisian shopkeepers started earlier than their London counterparts, and they had watched striped awnings being lowered, piles of fruit carefully arranged, vans delivering *baguettes* and *flûtes* of sweet-smelling bread, window displays of meat and poultry being laid out with the artistic flair of a still life. The conductor had laughed. "My God, it's like that scene in *Louise* when all the street sellers in Montmartre call out their wares! What a shame I can't sing Julien's aria!"

The café on Upper Regent Street was drab and smoke-filled, permeated by the acrid smell of overheated cooking fat. A portable radio, its speaker distorted, blared pop music. There was a large chromium urn which dispensed pale brown coffee, and a woman in a dirty apron offered a selection of sandwiches and pastries. Several early-morning patrons, their faces buried in newspapers, focussed their attention on topless girls and television gossip. Mark asked for a cup of coffee, and took it to a corner table away from the front window. Paris seemed very distant.

He had been waiting for about fifteen minutes when Tony Rossiter arrived. The older man nodded in Mark's direction, then walked to the counter and ordered coffee and a pastry. He was wearing a shabby raincoat over the same jacket and trousers, but had made some effort to improve his appearance with a change of shirt and tie. His unruly grey hair was combed back, and he had shaved, although patches of stubble still showed on his chin. He did not look in Mark's direction while he waited to be served.

"I didn't expect you to be so punctual." Rossiter sat down slowly. His coffee cup rattled, spilling liquid in the saucer. "I'm sorry if I kept you waiting."

"I have a number of other meetings this morning." Mark glanced at his watch. "I'll need to leave in less than an hour. Perhaps you should tell me what you want to discuss, and how it involves me."

"Yes, of course." The man smiled apologetically. "It was a bit of luck finding you at Covent Garden last night. I guessed you would be there, of course, but I hadn't expected it to be so easy."

"How did you know?"

"I saw your name this month in one of the magazines. Something about managing Cavalcanti, wasn't it?"

"I see." Mark had only recently taken on the conductor, and there had been a small reference to this in one of the London music journals. "Are you involved with the concert world?"

"Hardly." Rossiter stared at him, surprised. "I still have to read my way through the trade press. I thought you understood what I was saying last night." He lowered his voice. "I work for London Arts. You know what that means." He looked closely at Mark. "You really don't remember me, do you?"

"No."

"It was a long time ago, and we only met once." He smiled. "Of course, my hair was black in those days; not this grey thatch. I was working for Bill Warner. Do you remember him? He had the Scandinavian desk."

"I remember him." For a moment, a gesture by Rossiter caused a fleeting image in Mark's memory. He pictured a younger man's face with fewer lines, the skin less flaccid, and dark hair. It was like a blurred photograph. The man could have been Rossiter. "Yes, I think I can place you."

"I wouldn't blame you if you didn't. It was ten or twelve years ago. God, how time flies!" Rossiter had chosen a seat facing the door of the café, and his glance constantly slid in that direction, as though he was expecting someone. With an effort, he returned to Mark. "I remember when you left. There was quite a shake-up at the time. It interested me, because I was hoping for a transfer. I was getting a bit tired of life in the frozen North. When you moved on, I thought it might be a chance for me . . ." He left the sentence unfinished, his expression distracted by the memory.

"I hate to cut in on your reminiscences, but you asked to meet me because of something urgent."

"Yes." He still avoided Mark's eyes. "I'm sorry if I made it sound quite so dramatic last night. Things are inclined to become exaggerated in the small hours. It is important, God knows!"

"How does it involve me?"

"It doesn't, directly." Rossiter hesitated again. "I suppose I couldn't beg a cigarette, could I? I seem to have run out."

With an irritable gesture, Mark placed a packet of cigarettes and a lighter on the table between them. He noticed that Rossiter's fingers were trembling. "Why are we meeting?"

Rossiter inhaled smoke slowly. Finally, he looked at Mark. "Because you represent Emilio Cavalcanti."

"And?"

"I have pretty good reason to believe he's a courier. Either Cavalcanti or Alessandro. One of them is. Maybe, both of them. I think it's Cavalcanti." He watched Mark's face. "When you think about it, he's got the ideal occupation for the job: constantly moving about the world, jetting in and out of every major capital, East or West. The same applies to Alessandro. Their careers are tailor-made for it."

"Are you sure of what you're suggesting?"

"Yes, but I can't prove it—yet. That's where you come in."

"Why me? I'm not involved."

"You manage Cavalcanti, don't you?"

"Yes, but—"

"Which means that you know exactly where he's going to be, at all times: what countries, what cities, what dates. Who can keep better tabs on him than that?"

"That's nonsense! Cavalcanti's musical life is a matter of public record. There are dozens of people who can pinpoint a conductor's whereabouts any day of the week. You don't need me for that."

"You're better informed than anyone else I know, and I can stay in direct contact with you, if you'll agree. Besides, your . . . specialized background makes you—"

"But you've got the resources of the Department at your disposal. They have every kind of communication at their fingertips. Why come to me?"

"The Department doesn't know what I'm on to. They think I'm in Belfast at the moment."

"Why aren't you?"

Once again, Rossiter avoided Mark's eyes. "I wanted to stay on top of Cavalcanti and Alessandro. Having them together in London was an ideal opportunity."

"You're not making sense. What are you proposing to do: walk in and catch them red-handed? What proof have you got?"

Rossiter stubbed out his cigarette. "It started about six weeks ago, when Cavalcanti was here to conduct two performances of the Verdi *Requiem.* You may remember that Alessandro sang the tenor part."

"All right."

Rossiter stared at the table. "On both dates, some top secret documents disappeared. I have very good reason to believe that whoever took them passed them to one of those two musicians."

"Can you prove it?"

"Not exactly. I checked their movements following the London concerts. Alessandro gave a recital in Warsaw, and Cavalcanti conducted a series of concerts in East Berlin."

"So what? There's nothing unusual about either engagement. What proof have you that someone was passing them the stolen papers?"

"I'm not sure I want to give you those details at the moment."

"You're going to have to do a damn sight better than that! Why should I take your word for it?" Mark started to rise. "Why should I believe you? We may have met in the past. I remember someone vaguely resembling you. How do I know you're still in the Department? Can you prove it?"

Rossiter put out a restraining hand. "Please don't leave. I'm relying on you. If you want to check my credentials, there's a man called Sharpe. You could call him. He'll confirm who I am. Do you know who he is?"

"Yes, I know Quentin." Mark was thoughtful.

The man looked puzzled. "But he started long after your time. Did you say you know him? Have you ever met?"

"Yes. Our paths have crossed a few times."

"I don't understand."

"You don't need to. I'm simply saying I know him."

"I see. Well, you could call Sharpe and ask him about me. Actually, I'd rather you didn't."

"Why not?"

"Because he thinks I'm in Belfast. I explained. I'll be in bad trouble if he finds me here in London."

Mark spoke quietly. "I think you're in bad trouble already."

Rossiter was startled. "What do you mean?"

"I would have thought it was pretty obvious. You approached me surreptitiously at Covent Garden, trying to make sure that your presence wasn't noticed. Then you tried to arrange a meeting in the middle of the night, calling from a phone box, but you wouldn't come to the hotel. When we finally meet, you sit there scared out of your shadow that someone's about to spot you, and hand me a cock-and-bull story about an unidentified person whom you can't discuss but who you believe is stealing documents and giving them to either Cavalcanti or Alessandro. What person? To cap it all, you haven't told the Department what you know, and have gone absent without leave from a job in Northern Ireland. Bullshit!" Rossiter said nothing, and Mark stared at him, taking in the crumpled clothes and the clumsy attempt to shave. There was a thin film of sweat on the man's upper lip. "You know what I think?"

"What?"

"I think you're on the run." Rossiter was motionless, as though frozen. "You look as though you've been living in those clothes for several days; you shaved yourself with a dry razor; you're terrified of being spotted; and your story's got more holes in it than Dear Liza's bucket! In fact, the only part of your fairy tale that intrigues me is that you should have gone to such lengths to reach me. Why? I'm not involved in the Department's business, thank God, and I don't intend to get myself enmeshed again." He looked at his watch. "I haven't got much longer, so you'd better start explaining."

Rossiter was silent for a long time, staring at the greasy smears on the plastic surface of the table. At length, he ran a hand across the stubble on his chin and smiled ruefully. "I can tell you one thing: it's not much fun trying to shave in the front seat of a Volkswagen with no soap and a blunt razor!"

"Why not go to a public bath?"

"First place they'd look for me. For all I know, the Department's got the Metropolitan boys on the lookout, too." He seemed to relax. "I was going to slip into the men's room of one of the better hotels for a proper wash and brushup, but you can't do that in the middle of the night. The railway stations were another obvious place for them to be watching. There's a man staked out at my flat, and I don't have any close friends I can rely on. It will be easier during the day, but I couldn't risk staying out of sight any longer before talking to you. At least, my car's hidden away for the moment, but I'll have to dump it before long." He suddenly grinned rather boyishly. "Shit creek, here I come!"

For a moment, Mark pitied the man. In the past, he had faced similar circumstances. His voice was gentler. "Why don't you start again, from the beginning."

Rossiter helped himself to another cigarette. Lighting it, he smiled again. His expression was almost jaunty. "Sorry to pinch yours, but I've been out of them for hours, and I'm running short of ready money. I haven't risked using my cash card, in case they're watching out for it. I'm still hoping they believe I've gone to ground in Ireland, but it's probably wishful thinking. I'm trying to stay one step ahead of them, just like the manual says, but after a while being ultra-cautious makes you paranoid."

"How long have you been running?"

"About a week. I don't know how much longer I can keep going. To be honest, you're my last chance. I saw an advertisement for the opera house, and remembered that magazine piece about you and Cavalcanti." He sighed. "If you can't or won't help me, I may as well pack it in and give myself up. I'm too old for this kind of nonsense."

"I can't tell whether I can help until you give me a few facts to work on."

"That's fair."

"Let's start again. Have papers gone missing?"

"Yes. Everything I've told you has been the truth." He saw the expression in Mark's eyes. "It just wasn't the whole truth and nothing but."

"Who took them?"

Rossiter was silent again. Then he took a deep breath, apparently reaching a decision. "I did."

Mark looked at him. "That makes a hell of a difference." He gathered his cigarettes from the table. "The most sensible thing would be to turn yourself in."

"Would you at least hear me out?"

"I'll listen, if you want to talk. This time, try the whole truth."

"All right." Rossiter stared into space. "I suppose the only thing I can say in my defence is that I've made a bloody fool of myself." His voice was bitter. "I usually do."

"An Old Bailey judge might take it into consideration, but I doubt whether it would influence his sentence. What did you take?"

"Nothing vital. They were mostly NATO plans affecting the Baltic. They were the easiest things I could lay my hands on."

"Why, for God's sake?"

Rossiter bowed his head. "The oldest and most obvious reason in the world. For a woman. Spare me the sniggers."

"I'm not even smiling."

"Thanks." He looked up, and there was a spark of anger in his eyes. "You can also spare me the cliché that there's no fool like an old fool. I should have known better. The awful part of it is that half of me still thinks it was worth it. That's how stupidly besotted a man of my age can become!" For a moment, he stared at Mark. "She made me feel young again!" He blurted the words, unable to disguise their despair.

Mark looked away, keeping his voice impersonal. "Who is she?"

"Her name's Danuta. It's a pretty ordinary Polish name. Even now, I don't want to tell you the rest of it. God knows why I feel this loyalty after . . ." He closed his eyes. "The more I think about her, the more confused I become. I play mental games of hide-and-seek with myself:

pretend she didn't really lead me up the garden path; tell myself that she's in trouble and can't reach me; deceive myself into believing she really meant the things she said. I know it's ridiculous, but I can't help it. Pitiful, isn't it?"

Mark ignored the question. "You've only given me her name so far. Who is she?"

"She was working at the Polish Embassy when I met her. That was eight months ago. I've been back in London for the past two years." He grimaced. "They thought I was too old to be working as a field man. Too old!" He lapsed into silence.

"I thought you were supposed to be in Belfast."

"I am. I'm one of the senior advisers, these days. They ship me out from time to time when they want someone to dish out expert opinions—nothing too strenuous, of course! I pass on my words of wisdom, read them rules out of the book, and scurry home like a good little civil servant." He looked up. "I can see the derision in their eyes, the younger ones. 'Here's one of the old codgers from Head Office, to tell us how he won the war with a bow and arrow and a bent hairpin!' Christ! I'm fifty-seven years old, Mark. I don't feel any different. I'm not ready for the scrap heap yet!" After a pause, he said, "Could I have another cigarette?"

Mark passed the box across the table. "Keep them."

"Thanks." He lit one unsteadily. "Not much to show for fifty-seven years, am I? I can't even afford an effing pack of Silk Cut!"

"Maybe you should ease up on the self-pity."

"I know. I've spent too much time alone."

"Tell me more about the girl. You said she was working at the Embassy?"

He nodded. "I met her at a reception to launch some new export drive. They're always launching something. I suppose they've got a special budget that has to be used up, or they won't get it the following year. I've met quite a lot of Poles through my Scandinavian connections. They probably knew what I was doing, but they didn't seem to care."

"Perhaps. Maybe they didn't show it."

"To be honest, I didn't think about it. Listen, you know what sort of work we do. Half our time is spent gathering useless information for somebody's dead file in London. It's neither dangerous nor glamorous; just the routine putting together of bits and pieces of information that might come in handy. Most of us never see any real action. I never did. Christ, the most interesting thing I ever did was to take the car ferry from Copenhagen to Malmö!"

"You met Danuta at this reception?"

"Yes. She was working as a secretary in the Trade section. She made a joke about it. I think it was her sense of humour that first attracted me. The Poles aren't a very funny lot."

"What happened?"

Rossiter shrugged. "The usual sort of thing. I wasn't even trying to chat her up. She said she loved the theatre but couldn't afford London ticket prices on her salary. I asked her if she'd like to see a show, and she said she would, so I took her to a musical. I think I even asked her if it would be all right with her bosses if we went out together, and she laughed and said she wasn't planning to discuss it with them. It was all very harmless." Mark nodded silently, not wanting to disturb the flow of words. "We saw the show, and had dinner afterwards. Then I drove her back to her bed-sit in Earl's Court." He stared into space. "It was a nice evening. She told me how much she'd enjoyed it, and kissed me on the cheek before she ran into the house." Almost unconsciously, his fingers touched the place on his cheek that she had embraced. "I really enjoyed myself, too. We laughed a lot and made rather inane jokes. I remember thinking, as I drove home, that I hadn't had as much fun for a long time. It was so . . . innocent!"

"Where is home?"

"I own a small flat in Islington; bought it years ago, when the prices were still reasonable. When my wife left me, I didn't need very much, and the place was going for a song."

"You were married?"

He nodded. "That ended years ago. My wife got tired of hanging around a semidetached in Pinner waiting for me to show up from somewhere north of the border, so she moved in with an accountant from Enfield. I came home from a trip and found a note on the kitchen table telling me to sell the house and send her half the proceeds. I can't say I blamed her. She was a bright girl with a healthy appetite, and I was never around to keep her satisfied. We were all supposed to be terribly trendy in the swinging sixties. I don't think I ever was." He stopped suddenly. "I don't know why I'm telling you all this."

Mark smiled. "Because I'm a stranger. Why do you think bartenders hear so many life stories? Why don't you go on."

The interruption had made Rossiter self-conscious. He shrugged again. "You can probably put two and two together. I called Danuta the following week, told her I'd got tickets for another show, and we spent a second evening together. If anything, it was better than the first, but that's only natural, isn't it? You know how it is: you begin to understand each other, and share little jokes together. I teased her because her English was quaint, and she pretended to be offended." His face was sad. "It's all a kind of civilized mating dance. I was lonely, and she seemed to enjoy my company. I think she was lonely, too. It's not much fun living in London on her kind of salary." As he spoke, his eyes were lost in thought. "The third time we went out, I took her to a play. It was a thriller of some sort. Anyway, somewhere towards the middle of the second act, I found she was holding my hand. I liked that. Christ, I sound like a schoolboy! I pretended not to notice, but I was terribly conscious of her hand in mine. I can't even remember what the damn play was about." He closed his eyes. "God! I don't know why I'm saying all this. It sounds like something out of a bloody women's magazine!"

"No." Mark kept his voice neutral.

Rossiter leaned forward, his shoulders hunched. "I don't have to draw you a picture, do I? We had dinner, drank too much wine, and spent the night together at her place. It was incredible, that first night! It was as though we were made for each other. We seemed to understand each other's physical needs, as though we'd been lovers for years. From then on, she filled my life." He looked up angrily. "She became everything! We had to be careful, of course, because of her job and mine, but I couldn't bear to be away from her. I missed her desperately when she wasn't there. I thought about her constantly; longed to call her, if only to hear the sound of her voice. If there were nights we couldn't be together, I was in a sweat until I could talk to her in the morning. If she couldn't see me, I was convinced she was tired of me or, worse still, that she'd found someone else. We created secret anniversaries: the first time we met; the first time we made love . . . I tell you, I was hopelessly in love with her." He looked away. "In bed, we were so right for each other. God! When we made love, she used to cry out and say she couldn't take any more. She made me feel so . . . so virile! I was like a twenty-year-old again. It had never been as good with anyone else." He paused, embarrassed by his confession. "She said she didn't care about the difference in our ages. I was the one who worried about it."

"How old is she?"

His head was bowed. "Thirty-two. I'm old enough to be her father. No fool like an old fool! You see, I was going to ask her to marry me. I know it sounds ridiculous, but when you're obsessed like that, you don't think about the future. It didn't make sense, but I didn't care. When I talked to her, told her what I was thinking, she laughed and made a joke about it. She said we should just live for the moment, and enjoy it while we could. She meant it. I'm sure she meant it!" His fists were tightly clenched.

"What happened next?"

Rossiter spoke in a low voice. "The Embassy decided to send her back to Poland. Out of the blue. We were having dinner at my place, and she'd been quiet all evening. Then, suddenly, she said, 'They're sending me back to Warsaw at the end of the month.' I don't remember what I said. She just sat there at the table and started to cry. All I could do was watch her." He seemed to relive the moment, blaming himself for failing to find the right words of consolation. "It was then that I begged her to ask for political asylum. I never talked about my job to her, but I told her I had contacts who could pull strings. She wouldn't do it."

"Why not?"

"Her family. Both her parents are living in Poland, as well as two brothers. She was terrified that the authorities would arrest them and force her to return. Apparently, they'd already hinted that her family would be held to ransom if she ever tried something like that. I pleaded with her, but she wouldn't listen. All she would say, over and over, was that we'd both always known it would have to end one day."

Mark waited a moment before speaking. "You haven't explained about the papers."

"I know. We argued for hours that night. I begged her to drop out of sight and let me look after the details. God, after thirty years in the Department, it was the least they could do for me! She wouldn't agree. She was terrified of the reprisals they would take on her family. Then we talked about ways to extend her stay in London, and she said she had heard rumours in the office—some of the other girls were talking one day—that if an employee could latch on to classified information here, the Embassy would find ways to keep her in the country."

"In other words, if she could put the bite on a useful source, they would bend a few rules."

"Danuta wasn't like that." He spoke angrily. "For God's sake, I know her. She simply said she'd heard rumours." He stared at Mark. "It was my idea. I suggested it. Don't you understand?"

"What did she say?"

"At first, she wouldn't hear of it. She was frightened for my sake, but I persuaded her that there was no great risk. I could provide enough material to satisfy her people that it was worth keeping her in England without actually giving much away."

"And she agreed?"

"Not at first. It took all my powers of persuasion. I didn't care about the chances I was taking." He lit another cigarette. "Nothing happened for a few days. Then she told me she had spoken to the security man at the Embassy. She'd explained about me, and hinted that I often took documents home. She said she had enough on me to use blackmail, if necessary." He smiled. "I didn't care! They decided to extend her stay by six months. You've no idea what that meant to me. It gave me enough time either to persuade her to come over or to try to get her family out of Poland."

"And you never suspected her?"

He avoided Mark's eyes. "No. She couldn't have been lying. She couldn't!"

"Why didn't you tell the Department what was going on?"

"I wouldn't risk her safety. I know how the Department operates. They would have played along for as long as it suited them, and then thrown her to the wolves. You say you know Quentin Sharpe? What would her chances have been if he had known that he could use her without any liability?"

Mark nodded slowly. "You're right. What guarantees have you that the Poles aren't doing the same?"

"I haven't. That's the point. I still want to believe her."

"What did you do?"

Rossiter sighed. "I said I would arrange a drop, and asked her to choose a suitable place. She was frightened. I suppose she was afraid her people didn't trust her, and suspected that she might be playing a double game. For a while, it felt like a stalemate. Then, a few days later, she told me that the Embassy had come up with a plan of its own. We were to attend two performances of the Verdi *Requiem* at the Festival Hall, and go backstage after the concert. She would give the information I provided to a third party."

Mark sat forward. "Who?"

He frowned. "That's the trouble. She wouldn't tell me. She said it would be safer if I didn't know."

"What did you do?"

Rossiter smiled weakly. "I started to panic. It's one thing to say you'll deliver classified documents, but it's another when it comes to the crunch. I kept delaying, telling myself I'd do it the following day; there was still plenty of time. I had to do it. I'm not very brave, but I couldn't bear the thought of losing Danuta."

"You've explained that."

"All right. You don't have to rub it in, for God's sake!" He checked himself. "I'm sorry. My nerves are a bit stretched. I waited until the day of the concert. I intended to xerox a couple of pages I'd selected earlier. They were the current dispositions of vessels between the Kattegat and the southern area of the Baltic, with emergency plans for the CIC in case of an attack." His voice was pleading. "The information wasn't vital. If you know anything about that part of the world, you'd be aware that naval movements can be monitored relatively easily. Besides, every few weeks, operational plans are changed. I knew what I was doing. I may have been desperate to help her, but I wasn't prepared to give them anything critical. The idea was to establish her value to her bosses."

"So you made a xerox?"

His face seemed to crumple with the memory. "No. The bloody machine broke down that morning. It's always doing that! It was out of commission until three in the afternoon. We spend more time repairing it than using the damned thing! Every time I went to the copier, there was a queue of secretaries waiting to use it. I couldn't risk them seeing what I was doing, so in the end I had to take the originals."

"But that was stupid! Your name would have been the last one on the cover when it was signed out to you."

"I know, but I hoped the missing pages wouldn't be noticed until later. The file circulates regularly, and I gambled that their absence wouldn't be reported until there were other names on the cover."

"We'll get back to it. What happened at the concert?"

"It was simpler than I expected. I met Danuta in the foyer, and we went inside. I can't say I really liked the music. I don't have much of an ear for it, but it seemed rather long and noisy to me. I suppose I was too worried, conscious of that bloody envelope sitting in my breast pocket. I hardly listened, most of the time. When it was over, we walked down to the front of the auditorium, on the left-hand side of the stage. There's a door by the bottom exit, and a crowd was waiting to go through. Danuta seemed to know her way. We walked to the back of the hall, where there's a kind of wide corridor outside the dressing rooms for the conductor and soloists."

"I know the layout."

"I suppose you would. The corridor was packed with people waiting to see the solo singers, and there was another line at the far end, by the conductor's dressing room. As you know, the greenroom lies beyond that, and most of them were going in there. I suppose it's easier to wait in the proper reception room until the conductor's changed and come out."

Mark nodded. "What did you do?"

"I slipped the envelope to Danuta while we were working our way

through. I didn't realize the place would be so busy. It was worse than the
Tube during the rush hour! She went ahead of me to the conductor's
dressing room. I wasn't far behind, but there were dozens of people politely
pushing and shoving each other out of the way. You say you know the
layout?"

"Yes."

"Then you'll remember that there's a dreadful bottleneck by the conductor's door, with one lot aiming past it for the greenroom while the others
are waiting for the dressing room. To make matters worse, there's only the
one door in and out of the greenroom, so that people going in have to
elbow their way past others coming out, and get past the line standing by
the dressing room. On top of that, musicians carrying instruments were
milling round in the crowd, trying to go through an exit door, and there
were dozens of members of the chorus meeting friends and relatives. It was
a mess!"

"Where did you go?"

"When I saw Danuta go into Cavalcanti's room, I decided to wait for
her in the corridor. There were so many people bumping into each other
that it was easier to stand against the wall and let them pass."

"How long was she gone?"

"Hardly any time at all. She came out, and we walked back to the front
of the hall. The whole thing probably took no more than five minutes from
the moment we went backstage. I tried to say something to her, but she
just nodded and walked on. She wouldn't talk about it."

"And you're sure she went into Cavalcanti's dressing room?"

"Positive. There was a card with his name on it stuck to the door."

"Did you see inside?"

"No. She went in quickly and shut the door behind her."

"Then you don't know whether she actually gave the envelope to Cavalcanti."

"No. I told you, I can't prove anything."

Mark lit a cigarette. Rossiter's story was plausible, and his description of
the backstage area was accurate. "Where does Alessandro come into it?"

"At the second concert, two days later. This time, I managed to make a
xerox. I don't think anyone saw me do it. When we went backstage, it was
just as before, with the same rugby scrum to fight our way through. The
only difference was that, as Danuta went into the dressing room, Alessandro pushed past a whole lot of people and went in behind her."

"They were in there together? How long?"

"A minute or so; not very long. He came out and went back to his dressing room, and Danuta came out a few seconds later."

"Did you ask her about it?"

"I tried. This time, she just said, 'Everything is good,' or something like that, and we went home. I asked her again, but she wouldn't discuss it. All she would say was that I shouldn't worry." His voice was lowered. "She was very passionate that night."

"Why do you think Alessandro's involved?"

"He could have been watching Danuta and followed her inside. The first time, he could have been waiting in there already. I don't know. I think she went to see Cavalcanti, but it could have been Alessandro."

"What happened next?"

"For a while, nothing. When I questioned Danuta, she said they were checking the documents. They weren't very impressed with them, but they would tell her if they wanted more. It was amazing. She behaved as though nothing had happened. She simply wouldn't talk about it. I couldn't get through to her." He paused. "That was about five weeks ago. I was shit-scared about the missing pages from the file, but as each day passed and nothing was said, I began to relax. Then, about ten days ago, everything went wrong."

"How?"

"Quentin called me to his office, and asked me to do a job in Northern Ireland. It involved contacting . . ." He hesitated. "That part doesn't matter. I had to be away for four or five days, depending on the situation when I got there. I wasn't very happy with the idea. I didn't want to leave Danuta, but I couldn't tell Quentin that, so I said I'd leave the next morning. As soon as I could get out of the office, I found a public phone and called her. I never rang from within the Department." He was silent.

"What happened?"

"She'd gone. I called her extension at the Trade section, and another woman answered. When I asked for Danuta, she said she didn't work there. I asked what that meant, and had she been transferred to another section. After a long wait, a man came on the line. He said Danuta was no longer at the Embassy, and that he'd be pleased to help me. He started to ask all sorts of questions—who I was and why I wanted to speak to her—so I hung up. God, it felt as though my whole world had collapsed! I took a taxi to Earl's Court. I had a key to her room." He closed his eyes. "There was nothing."

"What do you mean?"

"The room was empty. All her things had been removed. It was as though she'd never lived there. I thought I was going mad! I had no idea how or where to start looking for her. I didn't even know her family's address in Poland. I haven't heard from her since." He seemed to withdraw into himself.

"Has anyone from the Polish Embassy tried to contact you?"

"No, I don't think so. I don't know. I left for Ireland the next day. They wouldn't have known where to find me. I haven't been back to my flat."

"Why not?"

"Because, a couple of days after I arrived in Belfast, the shit hit the fan."

"The missing pages from the file?"

He nodded. "Quentin called me. He was very friendly when he came on the line. God! You should always be wary of that man when he's pleasant. He wanted to know how things were going and whether I'd been in touch with the people he'd sent me to see. I was noncommittal. Then he asked whether I could come back earlier, because something else had come up. I told him I might need more time, and he started to get ratty. By the time we finished, he was snapping instructions, and told me to report back within twenty-four hours."

"Did he mention the file?"

"No, but I decided to take a few precautions. I called Jock Fraser in my office, and told him I'd just had a bollocking from Quentin. I asked him whether he knew why he was in such a bloody mood." He looked at Mark. "According to Jock, the gossip was that Quentin had found a mole in the organization. Fraser didn't know much about it, but he was irritated because Quentin had put a hold on all the files in one section and was having them checked." He gave a wry smile. "The file I used was in that section."

"What did you do?"

"Panicked. Christ! You'd think that, after all these years, I wouldn't lose my nerve. I was going crazy, trying to learn what had happened to Danuta and what to do about it, and now it was only a matter of time before Quentin and internal security caught up with me." Mark nodded silently, to avoid interrupting. "I dropped out of sight. I cashed a large cheque and told the Belfast office I was going South under cover. Then I boarded the night ferry to Liverpool. I don't think they spotted me. I took the train back to London and picked up my car. I keep it in a lock-up a few streets away from my flat."

"And the flat is being watched?"

He nodded. "Thank God I was careful! There were two of Quentin's heavies watching the front of the house, and a third at the back. I phoned Quentin from a call box and told him I was in Dublin, but I don't think he was convinced. Three hours later, I spotted the security men still waiting at the flat. Since then, I've been on the move. I stayed at a couple of cheap hotels for several days, but my money started to run out. I told you, I'd just about decided to pack it in, when I saw the Covent Garden sign and remembered the piece about you and Cavalcanti."

Mark lit a cigarette slowly, using the time to think. "Suppose I decide to help you, what are you going to do?"

"Get out of England. I've got a little money stashed away in . . ." He checked himself. "I did a little buying and selling over the years; nothing very illegal, but it seemed a shame not to take advantage of the situation, especially when the government was hanging on to most of my income here."

"How long will that last?"

He shrugged. "Not long, but maybe enough time for you to come up with something that will help me. Cavalcanti doesn't know your background, which could make him careless. I'll call Quentin once I'm out of here, and tell him the whole story. I doubt whether it will make any difference, but it might offer a few extenuating circumstances. If we can actually pin down Cavalcanti or Alessandro he might make a deal. He's senior enough to drop charges and let me resign. I'll lose my pension, but it's better than the alternative." He watched Mark. "Will you help?"

"I'll think about it. I have to be with Cavalcanti and Alessandro for the next few weeks, not that it means much."

"But that's perfect! At least you can keep an eye on them while I start digging. There's one other person that I have to talk to here who could give me a lead, but I don't think I'll learn very much. After that, I have to start looking for Danuta."

"How will you go about that?"

"I don't know. Call the Embassy again; tell them I'm a friend of hers. It's worth a try, isn't it?"

"I'm not sure. If everything you say about her is true, you may find the Poles are after you, too."

"What do you mean?"

"They could have been using her to put the screws on you. She could have been telling the truth all along. It's sometimes easier to blackmail you than to depend on your emotional attachment to her. For all you know, her room was bugged, or you were photographed with her at the Festival Hall. Once they've set you up, it's simpler to get her out of the way, willingly or otherwise, and put the pressure directly on you."

"Which means that she is innocent." His voice was impassioned. "I've got to find her!"

"I'm only guessing. Don't jump to conclusions."

"But you will help?"

"I'll keep my eyes and ears open. I can't guarantee more than that."

"It's all I'm asking for." He looked at his watch. "I'll call you later today and tell you what I've learned."

"How are you going to leave the country?"

"I've worked out a route. When I'm ready to go, I'll use my cash card one last time, and make a bolt for it. I'll tell you before I do. After that, I'll contact you in Switzerland." He hesitated, glancing towards the woman serving at the counter. "I'm afraid I didn't pay for my coffee."

"Don't worry." Mark stood. "When will you call?"

"Sometime this afternoon. Will you be at your hotel?"

"Probably. I have to talk to my office."

"Good. If you're not there, I'll leave a message." He looked embarrassed. "I suppose you couldn't lend me a fiver, could you? I'm almost out. I'll send it back when I get to . . ." He hesitated. "When I'm out of here."

"All right." He handed Rossiter the money, then walked over to the counter to pay.

When Mark turned back, the table at which they had been sitting was unoccupied. Rossiter had gone. The door to the street was slowly swinging shut. Mark walked over to the window. The pavement outside was now crowded with commuters hurrying to work. In the bright morning sunshine, there was no sign of a man in a shabby raincoat.

FOUR

"BLOODY TYPICAL!" Joshua Levin stared morosely out of the window of his office. "He asks for a special early meeting and then doesn't show up. Why do film producers think the whole world revolves around their personal needs?"

Diana came into the room carrying two mugs of coffee. "Wolfgang just called, to say he's been delayed. It was something to do with a problem in his Frankfurt office. He says he's very sorry and will be here as soon as he can." She handed one mug to Mark and placed the other on Levin's cluttered desk.

"Marvellous! Meanwhile, we sit here and twiddle our thumbs. Oh well, they also serve who only stand and wait, I suppose. If it's not Frankfurt, it's New York." He relapsed into moody silence.

Diana grinned at the record producer, who was slouched in his chair, his feet on the desk. "You're not standing, and Wolfgang was very correctly polite, which is more than you can say for our distinguished leaders in the Big Apple. Anyway, we can use the time to sort out a few details before he arrives." She turned to Mark. "Has your office arranged any hotels in Geneva?"

"Yes. Rudi will telex all the details in the next few days. He's super-efficient. I understand he's made a deal with the Hilton at special rates for the whole period. It's a pleasant walk from there to the hall, and I live just round the corner, if anyone needs a lift."

She grimaced. "I can't really imagine the great Alessandro walking any-where. It's bad for his image, let alone his big flat feet. What about Bianca Morini?"

"She'll have her own car and driver." Mark smiled. "The last time, it was a white Rolls-Royce."

Joshua looked up. "Christ! New York will shit a brick!"

"Don't worry, she won't charge you. It's one of the little comforts Ettore likes to provide wherever she goes. Does New York give you a hard time? American companies are usually rather lavish."

Joshua exchanged glances with Diana. "They question every bloody penny we spend, unless they're in town. Then the sky's the limit, as long as we remember to pick up the tab. Greg Laufer's one of the last great spenders, provided it's someone else's money. He fancies himself as an expert on wine these days, and his last visit put paid to half my entertain-ment budget. I take it you know our delightful vice president?"

"All too well, unfortunately. We've had frequent dealings." Laufer, in charge of International Artists and Repertoire for Magnum Records, was a familiar figure in the record world if only because his lack of musical knowl-edge, tactless comments and tasteless behaviour were the subjects of innu-merable humourous anecdotes. "On the other hand, I think I prefer deal-ing with him rather than his awful vice president for business affairs."

"Larry Austerklein? He's not so bad, as long as he's not making a deal. He just can't resist the challenge of trying to rip off everyone in sight. It goes with being a New York lawyer."

Diana laughed. "What a charming couple! As a newcomer to the organization, I can't wait to meet them!"

"I'm not exaggerating, believe me." Levin sipped his coffee. "I don't even mind Laufer's dreadful shirts, with the ties that run off two number eight batteries. It's the man's arrogance that gets me: all those lectures on something he just read in a book." He sighed. "At the moment, he's the world's foremost authority on opera, God help us! I'll swear he reads the names up in Kobbé before each meeting, so that he can sound like an expert. Just don't carry the conversation beyond that, although he's very good at covering up with the latest show-biz buzzword. Our Gregory doesn't like competition."

Mark nodded. "But he's very successful. After all, Magnum Records is a major company, with probably the best international distribution."

Levin scowled. "But what do we distribute these days? Pop records masquerading as classical: New Age music, tenors singing rock 'n' roll, jazz musicians playing scrambled classics. Half our activities are concentrated on the bloody crossover market."

"They sell. Mr. Laufer can cry all the way to to the bank."

"I suppose so, but in ten years' time we'll have a catalogue filled with obsolete trendies that nobody wants, instead of a lasting collection that people will return to again and again. You know, it used to be that the classical department was the poor relation of the company. Now, the classical record—I mean the real classical record—is in danger of being the poor relation of the classical department."

"It's not as bad as that, Josh." Diana patted him on the shoulder. "You're about to produce a new *Tosca*, aren't you?"

The producer grunted. "Only because the latest toy is a video disc, and Greg Laufer can make a cheap deal with Wolfgang."

"Why cheap?"

"Because Wiesman must have a soundtrack for his film. Why do you think Greg's so interested? It means that he can have a complete *Tosca* and bargain for the home video rights. He can't lose. For the past five years, he's only been prepared to make an opera if somebody else puts up the money. He doesn't want to invest Magnum money."

Mark lit a cigarette. "I would have thought it suited both sides. You get your opera, and Wolfgang gets his film."

"Perhaps. I'm not happy about Simon Vincent. He's already spoiling for a fight. If I'm going to make a decent recording, I can't have him interfering every five minutes."

Diana laughed. "I wouldn't worry too much on that account. Signor

Alessandro made it very clear that he's not too bothered by anything Vincent has to say. Mark and I walked in on a lively little discussion in his dressing room last night, while you were dazzling Miss America."

Levin remained unconvinced. "I hope you're right. As far as I'm concerned, the future's not very bright. The final decisions on casting will be left to the film people and, if we're not careful, interpretation will be decided by directors and cameramen. We're losing control." He turned to Mark. "I miss the old days, when all we had to do was go after a great performance, no matter what it cost."

"Of course, but in those days, it didn't cost very much."

"Not necessarily. It's all relative. The people at the top believed in what we were doing. Now, I have to fight for every bloody session, with New York breathing down my neck, questioning every item. We just don't speak the same language. I'm a producer, for God's sake, not an accountant! To hear them talk, you'd think I was supposed to make music by the yard, like a sausage machine!"

"You sound very disenchanted."

"Not really. It's fine, once we get started. They don't know enough about it to interfere. I just can't be bothered with all the red tape." He shook his head slowly. "We're coming to the end of an era, in the same way that the great film studios in Hollywood did. It's even worse in the pop field. They don't have A and R men anymore; just a bunch of lawyers who buy tapes from outside producers. They wouldn't know whether the music was good or not. The marketing and promotion people decide that for them. Nobody inside the company wants to know about music, except when it affects the bloody bottom line. They wouldn't recognize a good song if they tripped over it!"

Diana smiled. "Oh Lord! Somebody's in a filthy mood today. I wonder if it could be anything to do with a hangover from too much wine last night!"

"Piss off!" Levin smiled at her as he said it. "I just wish you could have seen the industry as it was when I first came into it. That was almost before you were born! We used to have such fun. Now, we spend our time watching clocks like a bunch of bloody civil servants. Anyway, there's no need to be so smug just because you only drink Perrier."

"I happen to prefer it, especially when I see what alcohol does to some of us the morning after. Drink your coffee." She turned to Mark. "I'm still trying to remember where I saw that man before."

"Which one?"

"The man who was talking to you at the bar in the opera house. I'm sure I recognized him."

Mark kept his voice neutral. "You've probably seen him before at a concert or an opera. After a while, the faces of strangers start to look familiar, because they're regulars like yourself. It's always happening to me."

"I suppose so. Did he tell you his name?"

Mark frowned, as though trying to remember. "Ross, or maybe Rossiter —something like that. I'm terrible with names. I shall have to develop Craig Layton's habit of repeating them when I'm introduced."

Levin rose from his chair and paced across the room. "Where the bloody hell is the man? I've got a busy day ahead, and I can't sit around here waiting for him to honour us with his presence."

As if in reply to his question, there was a knock on the door, and a secretary ushered in the film producer and his public relations man. Wiesman was dressed in a double-breasted blazer and grey slacks. His Gucci tie exactly matched the colour of the jacket.

"My dear fellow, I'm most frightfully sorry to keep you waiting." The room was suddenly filled with the aroma of his after-shave. "There was a minor crisis in my Frankfurt office, and they wouldn't let me go." Without waiting for Levin to speak, he turned to Diana. "Do you think Craig could send a couple of telexes? We've only just finished drafting them, and I didn't want to waste time at the hotel." He smiled disarmingly.

"Certainly." She gestured towards the anteroom. "If you'd like to give them to my secretary, she'll send them." The American departed, and Mark could hear him greeting the girl in the outer office with richly modulated tones.

Wiesman concentrated his attention on several framed record awards on the wall of the office. He smiled at Levin. "I see you have a large collection of trophies."

Joshua shrugged. "They're always handing those things out." He looked pleased, nevertheless.

"Let's hope you will add *Tosca* to them. With a team like the one I have assembled, it shouldn't be so difficult. I think I've picked you a winner."

The record producer exchanged a dark glance with Mark. "I would have said it was a joint effort. Most of the artists were recommended by us."

"Of course." Wiesman smiled again. "Speaking of joint efforts, that's one of the reasons why I wanted to talk to you this morning. My budget is running dangerously high. I mean, it's wonderful to have such a hand-picked cast, but it's also extremely expensive. I'm not happy with the contract from New York."

"Why is that?"

Wiesman settled himself in an armchair. "I'm working on a budget of four million dollars, not allowing for overage. Now, your Mr. Laufer agreed to put up an advance of three hundred thousand for the home video rights, but he wants to deduct the cost of making the recording from the advance."

"That sounds about right."

"Perhaps, but according to a letter I received this morning, the taping will cost that amount, which means that I am giving him the home video rights for nothing. So instead of an advance, I will receive no money at all, and he won't pay any royalties on video sales until he has recouped his entire investment, irrespective of what he receives from normal record sales. That doesn't seem right."

"You'll be getting a free soundtrack."

Wiesman laughed uneasily. "No, I won't. It's costing me three hundred thousand." He turned to Mark. "I was counting on most of that money as part of my budget. Now it appears that I'll receive none of it, even though I'm paying out an additional fortune to the cast for filming."

Levin ran a hand through his curly dark hair. "I'm afraid I don't know anything about the deal with New York. I wasn't involved."

"Can't you discuss it with them?"

"They wouldn't listen to me. I'm only involved with producing the tapes."

"Yes, I understand." Wiesman looked perplexed. "My problem is that I'm now short by at least two hundred thousand. I was given to understand that Magnum was paying that up front. At the time I reached an agreement with Mr. Laufer and Mr. Austerklein, they indicated that the recording would be in the region of one hundred thousand." Levin's eyebrows were raised, but he said nothing. "What would happen if I cancelled the project?"

There was an uneasy silence. Joshua cleared his throat. "I assume that New York would have to decide whether it wants to make the recording. You'd have to ask them."

Wiesman shook his head. "To be honest, we're too far into it to do anything as drastic as that. I have signed contracts with cancellation clauses. I can't afford not to go ahead. Laufer seems to have waited until the last moment to tell me that the recording costs are now three times his original prediction."

"Have you signed the contract with him?"

"Not yet." He sighed. "I'll have to fly to New York tomorrow and see whether I can adjust the terms. In the meantime, you should continue as

planned. We have another problem to resolve. Alessandro informed me last
night that he won't be available for two days of the first week in Geneva."

Joshua stood. "That's impossible! The sessions have been arranged
around him. I can't change the schedule now."

"I'm afraid you'll have to. He insists that he has to go to Budapest to
pick up some sort of Liszt award. He made a recording—"

"But that's ridiculous! Anyone who records anything by Liszt gets one of
those." He pointed to two framed diplomas on the wall. "They hand those
things out like toilet paper! He can't just walk out like that." He turned to
Diana. "What do we do now?"

"You'd better let me have a look at the schedule and see if we can work
around it." She remained calm. "If he stays an extra day or two, we can
probably catch up. It's a nuisance."

"It's a bloody disgrace! How can he do that sort of thing, and all for
some lousy Hungarian award?"

Diana sat on the edge of a chair. "He's probably paying off an old debt.
He made his first recordings in Budapest."

Mark looked up. "Really?"

She nodded. "The Hungaroton people gave him his start. They told me
about it the last time I was there."

"In Budapest?"

"Yes. I used to work for a public relations agency that handled publicity
for a number of Eastern European artists, including several Hungarians.
They invited me over to attend some recording sessions. As a matter of
fact, that's how I came to meet Josh. He was visiting at the same time, and
we met at the studio. What a lovely city. I had the most beautiful room in
the Intercontinental, overlooking the Danube."

Wiesman smiled. "You should have stayed at the Hilton. It's supposed to
be the best in Europe. When I think about it now, I'm sorry we didn't
decide to record our soundtrack there. It would have cost us a great deal
less." He looked at his watch. "I'll have to leave shortly, if I'm going to
catch my plane. While I'm gone, do you think you could arrange planning
meetings with Alessandro, Cavalcanti and Simon Vincent? I would like
everything to be agreed and prepared before they arrive in Geneva."

Diana wrote on a notepad. "I'll see what I can do. I don't know whether
Simon and Signor Alessandro are on speaking terms at the moment. Perhaps we should arrange for Alessandro and Cavalcanti to meet first, and
bring Simon in later."

"Whatever you think is appropriate."

Levin returned to his desk. "I won't join them at this point. They may as well sort out their problems first. I would have thought they'd already done that during the performances." He glared at Wiesman, as though blaming the film producer for Alessandro's intended absence. "Anyway, I've got too many other people to see before we leave. Graham Budd needs to discuss the setup."

"Who is he?"

"The sound engineer. We have to work out how to fit everyone on the stage. It involves building an apron out over the first ten rows of seats, but he's worried about accommodating the chorus as well."

Wiesman looked puzzled. "If the stage is not big enough, why are we recording there?"

"Because Victoria Hall is one of the finest recording locations in Europe. It has the best acoustics, but it's cramped for space. We're used to extending the stage there."

"That must be expensive."

"It is, but we have no choice. We managed to block off a long period for the sessions, but we still have to take the apron down and reassemble it again. There were a couple of concerts that had been booked before we reserved the time. Do you want to see Diana's schedule of sessions?"

"Not really. I would not make head nor tail of them, but I would be grateful if you would send copies to Frankfurt." He frowned. "It's a nuisance. I was hoping to spend the next few days in Frankfurt before going on to Geneva. Now I'll have to divide my time between there and New York. I have half a dozen irons in the fire at the moment."

"Really? I would have thought that *Tosca* was enough of a handful."

"Not at all. If you want to stay alive in the film business, you have to keep any number of productions going at the same time. It takes anything up to three years to develop a film or a television programme, and only about one in ten gets to the point of final production." He turned to Levin. "Do you think Laufer might reconsider his offer?"

"To be honest, no. He takes pride in being a hardheaded businessman." The record producer hesitated. "You've probably thought about this already, but it would be advisable to insist on an accurate costing for the recording. Three hundred thousand sounds a little high to me. I would have estimated closer to two, especially as the leads will be receiving advances against future royalties, so their fees can't be charged against you." Levin stared out of the window. "I'd be grateful if you wouldn't mind not mentioning that I suggested it."

Wiesman nodded silently. Then he rose from his chair. "I'd better leave if I'm going to make that Frankfurt flight."

Diana said, "Can I call a cab?"

"No, thank you. My driver's waiting downstairs." He shook hands with each of them and departed.

When he had gone, Joshua smiled. "Poor fellow. His financial problems seem to have reduced him to his last chauffeur!"

Katya Philips drove Mark to a small Italian restaurant on Walton Street, leaving her car parked on a yellow line.

"I always leave my press card in the window."

"Does it work?"

She laughed. "No."

She was dressed in a severely cut tailored suit with fashionably padded shoulders that were only slightly less exaggerated than an American football player's. It also emphasized her slim, athletic body and long legs. Crossing the street, she clung to his arm possessively.

The headwaiter treated Katya like a very distinguished guest and led them to a reserved table at the back.

"I do hope you're going to have a drink. The current vogue for mineral water strikes me as a little too austere. Or shall we order wine straight-away?" She beckoned to a waiter without waiting for Mark's reply. "By one o'clock, I need something a little stronger than Perrier."

"Pressure of work?"

"Not enough sleep. I don't normally go to those dreary receptions, but I wanted to meet Antonio Alessandro before he starts the recording. He interests me."

"As part of your background research on Bianca?"

"Not entirely, although it will be amusing to hear his side of that old fight story." She leaned forward, placing her hand on Mark's. "I spent this morning talking to a colleague in Milan. According to him, there's more to Signor Alessandro than meets the eye. He appears to have some rather unsavoury associations."

"I don't know very much about him, except that he's become one of the world's greatest tenors. Our paths haven't crossed very often."

"From what I hear, Alessandro wouldn't be the best person to cross, one way or the other." She lowered her voice. "According to my friend, he hangs out with some very questionable characters of Sicilian descent."

Mark smiled. "The Mafia? I wonder if that's really true. People are inclined to assume that every successful Italian has connections with the syndicate."

"Perhaps, but his career was sponsored by a wealthy patron from

Palermo, and he makes regular visits there between engagements. It's an interesting thought."

Mark laughed. "People get carried away. I sometimes have the impression that every Sicilian carries a *lupa* in one hand and a copy of *The Godfather* in the other. There must be one or two who earn an honest living. Besides, I heard this morning that the Hungarians started him on his recording career. He made his first records in Budapest."

"Really? Why would he go to Eastern Europe?"

"I don't know." Mark was thoughtful. "They must have asked him first. When it comes to his underworld connections, are you sure you're not just intrigued by the prospect of a good story?"

Katya settled back in her chair. "You could be right. I'm a newspaper-woman at heart, despite last night's outburst, for which I apologize again. I think it's a reaction to London's musical life."

"I thought you were extolling its virtues yesterday, when you were asking me why I should live in a village like Geneva."

"Oh, London's all right. It's probably the centre of the musical world, if such a thing exists. It's just the English who irritate me, with their everlasting patriotism. I can't stand the way they become watery-eyed every time someone mentions Elgar or Benjamin Britten. Let's face it. They wrote some good pieces, but they hardly stand up to their more distinguished contemporaries. I once wrote an article saying that the last truly great British composer was Purcell and that it was about time we stopped lionizing every local hero. You should have seen the number of letters I received from Disgusted of Tunbridge Wells. Anyone would think I'd suggested incest in the royal family!"

"At least you provoked a few readers."

"I suppose so." She watched him in silence for a moment, employing her trick of concentrating her gaze. "What about Bianca Morini? Are you going to give me a few provocative tidbits about her?"

"No. She'll probably do that herself."

She pretended to pout. "That's not very chivalrous. Have you known her for a long time?"

"Five or six years. I was lucky. My partner Abe in New York took a chance when he passed her on to me. She could have chosen any manager she wanted."

"But she asked for you." Katya smiled. "I wonder why."

"Because Abe recommended me, and she trusts his judgement. He's managed her for fifteen years, almost from the beginning of her career."

"And it was nothing to do with being a tall, handsome Englishman?"

"No. Besides, Bianca can select any number of them, too, if she feels like it."

"She still chose you. How well do you know her?"

Mark shrugged. "She's a good friend. We talk at least once a week; otherwise, she thinks I'm neglecting her. She's also a great artist and a complete professional in everything she does. I think you'll understand that better when you meet her and see her in action."

Katya's gaze was unblinking. "How good a friend?"

Mark smiled. "I think your journalist's instinct is getting the better of you again. If there was anything between us, you wouldn't expect me to tell you, would you?"

"You never know. Men can be very vain sometimes." She returned his smile, revealing very even white teeth. "It was worth a try. Weren't you ever tempted?"

Mark did not reply immediately. There had been a time, a few years earlier, but that was long past, even though Bianca occasionally suggested reviving old passions. "What else would you like to know about her?"

"Oh, the usual sorts of things, I suppose, unless you're going to reward me with one juicy item." Mark shook his head. "I think I told you, I'm a little nervous of meeting her. Coming face to face with a legend—especially a beautiful one—makes me uneasy. Why don't we order our lunch."

The food was good, and Katya proved to be both charming and witty. After a few further questions about Bianca, she seemed to lose interest, and talked instead about London life, colouring the conversation with funny anecdotes and astute observations. She was intelligent and amusing, and Mark enjoyed the virtuosity of her conversation. It was easy to understand why a younger woman like Diana found her so formidable. The time passed quickly.

As she drove him back to the hotel, Katya glanced at Mark through half-closed eyes. "I must congratulate you."

"Why?"

"We've spent the last two and a half hours together and, in the nicest possible way, you've avoided telling me anything, either about yourself or about La Morini. I have the feeling that you'd make a very good friend. For one thing, I'd know that if I had any secrets, they'd be safe with you. That's a compliment, by the way."

"Thank you. Actually, I was having too much fun being entertained by you. It wasn't deliberate on my part. For all I know, I gave away a dozen sacred confessions."

"Not one. I'm glad we had this opportunity to talk. I thought you were going to turn me down when I suggested lunch."

"Why so?"

"My damned job. Unfortunately, my reputation sometimes precedes me. You'd be surprised how many beautiful friendships find themselves nipped in the bud because my new acquaintances get cold feet. It's rather depressing."

"I'm sorry."

"It's my own fault. I can't resist a good story. If you want to know the truth, some of it's bravado. Most of the time, I'm more than a little bit insecure. Anyway, thank you for being such an attentive listener." She drove in silence.

At the entrance to the Westbury, she parked the car in a small space between two Mercedeses with Middle Eastern number plates. The doorman eyed her disdainfully. "The trouble with Italian food is that it makes me sleepy."

"Especially when you wash it down with good wine. Thank you. I enjoyed it very much."

Katya stretched sensuously, and the car's safety belt, drawn tightly across her body, emphasized the curves of her breasts. "It feels like a good time to take a little siesta." Her eyes met Mark's and he was again conscious of her unwavering stare. "What do you think?"

"I wish I could, but I have a list of calls to make that will take me halfway through the night."

Her voice was soft. "What a shame. I hate to leave, but I'd better get back to my steaming typewriter. When are you leaving London?"

"Tomorrow."

"Then we'll have to catch up in Switzerland."

"I'll look forward to it."

"I'll call you when I get in." She leaned her cheek against his for a moment, then busied herself with starting the car. "You'll have to show me all round Geneva."

"With pleasure." Mark laughed. "And in the afternoon, we'll find somewhere else!"

The concierge in the Westbury seemed disappointed to report that there were no telephone messages, and Mark went up to his room. Apparently, Rossiter had not called back. He phoned his Geneva office and asked for Rudi.

"Mr. Holland, I am so glad that you have called!" For a moment, Mark had the impression that, when he came on the line, Rudi stood to attention, clicking his heels. There was something ruthlessly correct about everything he did. "Madame Morini phoned from New York a few minutes ago. She wondered why she hadn't heard from you."

"I was planning to ring her this afternoon. Is anything the matter?"

"She did not mention anything, but she said she was anxious to speak to you."

"All right. Are there any other messages?"

"One or two, but they can wait until you return tomorrow. I will of course meet you at the airport."

"You don't have to bother."

"It is my pleasure." As the senior member of Mark's small staff, Rudi considered the chore a privilege to which he was entitled. "I have the details of your flight."

"Fine." Mark knew that Rudi would be waiting at the arrivals door, almost at attention, with a file of papers, neatly arranged, for him to read in the back seat of the car while Rudi drove at a stately twenty miles an hour, meticulously observing all the traffic regulations. He preferred the local taxi drivers, most of whom raced into town ignoring all the rules. It was the only time the Swiss seemed to lose their traditional sense of decorum.

As if reading Mark's thoughts, Rudi added, "I have put together the most important correspondence in a file for you to have a look through on our way into town."

"Good. The people from Magnum Records were asking me whether you've managed to look after the hotel reservations."

"Of course." Rudi sounded surprised. "I have prepared a special schedule, listing all the arrival and departure times. Frau Emmi is typing it for me now, and I will send a fax this afternoon."

"Thank you." If Mark knew Rudi, he had probably listed the numbers of the rooms. "We may have to make a few changes. I understand Alessandro intends to make a side trip during the first week."

"I will make a note of it as soon as I have all the details." Rudi clicked his tongue disapprovingly. "Miss Nightingale will have to rearrange the recording schedule."

"Yes. She's already doing it. There is one other thing I'd like you to look after. Can you have a look at Emilio Cavalcanti's biography and see if it needs bringing up to date?"

"Cavalcanti? I prepared one only a few weeks ago."

"I know, but the film people are hoping we can prepare something a little more extensive about him. You know how they like to go into every detail, from his childhood onwards. By the time the film is released, Craig

Layton—Wiesman's PR man from New York—will want to produce a whole book of information. Do you know anyone who can give us some more detailed background?"

"I'm not sure. Let me look in the file." There was a pause while Rudi made his search. "I seem to remember talking to a man from Rome about the maestro. He worked for one of the newspapers. I remember because, at the time, he hinted that he had information about the conductor that was not generally known."

"Really?" Mark sat forward. "That's interesting."

"I am not so sure. I rather ignored his comments. He seemed to be suggesting that I should pay him for the information. You know what Italian journalists are like." Rudi's disapproval was apparent. "Would you want me to call him?"

"Yes, I think you should. We might even see how much money he wants."

"You think we should pay him?" Rudi was shocked.

"It might be a good idea. If we're going to be working regularly with Cavalcanti over the next few years, I would like to know everything about him, including any less favourable stories."

"Why?"

"For his protection. It's probably nothing more than some minor affair with a woman."

"Perhaps. The man seemed to be suggesting something of a political nature." Though reassured, Rudi was unconvinced.

"Then there's all the more reason to find out what he's selling. If we're going to look after Cavalcanti properly, I'd sooner not have to deal with unexpected surprises."

"Yes, of course."

"Give him a call and see what you can find out. After all, if it's nonsense, we'll know how to deal with it."

"Very well. I'll try to reach him this afternoon."

"Thank you, Rudi. I'll see you at the airport tomorrow." Mark pressed down on the telephone receiver, severing the connection. No doubt, Rudi's expression at the other end suggested that he had just encountered an unpleasant smell.

Mark checked in his address book for Bianca's latest New York telephone number. Like so many successful artists, she was forced to change her unlisted number frequently because it became known by too many people. It was a constant game of hide-and-seek between the famous and those seeking them out.

He was about to lift the receiver again when the phone rang. A woman's voice spoke. "Mr. Mark Holland?"

"Yes."

"Hold the line, please." She was gone before he could ask who was calling.

After a moment, a man spoke. His voice was vaguely familiar, but Mark could not immediately place it. "Mark?"

"Yes."

"You do have an uncanny knack for showing up at the oddest times." The man chuckled softly.

"Oh?"

"I'm very curious to know what brings you to London."

Mark frowned, feeling slightly irritated. "I'm afraid you have me at a disadvantage. Your secretary, if that's who she was, didn't tell me who was calling."

"And you don't recognize my voice?" His tone was almost bantering.

"No." He knew the voice, but he could not identify the caller.

"I'm disappointed." There was a pause. "This is Quentin."

A pulse seemed to be beating in Mark's temple. "Quentin Sharpe?"

"That's right. I'd prefer to stick to first names, if it's all the same with you."

"Why are you calling?"

"I told you. I want to know why you're here."

For a moment, Mark felt a surge of anger, but he controlled his voice. "My work. One of my conductors has been appearing at Covent Garden. I came over to hear him."

"I see. Is that all?"

"Well, there have been some meetings about a film he's going to make. Why the questions? In fact, why the call?"

"Perhaps I'd better come over and tell you about it. It's not the sort of thing I'm anxious to discuss on the phone. Do you think you could stay at the hotel for the next half hour or so?"

"If necessary. Would you mind telling me what it's about?"

Quentin's voice was casual. "It involves a fellow called Tony Rossiter. Do you remember him?"

Mark hesitated. "Rossiter? I'm not sure. The name rings a bell. It's been a long time. I seem to remember a man called Rossiter who had something to do with Scandinavia. I can't say that I recall anything more than that. Is he the one?"

"Yes." Sharpe did not add anything.

"I doubt whether I can offer very much more than that. I don't really remember him."

"That's funny. He seems to remember you."

"How is that?"

"He has a piece of paper with your name and hotel telephone number written on it. What do you make of that?"

"I'm not sure."

"Perhaps we can talk about it when I see you."

"If you want to know, why don't you ask Rossiter?"

"That would be a little difficult, I'm afraid." Quentin sounded almost cheerful. "You see, he's dead."

"What?"

"Somebody killed him: shot him through the heart at quite close range, as I understand it. It happened outside a pub in Bruton Mews. That's just around the corner from your hotel, isn't it?"

"Yes."

"Then I think you can understand why we're curious about that piece of paper in his pocket." Mark did not reply. "You'd better wait in your room until I arrive."

Before Mark could reply, Quentin had hung up.

FIVE

QUENTIN SHARPE had been a handsome, almost effeminately pretty young man: pale-skinned with chiselled features, wide-set eyes and a sensual mouth. He had not aged well. Mark suspected that too many sunless hours behind a desk, working under pressure, were the cause of his sallow complexion and the dark patches under his eyes. His receding hairline, tinged with grey, suggested premature middle age, and the lines on his face cut deeply into the sides of his nose and mouth, giving him a permanent expression of disillusionment. He was dressed in a charcoal-grey suit, which added to his generally sombre appearance.

He nodded curtly to Mark as he entered the room and walked across to the telephone, where he dialled a number. After a moment, he spoke into the receiver. "I'm in his room at the Westbury. . . . I don't know. . . . It depends on what he has to say for himself. . . . I should be back within the hour." Quentin glanced at Mark, his face expressionless. "He may come back with me, in which case you know the procedure." He replaced the receiver without speaking further.

Mark lit a cigarette. "If that little speech was intended to make me feel nervous, it didn't work. What do you want, Quentin?"

Sharpe settled himself into an armchair. "I would have thought that was patently obvious." He tried to smile. "What the hell are you up to?"

"Not a damn thing."

"You don't expect me to believe that."

"I don't really care, one way or the other. I didn't invite you, and I'm no longer involved with you or your organization. That ended a long time ago."

"Oh?" Quentin's eyes narrowed. "I'll need some better answers than that. As for your invitation, I would prefer to think that you were simply being cooperative on a matter of national security."

"Bullshit!"

"Spare me the schoolboy language, Mark. You have some explaining to do. A murdered man—someone you haven't seen in more than ten years—has your name and telephone number on a scrap of paper in his pocket. Why? He died within a hundred yards of this hotel. What do you know about that?"

"I don't know the answers to either question."

Quentin gestured irritably. "Let's not waste each other's time. What was your connection with Rossiter?"

"I didn't have one."

"Your name and number didn't get there by accident, for God's sake."

"I didn't put them there. If there was a connection between us, Rossiter made it."

"Very well." Quentin took a deep breath, showing exaggerated patience. "Perhaps you had better start by telling me where you were at two-thirty this afternoon."

"I was having lunch at an Italian restaurant in Kensington with a music journalist called Katya Philips. She drove me back here at about three o'clock. She can confirm that; so can the doorman and the concierge downstairs. I assume from your reference to national security that Rossiter was still working for you?" Quentin nodded. "Then you know more about his activities than I do."

"That remains to be seen. When did you speak to him?"

Mark hesitated. Quentin's men could easily check the hotel operator for phone messages. He wondered whether they kept a record of them once they had been delivered. At length, he said, "What makes you think I did? I want to know a little more before you cross-examine me any further. Exactly what happened to Rossiter?"

"I've already told you. Somebody murdered him outside a pub in Bruton Mews sometime after two this afternoon."

"In broad daylight?"

Quentin nodded. "It's a very popular place at lunchtime. On a sunny day like today, the patrons spill out into the street."

"Then there would have been dozens of witnesses."

"They may not have known what was going on. There's always a crowd. People stand around the mews or sit on whatever's handy. It's not a very busy back street. The mews itself mostly consists of garages and offices, but it looks vaguely quaint. Visitors like it because it has a kind of Old World air in the middle of town. A lot of tourists go there to soak up the local atmosphere. Anyway, Rossiter was found sitting on the steps of the building next door to the pub, leaning against the wall, with a tankard of beer on the ground beside him. He looked as though he was dozing in the sunlight. When the barmaid was collecting glasses at closing time, she tapped him on the shoulder, and he keeled over. You can imagine the hullabaloo that followed."

"But somebody must have seen or heard it happen."

"Not necessarily. The killer held a silenced revolver against Rossiter's body. It would have made very little noise. Any kind of distraction in the mews—a lorry trying to get through or an unusual car going past—would have given him time to pull the trigger without causing attention. We found one man who was there at the time. The only thing he could remember was that a rather flashy Ferrari drove past at one point. It was the latest model, and everyone watched it. I imagine it had one of those noisy engines that would have covered most other sounds."

"It was still a hell of a chance to take."

"Yes." Quentin was thoughtful. "It suggests that whoever did it had nerves of steel or was in a panic and had to get rid of Rossiter quickly."

"Any particular reason for that?"

"There could have been." Quentin looked up quickly. "Why do you ask that?"

"I don't know. I just have the impression that his death doesn't entirely surprise you."

Sharpe smiled coldly. "That's very astute of you. You haven't told me yet whether you spoke to Rossiter or not. Did you?"

"Yes."

"I thought as much. When?"

"Last night, and this morning."

"Well, now we're getting somewhere. I don't know why the hell you couldn't have said so in the first place." Quentin watched Mark in silence. "What did he tell you?"

"That he was on the run from you."

"I see. Did he tell you why?"

"He believed you'd caught him with his finger in the classified files. He knew his flat was being watched, and he didn't think he'd fooled you into believing that he was still in Ireland." Quentin remained silent, his eyes never leaving Mark's face. "He was preparing to duck out of the country."

"Where to?"

"He wouldn't tell me. He was going to call when he'd reached a safe place."

Quentin seemed to relax, perhaps because his curiosity was aroused. "Why did he come to you?"

"It was almost by accident. He was running out of time and money, and remembered seeing a piece about me in one of the music magazines. So he played a long shot and found me last night at Covent Garden."

"What exactly did he tell you?"

"That he'd stolen some NATO documents and passed them to the other side. He was pretty certain that you had guessed what he'd done, and was going to make a break for it before you grabbed him." Mark stared at Quentin. "He knew that he was finished if you got him first."

For a moment, Sharpe looked surprised. "You're not trying to suggest that we . . ." He laughed uneasily. "For God's sake, Mark, we wouldn't do anything as drastic or clumsy as that!"

"I suppose not. It depends on the circumstances."

"Don't be stupid. If we'd spotted Rossiter, we would have pulled him in for questioning. I need to know why he did it, and who he was working for. We're hardly going to risk the publicity by assassinating him in front of God knows how many witnesses. Why would we? Besides, if we really wanted him out of the way, there are plenty of more sophisticated means than a silenced revolver in the middle of a London street. We're not that amateur."

"That's true." Mark paused. "It was a very amateur job."

"And you know damn well that it would have made no sense for us to have done it. What are you trying to do: twist the knife in an old wound?"

Mark smiled. "Something like that. I wanted to see your reaction."

"I hope you're satisfied." Quentin watched Mark with distaste. "I always forget how much you hated us. All right, let's put a few cards on the table. How much did Rossiter tell you? Did he mention the Polish girl?"

Mark was surprised. "You knew about her?" Sharpe nodded. "Why the hell didn't you tell him? It might have saved his life."

"What the hell are you talking about?"

"Danuta. His Polish girl. She was the cause of all this."

"Are you sure?"

"Positive. Why didn't you tell him you knew about her?"

Quentin was suddenly subdued. "It didn't seem necessary. He was hardly being very discreet about her. When she moved in with him, we had a quiet talk to the Polish Embassy and suggested that it might be wiser to move her on. They agreed." He smiled briefly. "We don't spend all our time picking each other off these days. Ever since *glasnost,* our relationships have become a great deal more civilized."

"So Big Brother now wears kid gloves, and you turn the poor bastard's life upside down without even bothering to advise him. Jesus, Quentin!"

"He shouldn't have got himself involved with her in the first place. The Poles were doing us a favour when they said they'd ship her back."

"They didn't move her out immediately."

"How do you know that?"

"Rossiter told me. At first, she was supposed to leave by the end of the month, but she was then permitted to stay on for a while."

"Yes." Quentin was silent for a moment. "They asked if she might remain a few weeks longer. It was something to do with completing an assignment she'd been given. We saw no harm in it. A few weeks either way made little difference."

"Your civilized friends double-crossed you, Quentin. She fed Rossiter a story about persuading her bosses to let her stay in England because she'd made contact with a man who had access to classified information. They knew that already, but he believed it would buy her additional time in London. He was hoping to persuade her to defect. That's why he stole the papers and gave them to her."

Quentin had paled slightly. "The bloody fool! He couldn't have believed a hoary old gambit like that."

"He did. The problem was that he loved her desperately. He wanted to believe anything that might keep them together. From what he said, I think she loved him, too. It's just possible the Poles were playing them both off against each other. If it's any consolation, he was careful to steal documents of little real value. Despite the way he felt about the girl, he was trying to stay loyal."

"He should have told us. We would have helped."

"He didn't trust you, Quentin. I think I can understand that."

"Thanks. How the hell did he hope to get away with it? He left a trail a mile wide. It was almost as though the idiot was hoping to get caught."

"The xerox machine broke down. I understand it does that quite frequently. You should tell Accounting to invest in a more expensive, reliable model."

"What the hell are you talking about?"

"I'd better explain, from the beginning. You'll also understand why Rossiter got in touch with me."

Quentin suddenly grinned. "About bloody time!" When he smiled, some of his boyish good looks returned.

Mark spoke slowly, piecing the story together as Rossiter had told it that morning. Quentin listened in silence, his body immobile, as though forcing himself not to interrupt. At one point, he raised his hand.

"I don't exactly follow the part backstage at the Festival Hall. Where did the girl go, and where was Rossiter at the time?"

"She went into the conductor's dressing room and shut the door, while he waited in the corridor outside."

Quentin frowned. "I've been to the hall a few times, so I know roughly where everything is. Why didn't he wait in the greenroom at the back?"

"Presumably because the place was very crowded, and he wanted to get away as quickly as possible. Rossiter didn't like what he was doing, Quentin, but the girl meant more to him than a couple of NATO plans that would shortly become obsolete. It's always congested by the greenroom, with people trying to go in and out at the same time. He thought it would be easier to wait in the wide corridor outside, facing the other dressing rooms."

"I see. So the girl went to Cavalcanti?"

"Probably. He didn't see what happened. He thought it had to be Cavalcanti, but it might have been Alessandro. On the second visit, Alessandro followed her into Cavalcanti's room, and they were in there together for a minute or two. It occurred to Rossiter that the tenor might have been there already on the first visit, waiting for her."

"So it's got to be one or the other, or even both of them."

"Probably, but not necessarily. Those dressing rooms are often full of visitors and hangers-on; anything from friends and admirers to students and autograph hunters."

"Not to mention managers?"

"True. Alessandro's manager lives in New York, and I don't think he was there. I manage Cavalcanti, but I was in Amsterdam with Konstantin Steigel that week."

"What a pity. I might have had a reliable witness!"

"The only thing that makes it less likely for a casual visitor to have chosen the dressing room as a meeting place is that whoever met Danuta chose the same place both times. Not many outsiders would go to both performances of the *Requiem.*"

"Then we'd better stick close to our two Italians. Do you know where they're going to be for the next few weeks?"

"Yes, as a matter of fact, I do. Geneva. They're recording the soundtrack of an opera film for a German production company. Bianca Morini will be singing Tosca."

Quentin smiled. "Right on your doorstep. That's very convenient."

"Why?"

"Because you'll know exactly what's going on. You can keep an eye on both men for me. With your training and—"

Mark raised his hands. "I'm not involved in any of this."

"Oh, for God's sake, of course you are! You were the last person to talk to Rossiter. Don't you care about what happened to him?"

"In the first place, I wasn't the last. There was the man who sat next to him outside the pub and pulled the trigger."

"Man or woman."

"All right, but you know what I mean. In the second place, Rossiter meant nothing to me. I wouldn't have known him if he hadn't identified himself when we met."

"Somebody murdered him." Sharpe spoke softly.

"I've known a lot of men who have died, one way or the other, Quentin. Working at the Department gave me more than my full share. I felt sorry for the poor devil when he told me his pathetic little love story, but not sympathetic enough to want to find myself working for you again." He paused, frowning.

Quentin was watching him curiously. "What's the matter?"

"I don't know. There's something about Rossiter's story that doesn't quite fit, but I'm not sure what it is. I was mentally picturing everything as he described it, and I meant to ask him something, but it slipped my mind at the time. Now I'm damned if I can remember what it was."

"Do you want to go back over the story again?"

"No, I don't think it would help."

"Was it important?"

"I don't think so." Mark smiled. "If I could remember what it was, I'd know."

At that moment, the telephone rang. Mark made no move to answer it, and the instrument continued to sound insistently. It seemed loud in the silent room. At length, Quentin gestured irritably.

"You'd better pick that up."

"If you like." Mark waited a moment further. "The hotel will take a message, if you prefer."

"I can't stand the bloody noise. Get rid of them quickly, will you?"

Mark lifted the receiver. "Hello?"

"Marco, darling, why haven't you called me?" It was Bianca Morini, using her best reproachful voice.

"I was just about to call you, Bianca." Across the room, Quentin's eyes were raised to the ceiling with an expression of impatience. "Can I call you back in a few minutes?"

"Why don't we talk now?"

"I'm in the middle of a rather complicated meeting."

"In your bedroom?" She chuckled. "Have you got a woman, *caro?* What is she like? If you are making love, you should have asked the operator to hold all the phone calls. It can be very embarrassing. You know, I was once in a hotel in San Francisco, with this beautiful young stage director—"

"No, Bianca, it's nothing like that." Quentin looked puzzled. "We're discussing business."

She laughed. "If you say so, Marco, then I will believe you. You never discussed business in my bedroom. Do you remember that time?"

"Yes, very well."

"That was a long time ago, *caro.*" She sighed, and Mark could picture the legendary Morini bosom heaving sensuously. "Maybe too long. The next time we have to discuss my career, I think I will arrange to meet you in your room. What a lovely way to make plans! How is the opera going? Is Cavalcanti good?"

"He's excellent. I think you'll like him. He's one of those conductors who watch the stage and memorize the score." Mark was conscious that Quentin was listening attentively.

Bianca purred. "He's very handsome. I will have no difficulty remembering to keep my eyes on him. Is that stupid wife of his going to be there?"

"I don't know. Probably."

"I don't like her. She is a fat little peasant girl who pretends to be bored all the time. Her idea of an intellectual exercise is to go window-shopping for a new dress that will not fit her."

"I didn't know you'd met the Cavalcantis." Quentin was leaning forward, watching Mark's face.

"I haven't, really. He and his little sausage lady were staying at the Principe in Venezia when I was there last year. He came over to my table one afternoon when I was having coffee with Ettore. I liked him. He is very bright, and I think he has what you call a roving eye. I adore intense, passionate men."

Mark laughed. "So I've heard!"

Bianca ignored the comment. If anything, she accepted it as a compliment. "We talked for a few minutes, but the butterball lady wanted to go shopping, and kept tugging at his sleeve. I think she was becoming jealous."

"I wonder why."

"Ah, Marco." The reproach returned to her voice. "I was only flirting a little. Besides, I would not embarrass my darling Ettore. That would be in very bad taste. Now, tell me a little more about *Tosca*. Did Antonio behave himself? He can be very difficult. You had better warn him that if he so much as blinks an eye during my arias, I will use the knife on him instead of poor old Belasco. He is such a dear man! How was the American girl? I heard she has a good voice but a flat chest. Imagine Floria Tosca without a suitable *balcon!* American women spend too much of their time jogging, *caro.* They want to look like men. Italian audiences would laugh them off the stage!" Quentin was looking at his watch impatiently.

"I'll have to tell you all about it when I call back, Bianca. I'm keeping my guest waiting."

She giggled. "Is she very pretty? Just think how excited you are making her! I think maybe anticipation is more erotic than sex. Is she breathing quickly?"

"No, *he's* not, and he's growing rather impatient. Will you be there for a while?"

"I am still in bed. How long will you be?"

"About half an hour."

"Only half an hour? If that were me, *caro,* you would hardly be in your stride."

"Bianca, you're impossible! I'll call you back as soon as I can. *Ciao!*" Mark replaced the receiver.

"What did she want?"

"Nothing in particular. Whenever Bianca is left alone for more than a few minutes, she picks up the telephone and calls someone. It's a kind of therapy."

"What did she say about Cavalcanti?"

"Very little. Apparently, she met him socially last year at her hotel in Venice. They've not worked together professionally."

"Doesn't that make him an unusual choice for the film?"

"Not entirely. Films and records are put together by combining the most interesting names. Bianca and Alessandro have worked together before, of course, and Cavalcanti is the most exciting of the younger conductors. The film will be a big break for him."

Quentin settled back in his chair. "And us, I would say. I like the idea of having them all in the same place for the next few weeks. We were talking about your part of the operation."

"And I was saying I didn't have one. Look, Quentin, if you want to cover the situation, you can send one of your own people over. Why drag me in?"

"Because I don't have all the manpower in the world, or the budget, for that matter. You're right there." He raised a well-manicured hand. "Forget the speech about not being involved. You are. How did you leave things with Rossiter?"

"He was going to call me. He said he wanted to follow up another lead, and was going to make one last effort to find Danuta before leaving London. Finding her meant more to him than anything else."

"Yes." Quentin was pensive. "I wonder whether one of our Polish colleagues met him in Bruton Mews. After all, if they've already moved the girl out, they didn't expect him to supply any more information. Perhaps they were tidying up."

"The same thought occurred to me. Why choose such a risky way of doing it?"

"I don't know. Maybe he threatened to spill the beans if they didn't produce her. If he had promised to make a loud noise in the right quarters, it could have caused an embarrassing situation for them." He shook his head. "At the same time, they could have invited him to a more secluded meeting place. They could have offered to take him to meet her anywhere they chose, and . . ." He clicked his fingers softly to complete the sentence.

Mark looked at him. "When it comes down to it, Quentin, you all graduated from the same training school. I think you're right. Rossiter's death was the work of either an amateur or someone in a hell of a hurry, or both."

"So we can probably rule out the Poles. It would be a little naïve to assume they're as unprofessional as that. Who else do we look for?"

"I'm not sure."

"Wouldn't the most likely person be the courier to whom the girl handed the papers? There was no guarantee that she hadn't told Rossiter whom she was going to meet."

"Yes."

"Which brings us back to our Italian conductor." He paused for a moment. "Perhaps I should have said *your* Italian conductor, since you manage him. Is he good? I heard what you said on the telephone, but you didn't say very much about him."

"He's very good. He's still quite young, but most people feel that he's the best of his generation." Mark smiled. "I'm not trying to sell him to you!"

"But he is going to be very important for you in the next few years, let alone a lucrative income earner. I understand the top musicians earn formidable amounts these days."

"I know what you're trying to say, Quentin. You don't have to dot every bloody *i.*"

Sharpe's smile was vulpine. "Good. If nothing else, you can look on it as protecting your investment. Presumably, you'd like to prove he's innocent."

"If he is."

"You mean you're not sure?"

"I mean I don't know. My only reason to question Cavalcanti's involvement in this whole affair is a convoluted and complicated story, told to me this morning by Tony Rossiter—"

"Who had the misfortune to come to a sticky end at lunchtime." Quentin looked again at his watch and stood. "I have to go. I'm not asking you to work for us, Mark. I'm simply suggesting you keep your eyes and ears open while Cavalcanti and Alessandro are in Geneva. If anything happens, call me. Isn't that reasonable?"

"It always starts out by being eminently reasonable, Quentin!"

"I'm not proposing anything more. I give you my word. If you happen on something, just call. Don't try to sort it out by yourself." He smiled. "As you mentioned rather forcibly, you don't work for us anymore. Why don't you look on it as defending the good name of Signor Cavalcanti? In that way, you'll be working on his behalf instead of ours. Isn't that what a manager's supposed to do?"

"You have a charming way of enlisting help!"

Quentin reached into a pocket. "I'll give you my card. There's a number you can call at any time, and someone will find me almost immediately."

"I've used it before."

"I know. I must leave you. I have a little homework of my own. Officially, Rossiter was still working for us." He glanced at Mark. "We only have your word for it that he was ever a traitor. Will you call me before you leave?"

"If you wish. I'm not planning to check in at regular intervals. We're not going back to the old days, Quentin."

"Agreed." Quentin laughed. "At your age, you probably wouldn't pass the physical!"

Mark grasped the handle and pulled the door of his room open. He was confronted by a man standing directly before him, his hand raised as though about to knock on the panel. It was Emilio Cavalcanti. He seemed slightly taken aback by the force with which the door had been opened.

"Oh. Excuse me, Mr. Holland. I was just coming to see you. I hope I am not disturbing you."

For a moment, Mark was silent. Cavalcanti was close enough to have been listening behind the closed door. It was also unusual that he had not used the hotel house phone to announce his arrival. Mark hoped that his surprise was not apparent. "I was just finishing a meeting." He turned. "May I introduce Mr. Sharpe of London Arts." His eyes met Quentin's. "This is Emilio Cavalcanti."

Quentin showed no reaction. "How do you do." He held out his hand. "I believe congratulations are in order. Your *Tosca* has been a great success."

"Thank you." Cavalcanti scarcely acknowledged the compliment. He seemed distracted.

"I'm sorry I didn't have the chance to see it. Perhaps next time?" Quentin smiled politely, walking through the open doorway.

"What?" Cavalcanti looked up. "Oh yes, of course. I hope so."

"Goodbye, Mark." Quentin waved casually. "I expect we'll be in touch." He nodded to Cavalcanti and sauntered towards the lifts.

Mark turned to the conductor, who was standing at the window. "I wasn't expecting to see you."

"No. I had arranged another meeting. I tried to call you from downstairs, but your line was busy. I hope you do not mind my arriving unexpectedly like this. My reason for being here is that I am supposed to meet Antonio Alessandro. He wanted to discuss the first act."

"Are there problems with it?"

Cavalcanti smiled, but he was ill at ease. "Always problems! We never seem to hit upon the right tempi. You know, all the way through the rehearsals—and he only gave me four—he kept changing his mind. At

'*L'arte nel suo mistero,*' he asked me to make a little accelerando. The next time, he complained that I was going too fast for him. I'm sure I wasn't. Poor old Silvio, who was singing the Sagrestano, was becoming more and more confused. The same thing happened in half a dozen other places. I have never had difficulties like that before. In fact, I think he was doing it deliberately, to make me feel insecure."

"He probably was."

"It makes no sense. Anyway, I spoke to him at the party, and we arranged to meet this afternoon, to make a few decisions. It may not help, but I want to show him that I care."

"Did you bring the score?" The conductor was empty-handed.

"No, I memorized it long ago. If there are changes, I will remember them. I have lived with *Tosca* for a long time." He paced across the room. "When I arrived, I called Alessandro, but there was no reply. The concierge checked the dining room and the lounges for me, but he is not in the hotel. I don't like being treated like that. I am not a student!"

"He must have forgotten."

"The doorman said he thought he had seen him go out half an hour earlier with his lady friend. He probably took her shopping for fur coats!"

"They could be back by now. Shall I try his room?"

"No. If he cannot keep an appointment, he can wait until I am free."

"Did he behave like this last time, when you were here for the Verdi *Requiem?*"

"No, he was quite reasonable, considering the very short rehearsal time we were permitted. You know how it is with London orchestras. They give you one or two rehearsals, and still expect a polished performance. I was able to work with the choir a few times, and Alessandro came to the piano rehearsals. Of course, on that occasion, he did not have that woman with him."

"Oh?"

"His wife was there. Perhaps we should persuade her to come to the sessions in Geneva."

"I don't think I can guarantee that. We might ask Wolfgang Wiesman to extend an invitation, but he's already got enough budget problems on his mind. I have the feeling that Signor Alessandro expects to have female company at all times. His dressing room is usually packed with admirers. It goes with being a tenor. Do you have the same problems?"

The conductor looked up sharply. "With women? No."

"But you must find yourself occasionally besieged by female fans, especially after concerts. You have a very glamorous profession." Mark could feel himself smiling falsely. "Isn't your dressing room invaded from time to time? Even poor old Konstantin Steigel, who's nearly eighty, is an object of near-adoration after a concert."

Cavalcanti nodded briefly. "It sometimes happens." He smiled. "There was a woman in Paris who announced she would not leave until I gave her a lock of my hair. I was afraid she was going to produce a pair of scissors and claim her prize. Fortunately, Maria was with me, and chased her away!"

"I didn't realize you needed a wife to beat off the marauders." Mark waited fractionally, and asked casually, "Was she with you for the *Requiem* concerts?"

"No." His face was suddenly blank.

"You're lucky your French fan didn't follow you across the Channel, brandishing her scissors. I seem to remember there was a woman who followed Pierre Boulez wherever he went, and attended every concert. It must add a certain drama backstage, although Londoners are inclined to be more discreet. Did they leave you alone?"

"Mostly."

"No strange ladies looking for adventure in the conductor's dressing room?"

The conductor smiled nervously. "Not that I remember." He hesitated. "Are we speaking confidentially?" Mark nodded. "I am a little embarrassed to mention this, but you seem to understand the problem. You see, Maria can be very jealous. Sometimes, I think she is convinced that I am constantly unfaithful to her. She does not trust me. That is why she often accompanies me. She does not love music deeply, but . . ." His voice trailed away uneasily.

"I'm sure she understands that you don't invite the attention you receive. It's one of the penalties of your profession."

"Yes." He remained uneasy.

"Is something wrong?"

"In a way. You see, although she will not say anything directly, I think Maria believes I was involved in a . . . liaison the last time I was here." He gestured helplessly. "I don't know when I was supposed to find the time. Between the soloists, the choir and the orchestral rehearsals, there was only time to eat and sleep."

Mark smiled. "Some of your colleagues seem to manage."

"I suppose they do."

"It must be tempting."

"Yes, yes." Cavalcanti began pacing again. "I am worried about this recording, Mr. Holland."

"I'd prefer it if you would call me Mark."

"Thank you. Please call me Emilio. I am glad you are here in London and we have the opportunity to get to know each other. You see, I am not experienced with recording and, working with Alessandro and La Morini, I do not want to appear incompetent. This film will make a considerable difference to my career if it goes well." He moved about the room restlessly. "Maria has got it into her head that I am . . . entangled with another woman. For this reason, she insists on coming to Geneva with me. I would much prefer that she stayed in Rome, so that I can concentrate on my work. It is very important. She does not believe that I spent my time in London alone."

Mark watched him in silence. "And did you?"

"I told you. I was extremely busy with all the rehearsals." Cavalcanti avoided Mark's eyes.

"You haven't answered my question, Emilio." Mark smiled. "As your manager, I can offer you the same privileged confidence as a priest. Are you sure you weren't seen with anyone?"

The conductor hesitated. "I may have been seen in the company of . . . of . . . someone, but that doesn't mean that there was anything between us."

"Was this after a concert?"

"Well, yes. Of course, I also gave an interview, but that was quite innocent." He looked at Mark. "You do not believe me?"

Mark shrugged. "I believe whatever you want to tell me. Who visited you?"

Suddenly, Cavalcanti became irritated. "I came here to ask for your help. I would prefer that you don't interrogate me. I am not in a witness box!"

"Of course not. I'm sorry if I gave that impression."

"No." He made an effort to control himself. "Please forgive me. I did not intend to be rude. It is just that I am very anxious at the moment. It has been a difficult time for me."

"Don't worry too much about the recording. Levin's very good, and you'll find Bianca completely professional. I spoke to her earlier, and she said she was looking forward to working with you."

"Really?" He was almost childishly pleased.

"She remembered you from Venice last year. I know she'll go out of her way to be cooperative." For a moment, Mark hesitated. Knowing Bianca's idea of "cooperation," it might be better if Maria Cavalcanti was present.

"I'm very relieved. Thank you for your help." His expression clouded again. "I wish I knew where that fool of a tenor was. He promised to meet me this afternoon."

"Are you sure you got the appointment right? He didn't by chance arrange to come to you? I know he's very arrogant, but you are the maestro after all."

"I didn't think of that! When he said we should meet at four, I naturally assumed that he expected me to come here. Oh God! Do you think he could have gone to the Connaught?"

"It's possible. You could give them a ring."

"No. It's easier to go back." Cavalcanti looked at his watch. "I am only a little late." He walked to the door.

"If you take a cab, you can be there in a few minutes."

"No. It's quicker to walk."

"Really?"

"Yes. I have timed myself before. You see, the taxis have to drive all the way round Berkeley Square, which is always full of traffic. It can take a long time. If I walk, there is a little street connected to the top of the square, and the hotel is just a short distance beyond. I know, because I have used it before."

Mark smiled. "You're getting to know London better than I do. I don't remember a shortcut like that."

"Yes. It is easy. After the traffic light, you turn to the right, and there is a little street which goes round the back. It is called Bruton Mews."

GENEVA

SIX

"I FINALLY FIGURED OUT what the hell's wrong with this place." Abe Sincoff gazed across Lac Léman at the substantial rows of solid buildings and the giant spout of a fountain that leapt from the water. "It's too goddamn spotless! I never saw a town that needed a little dirtying up so much. Jesus, I bet Geneva dogs even sweep up their own poops!"

Mark smiled. "You're just homesick for New York."

"You got it in one, kid. I belong in the Big Apple, and I hate to leave it. You know, my heart sinks every time the taxi heads for the airport. I'm being wrenched from my natural habitat. It's the centre of the civilized world already, so who needs anyplace else?"

"You call that dump civilized, Abe? The streets are full of garbage trucks and black plastic bags."

"Sure they are. Civilization needs a little refuse lying around. It's more comfortable. This place is so squeaky clean it makes me nervous!"

They were strolling across the Pont du Mont-Blanc, walking towards the centre of the city. It was a glorious summer morning and Abe, momentarily taken unaware by the heat, had conceded to the weather by taking off the jacket of his perennially dark suit and hanging it across his shoulders. Mark suspected that it made him feel like a European. He had also loosened his tie, tucking the end into his overstretched waistline. The sartorial changes had little effect. Wherever he was, Abe always looked like a New Yorker.

At his side, Myra Sincoff walked in silence, her face expressionless, offering no complaints. Myra seldom smiled. Carrying the burden of the Chosen People on her shoulders was no laughing matter, and anyway, what was there to smile at? Even when she had private thoughts, Myra ended them with a question mark.

Mark turned to her for support. "How do you put up with this philistine? One night in a luxury Swiss hotel, a huge breakfast and a beautiful view like this, and he's already pining for Manhattan!"

Myra shrugged expressively, and her pointed Sephardic features indicated a *Weltschmerz* that had long ago taught her not to struggle against the inevitable. "So what makes you think he's going to change? Luxury he already has in his own home, at no extra charge, and he eats like a horse wherever he goes." Her face darkened. "One of these days, he'll drop dead in the street!" She turned her attention on Mark. "You just sit and pick. If the food's so great in Switzerland, how come you're all skin and bones? You should have someone to prepare a proper meal for you."

Abe grinned broadly, the light dancing on his rimless glasses. Almost totally bald, and with a roly-poly face that was constantly animated, he looked like a beardless Jewish Santa Claus. "Don't start in on him, babe. He'll find himself a wife when he's ready for one." Myra sniffed disapprovingly. "He's still a kid." Abe winked at Mark. "I'm told there are plenty of nice Jewish girls in Switzerland."

Mark looked at his watch. "As a matter of fact, I'm on my way to see one in a few minutes." Myra became cautiously interested. "She called me earlier this morning to warn me that there's a problem with Emilio Cavalcanti."

Abe reached in a pocket for a Havana cigar, but a glower from Myra made him replace it. "What's up?"

"He wants extra rehearsals. He claims the orchestra isn't properly prepared."

"Is it?"

"It's difficult to say. They know the music well enough. There was a production of *Tosca* at the Opéra here this season. I think it's mostly nerves on Emilio's part. He's still worried about working with Bianca and Alessandro."

Abe shrugged. "Listen, he's got to start somewhere, so it may as well be at the top. A few extra rehearsals will give him confidence. So what's the problem?"

"Joshua Levin, who's producing the recording, doesn't want to spend the money. It's not budgeted."

"I thought it was being charged against Wiesman."

"Not anymore. Wolfgang flew to New York and persuaded them to stay within the two-hundred-thousand figure. Laufer will have to pay for anything extra."

"Which is hitting him where it really hurts." Abe chuckled. "He's smarter than I thought, unless our Gregory's going soft in his old age."

"Exactly. Emilio's demanded three rehearsals before the recording sessions, and I've been asked to talk him out of them. I'll see if he'll compromise, but I have the feeling that he can be very stubborn when he wants."

"He'll compromise, kid. That's what this business is about. Jesus, I once saw Toscanini start to tear a score apart when he was having one of those famous rehearsal tantrums of his. Then he remembered it was the only copy of the score available, and he quietly put it back on the stand. That's compromise!"

"Emilio's not Toscanini, in more ways than one. I'll see what I can do. What time does Bianca get in?"

"Around twelve. I said I'd meet her."

"I don't know if I'll be finished by then."

Abe grinned. "Don't worry, kid. I'll give her ass a little extra pat for you." Myra glared at him. "You can have her all to yourself later."

"Thanks, Abe, but I'd sooner keep you around as a chaperone. Ettore should be with her for the first few days."

"Then you have enough time to work up an alibi or go into training, depending on your preference." Abe sighed. "I must say, kid, if I was your age . . ." He caught his wife's eye, and left the sentence unfinished.

Mark laughed. "No, you wouldn't!" Abe and Myra had been happily married for nearly forty years, during which he had never strayed. "Are you going with him, Myra?"

"Nah." Abe answered on her behalf. "I'm just delivering her to the stores on the Rue du Rhône." He glowed. "My wife's a human currency converter. She'll have everything priced to the nearest dollar within twenty minutes."

"So what's to buy in Geneva?" Myra eyed her husband, unsure whether he was teasing her.

"You could try the shoe stores for a start. Isn't this the home of Bally?"

"Shoes I already have." Her pronouncement was final. When buying gifts for other people, Myra was generous to an embarrassing degree. Her own requirements seemed to be minimal. She turned to Mark. "And what's the name of this nice Jewish girl you're going to meet?"

"Diana Nightingale."

"Nightingale? What sort of a Jewish name is that?"

"An English one. Her family changed it."

"Were they ashamed?" Myra's eyes narrowed.

"No, they wanted to live in England. Nobody's permitted to be a foreigner there."

He found Diana in one of the chorus dressing rooms at the back of Victoria Hall. It had been converted into the control room for the recording sessions, and a large metal console, with complicated rows of dials and sliding knobs set in graduated tracks, dominated the space. It faced two king-size loudspeakers, between which there was a television set. The walls were draped with heavy material, and amid thick wire cables and junction boxes, various cabinets winked with green and red lights. Wooden crates lay open, displaying tools, spare parts and various additional pieces of equipment, and the room looked more like an electronic research laboratory than a studio, with few concessions to comfort. A row of hard-backed chairs lined the rear wall, to accommodate the performers for playbacks of the tape.

Diana was seated behind the console, absorbed in a sheaf of papers. She was dressed in a dark blue shirt and slacks which seemed to emphasize her narrow waist and generous breasts. She did not hear Mark enter the room.

"I seem to remember a line from Robert Burton's *Anatomy of Melancholy* about the nightingale dying of shame if another bird sings better." He pretended to look solicitous. "I hope you won't take it to heart when Bianca gets here."

Diana's face lit up with pleasure. "Hi!" He had forgotten how beautiful she was when she smiled. "I didn't hear you. I've been trying to work out the new schedule." She rose from her chair and hugged him, reaching up to place her cheek against his. They embraced like old friends. "It's lovely to see you again." She sounded slightly breathless, and the pressure of her arms increased momentarily.

"Is Joshua here?"

She nodded. "He's out in the hall with Graham, going over the microphone positions. They've been playing with the equipment for the past couple of hours, testing everything. Graham was here all day yesterday with his assistant, Jack, assembling this lot. It takes ages to put together."

Mark surveyed the banks of electronic machinery. "I won't even start to ask you how it all works."

She laughed. "That's just as well, because I haven't the faintest idea! Every now and then, Graham and Jack start to tell me, but I get lost somewhere around the first potentiometer. The only thing I know is that when you slide one of those"—she indicated the knobs on the console—"the sound gets louder. They dazzle me with words like 'groups of faders' and 'equalization,' so I just nod wisely and try to look intelligent. About the only other contribution I can make is that the tape machines are next door and the television set over there is so that Josh can see what the singers are doing during a take." Her arm remained around Mark's waist. Its presence pleased him.

"Which button makes the tea?"

"I'm not sure, but I have the sneaking suspicion that I do, when I'm not standing on the stage outside wearing headphones and pushing the singers from one square to another." She pointed to a desk with a microphone, to one side of the console. The score of the opera lay on it. "Josh sits over there, and he can talk to me through the phones while they're recording, telling me if he wants the singers to move. At least, that's the principle. I'm a bit nervous about the idea of giving the great Alessandro a shove when he's in full throat. I've never done this sort of thing before, so I hope I'm not going to make an idiot of myself. According to Josh, there's nothing to it, but he's been producing operas for years."

"You haven't been at Magnum for very long, have you?"

"Three months. I've attended quite a few sessions, but this is my first opera. Between the scheduling and the setting up, it's a nightmare. The builders arrived yesterday morning at six, to make the stage extension. By the time Graham arrived at ten, the whole thing was constructed. Talk about efficient!" She seemed keyed up, speaking rapidly. "After that, he and Jack set up their microphones and started to test everything. I never realized there was so much to do before it all starts. By yesterday evening, I was so exhausted I could hardly eat." She shook her head in wonder. "Now they're testing everything all over again, from the beginning."

"Presumably, it's insurance against breakdowns once the recording begins."

"Yes. Josh says that if you have to stop in the . . ." She paused, looking closely at Mark. "But you know all this already. You must have been to dozens of recordings before."

Mark smiled. "A few."

"Am I babbling? Oh Lord, here I am, explaining everything as though I know all about it, and you're letting me jabber like an idiot! I have the feeling you've been winding me up."

"Perhaps a little."

"That's mean! I suppose I'm suffering a few first-night nerves of my own. I thought the classical-music world was going to be a peaceful, uneventful life, like working in a museum."

"Not like your last job?"

"Well, hopefully a little less hectic, but I like the idea of all the travelling. I love to visit new places."

"I thought you did that before. Didn't you say you went to Budapest?"

She looked at Mark. "You have a good memory. I'm flattered. Anyway, that was a once-in-a-blue-moon trip. Most of my time was spent in a tiny office making phone calls or running errands for my boss. PR isn't always as glamorous as it sounds. This is much more fun, despite the wear and tear on the nerves."

"How is the hotel?"

"Very plush. I'm glad the company's paying! The rooms are very comfortable, but the decor's gross! Each floor's a different colour. Mine's entirely in a sort of prussic green plastic. Josh's is bright red. It rather put us off our breakfast."

For a moment, Mark wondered whether she meant that she had spent the night with the record producer. At Covent Garden, she had denied any great affection for him. He paused. Why did it concern him? "You should have eaten downstairs. There's a rather nice café overlooking the lake."

"I know, but Josh decided to hold a working breakfast. It made him feel like a businessman. Poor thing, he's hopelessly disorganized. I walked in on him this morning while he was arguing with Cavalcanti."

Was that a discreetly chosen comment? Mark was vaguely irritated with himself for being concerned. He hardly knew her. "What happened?"

"It seems that Cavalcanti took it upon himself to call the manager of the orchestra from Rome and ask him to make the orchestra available for extra rehearsals. He didn't even bother to tell us about it! Needless to say, the manager was only too pleased to oblige. The orchestra will be paid for it. Emilio had the chutzpah to book three rehearsals."

"Have you told him he can't have them?"

"No. Josh has asked him to meet us here this morning to talk about it. That's why I called you. Josh was on the phone to New York for nearly an hour last night. Mr. Laufer's furious. If we agree to the rehearsals, Magnum will have to pay for them. He practically threatened to fire Josh if we give in. When Josh talked to Cavalcanti this morning, the man was adamant, and said we'd have to find another conductor if he didn't have adequate time to prepare. He was getting quite ratty. Now Josh doesn't know what to do. Can you help him?" Her eyes seemed very large.

"I hope so. Emilio's very nervous about this whole project."

"He had no right to call the orchestra without at least consulting us first."

"Of course not. I'll talk to him about it."

"I had no idea he was so temperamental. He was quite different when he came to London for the Verdi."

"Did you meet him then?"

"Not in person. I sent some flowers to his hotel and spoke to him on the phone. He was tremendously tied up with all the rehearsals."

"How about the concerts?"

"No. I left that to Josh. I knew Emilio was coming back for the *Tosca* a few weeks later. There was an awful crush after the *Requiem,* and I was busy looking after Alessandro. That way, we divided the work between us."

"You sound like a good team."

She shrugged. "I'm still learning. According to Josh, Cavalcanti was very easygoing and relaxed. He seemed to revel in all the work. We thought this was going to be a stroll. Now, he's just irritable and bloody-minded."

"Is his wife here with him?"

"I think so. To be honest, I haven't had much time to check. I only arrived at lunchtime yesterday, and Rudi in your office has been looking after everything so efficiently that I haven't had to bother. Rudi's very good, isn't he?"

"Meticulously so."

"You don't sound very enthusiastic."

"He's excellent and invaluable, and as reliable as a Swiss watch. He never makes mistakes." Mark smiled. "I just wish he was a little more human at times. Efficiency like his makes me uneasy."

She giggled. "He is a bit pompous. When I said I thought I might go out to the airport to meet Madame Morini, he advised me in no uncertain terms that it was all being looked after and was quite unnecessary. He said that you and Mr. Sincoff would be there, and that there was no need for me to get in the way. I don't think he approved of my presence when the great lady arrives." Her smile broadened. "As a matter of fact, he made some sort of comment to the effect that I was hardly appropriately dressed for the occasion."

"That sounds like our Rudi! I'd better have a little talk with him."

"Oh, please don't. I'm perfectly able to look after myself, and I think he thought he was doing me a favour. The Swiss are formal, aren't they? I keep forgetting that *Arms and the Man* was written by an Irishman!"

"All right, but let me know if he starts to get too snotty. We'd better go and talk to Joshua before Cavalcanti arrives."

"Yes." She took his arm. "I'll show you the way, although it's easy enough. Just follow the cables." She stayed close to Mark, and he was again aware of her perfume. "You probably know this place better than I do. I keep forgetting this is your home territory. I've never been to Geneva before."

"You must let me show you around."

She smiled. "I'd like that very much."

In the auditorium, the orchestra staff was setting chairs and placing music stands in front of them. A wooden apron had been built which extended the stage a further twenty feet into the hall, over the first twelve rows of seats. At the back of the stage, there were risers for the chorus, and there was a large open space, whose floor had been marked out with numbered squares, for the singers. This was the sound "stage."

Joshua Levin was standing on the edge of the apron, watching as a white-haired man adjusted microphone booms over the space to be occupied by the first violins. Seeing Mark and Diana approach, he picked his way past the chairs.

"Hello. Thank God you're here." He shook hands rather formally. "Has Cavalcanti shown up yet?"

"No. Diana told me what's been going on."

"I hope you're going to help me sort him out. He can't order three rehearsals just like that. Why the hell didn't he call me?" The producer was angry. "It's bad enough having to contend with singers and the film people when I'm trying to work."

"I'll talk to him as soon as he arrives. He should have called you first, or at least talked to me about it."

"I tried to discuss it with him earlier, but he hung up on me. Does he have any idea how much it's going to cost?"

"I doubt it."

"Well, Greg Laufer does, to the last penny! He was yelling down the bloody phone for half an hour last night, threatening bloody murder. He's holding me personally responsible. I tried to explain, but he didn't want to hear. Nobody wants to know!" His voice was thick with self-pity. "Doesn't Cavalcanti realize that he'll have time to rehearse all he wants during the sessions? I've broken the opera down into ten- or twelve-minute segments for each three-hour session, so there's more than enough time to prepare the players, who've only just done the bloody piece in the opera house. For one thing, the singers aren't going to keep going for three hours on the trot. They won't want to do more than two or three takes of each sequence, or they'll lose the edge to their voices. We need the time between to let them rest, and he can work on the bloody orchestra."

"I know. I'll tell him. Didn't you explain the routine in London?"

Joshua gesticulated angrily. "He was never available to talk to me. I arranged two meetings on different occasions, and he cancelled both of them. It's impossible to work like this!"

"Diana was saying he was much better during the Verdi."

"He seemed perfectly relaxed when I met him backstage, and promised to set aside time to discuss the recording during the run of *Tosca*, but when it came to it, he was never there."

Diana stepped forward. "You were away for some of that period, Josh."

He shrugged irritably. "A few days, but that was during the early rehearsals. I was certainly available most of the time. I also had tapes to edit, but I was there when he needed me. The world didn't have to come to a standstill just because he was about to record his first bloody opera!"

Mark remained calm. "We'll sort it out. He's obviously very tense—"

"Who isn't?" Levin was not ready to be appeased.

"When we last met, I told him to rely on your judgement and experience. If you go through it step by step with him, I'm sure he'll understand."

"I hope so. Christ, I've produced operas all over the world, and we've never hit problems like these." Levin seemed to grow calmer. "My God, when it comes to playing, he should try working with a French orchestra. They make this lot sound like the Cleveland under George Szell. If Cavalcanti were working in Paris, *I'd* insist on the extra rehearsals."

"Are they that bad?"

"Oh, the French are famous for their lack of any sort of discipline. Let's hope that Barenboim knocks the new opera into shape. Listen, do you think you can talk Emilio out of those rehearsals? I've got a dozen things to look after."

"I'll try. Emilio's intelligent. Once he understands the situation, he'll settle down."

"I hope so. Now Laufer's talking about flying over to attend the sessions, which will be the last straw." He turned to Diana. "If he does show up, I'm putting you in charge of him. You'll have to use all your famous public relations charm on him, but I'd better warn you that he sees himself as God's gift to women."

"No, thank you!" She grinned. "I have a great idea. Why don't we get him together with Simon Vincent, and they can charm each other to death. Mr. Laufer always seems to have dreams of grandeur, so if we play our cards right, we can let him think he's about to become a movie mogul."

Levin nodded moodily. "It's worth a try. I'd better go back to Graham." He gestured towards the engineer, who was standing, arms akimbo, awaiting his return. "We still have hours of planning ahead." He turned to Mark. "After all, when it comes to the crunch, he's the one who has to make some sort of sense out of all this bloody chaos!"

Cavalcanti arrived a few minutes later, entering from the foyer of the theatre. He looked pale and rather tense, walking briskly. After nodding briefly towards Joshua and Diana, he took Mark's hand and led him aside.

"They have told you about my request?" He kept his voice low, and Joshua tactfully moved away to discuss a problem with the engineer.

"Yes."

"You don't look very pleased."

"I think you should listen to what Joshua Levin has to say before you decide anything."

"But I have worked with this orchestra before. Their ensemble is weak, and their intonation is often unacceptable. Mr. Levin cannot expect me to work with them until I am satisfied that they will play properly."

"I still think you should let him have his say, Emilio. He has only scheduled ten or twelve minutes of music for each session, and you have three hours to put it down. In addition, the singers will want to rest between takes, giving you additional preparation time."

"That is true."

"Why not let him show you the schedule?"

"Very well." For a moment, he stared at Mark. "I had expected you to support me in this."

"I will, if you're still convinced that you need the extra time. You may remember that when we spoke in London, I recommended that you discuss everything with Levin. He's very experienced and dedicated to his job."

Cavalcanti looked sceptical. "It is not just the extra cost that is worrying him?"

"That may be part of it, but I believe he knows what he's doing."

The conductor was silent for a moment, pursing his lips. Then he nodded. "Very well. We will talk." He walked over to the record producer.

A change had overtaken Joshua. He smiled easily and seemed very relaxed. "We seem to have misunderstood each other this morning. I hope you weren't offended." Diana handed him a file. "May I show you the recording plan we've scheduled? I'm sure you'll see how comfortably it works. You'll have all the time you need to sort out any problems with the orchestra."

Cavalcanti remained stiff. "But I don't want to be distracted when the singers are performing."

"You won't be. I give you my word." Joshua continued, explaining each detail, and the conductor listened attentively, his head bowed over the schedule. At one point, he smiled briefly.

"You are very persuasive, Mr. Levin."

"Well, I've recorded this orchestra before on a number of occasions.

You'll be surprised how the presence of microphones adds to their powers of concentration." He continued through the timetable, occasionally pausing to ask the conductor about a particular section of the score.

After twenty minutes, Cavalcanti placed a hand on Levin's shoulder. "You have made your point. I apologize. I am sorry we did not have this conversation earlier."

Joshua looked relieved. "As long as you're happy."

The conductor smiled bleakly. "That is asking a little too much, but I am satisfied. I have the feeling you know the score as well as I do."

Levin laughed. "That I can't claim, but I've certainly heard it a few times!"

"Will you tell the manager of the orchestra that the rehearsals will not be necessary after all?"

Joshua bowed, giving an exaggerated sigh of relief. "With great pleasure!" At his side, Diana grinned broadly.

"Thank you." Some of Cavalcanti's stiffness returned. "I am placing myself in your hands."

Joshua seemed a little embarrassed. "We won't let you down. Thank you for being so cooperative. Diana's also worked out how to fit in Alessandro if he misses a couple of days. If we leave out the Angelotti sequence, we can pick it up later." He smiled in her direction. "Everything's under control."

"I am relying on that." The conductor turned away.

Mark joined him. "I'll walk you down. Do you have time for a coffee?"

"No. I must work."

Diana said, "I'd love one. How about you, Josh?"

"Yes. I could use a break." The producer was visibly relieved.

In the street, the conductor again drew Mark aside. "I am disappointed."

"What's wrong?"

"I had expected you to offer more support when Levin was talking to me. You are my manager. It seemed to me that you were on his side." He spoke calmly, but his nostrils were flared. "In London, you cross-examined me about my personal life."

"It wasn't intended, and I'm sorry if you had that impression. I was trying to reassure you that I would help in any way I could. As far as today is concerned, I simply proposed that you listen to what he had to say. If you're still unhappy, I'll tell him that you must have some additional rehearsal time."

"No, it will not be necessary." He paused. "I do not like to make myself look foolish."

"I don't think anyone sees it that way. If anything, you've earned their respect by accepting the schedule. As Josh said, he won't let you down."

"No." Cavalcanti's face remained set. "I will accept your advice."

"Can I give you a lift back to the hotel? My car's parked just up the road, outside the office."

"No, thank you. Please don't worry. I will take a taxi to the hotel. We will talk later?"

"Of course. As soon as I see Bianca, I'll arrange a meeting with you."

"Thank you. I am looking forward to it." Cavalcanti walked away quickly.

Watching his departing figure, Diana moved closer to Mark. "I don't know what you said to him, but it certainly did the trick." She placed her hand on his. "Thank you."

Mark kept his voice light. "It's all a part of the service!"

As they crossed the road, a taxi drove past. Cavalcanti, deep in thought, was hunched in the back seat.

Diana looked at Mark. "Is anything the matter?"

"No."

"You were frowning."

"I was just preoccupied. Let's find that coffee. I'll introduce you to the manager of La Cave. That's the hangout for all the local musicians. He'll also keep you supplied with fresh coffee during the sessions."

"Lovely."

Mark took her arm, steering her across the road. He decided not to mention that Cavalcanti's taxi was travelling in the wrong direction, away from his hotel.

Diana was still watching him, her large, grey-blue eyes searching his face. "Are you sure there's nothing wrong? You're looking very serious."

For a moment, he was tempted to confide in her, but it was too soon. "I was thinking about something else." He smiled. "Believe it or not, I still have an office to run."

"I know. I was just thinking the same thing. When you get involved in a recording, it's as though nothing else in the world exists."

Mark left Diana and Josh at the stage door of Victoria Hall and walked the few blocks to his office on the Rue des Marbriers. Agnes, his pretty receptionist, seemed relieved to see him.

"Ah, Monsieur Holland, I am glad you have returned. Rudi has been asking for you every five minutes!"

"What's the problem?"

"I do not think there is one, but Herr Wiesman has installed himself in

Rudi's office to make telephone calls, and Rudi is not happy about it." She hesitated. "I told him to use yours. I hope that was correct. He seemed to think it would be impertinent."

"It was very sensible. I'll probably be in and out of here a lot of the time until the sessions settle down. Rudi doesn't like a change of routine, does he?"

Agnes gave a conspiratorial smile, revealing a large amount of silver amid her good Swiss teeth. "No, he hates any kind of change." She was a very attractive girl. It was a shame about the metalwork.

"I'll calm him down. Thank you for looking after everything so efficiently, Agnes."

"It was no trouble." She looked pleased, and raised a hand to settle an imagined stray hair. Mark wondered whether she realized it was a very feminine gesture.

When he entered his office, Rudi looked up guiltily, as though caught in an illegal act. He half rose from his chair.

"I hope you do not mind my being in here. Wiesman insisted on using my phone, and I needed to make calls of my own."

"No problem."

"I don't see why he couldn't use the phone in his hotel." Rudi sniffed. "He has been talking for hours."

"Film producers set up camp wherever they go. It's an occupational habit."

"I doubt whether he'll offer to pay for the calls. I needed to check whether Madame Morini's flight was on time."

"Abe Sincoff will have done that already. He's going out to meet her." Rudi looked relieved. On one occasion, he had met Bianca, and she had asked him about his love life, which had embarrassed him painfully. Since that time, he had rather pointedly avoided her.

"Apparently, she is staying at the Hôtel des Bergues. I had booked her into the Hilton with the others, but she made her own arrangements." He seemed slightly offended.

"She always stays there. By the way, did you ever contact that journalist who was offering to sell you information about Cavalcanti?"

"Yes. He didn't have anything to sell."

"Really?"

"Well, he tried to interest me in some photographs of Cavalcanti with some woman. From what he said, they were very compromising, but I assumed you wouldn't be interested in anything like that."

"No. Did he say who the woman was?"

Rudi shrugged. "Some minor Italian contessa, as I understand it. The pictures date back to the time when Cavalcanti was an ardent supporter of the Left. I think he deliberately posed for them to show how decadent Italian society women had become. He was little more than a student at the time. As a matter of fact, I don't think the journalist really expected me to buy them. He'd already offered them all over the place without any success. You know what Italians are like." Rudi clearly didn't approve of Italians. "He did let slip one interesting fact, though. Signor Cavalcanti and his wife were separated from each other for about three months."

"When was that?"

"A year or two ago. This journalist, who's little more than a gossip columnist, said that they hushed the matter up. The official story was that Cavalcanti was working with the opera in Naples for three months, but according to him, there was another woman in his apartment. Whatever it was, he returned home at the end of the season, and nothing further was said." Rudi looked superior. "Italians always fancy themselves as ladies' men."

"So it would appear. It's certainly true in the case of Alessandro."

Rudi looked smug. "Ah, that's another matter. I also learned quite a lot about him."

"Oh?"

"Yes. It seems that Signor Alessandro isn't all he appears to be."

"How is that?"

"Well, if my source is correct, he's a Russian." Mark looked up sharply. "At least, he comes from Georgia, which is more or less the same thing, isn't it?"

Mark was thoughtful. "More or less. What's the story?"

"His real name is Antonio Alessandro Abashili, and he actually comes from Tbilisi. His family left the country illegally. Apparently, they walked across the border into Turkey. It's not very difficult in that region, although you have to be tough to make the journey across the mountains."

Mark nodded. "When did this happen?"

"Years ago, when Alessandro was about sixteen. The family settled in Turkey and lived there for a number of years before they moved to Italy. My journalist wasn't too sure of all the details, but he thinks they made contact with a family in Sicily, and finally showed up in Palermo." Rudi lowered his voice slightly. "I think he was hinting that Alessandro's father was mixed up with drug trafficking."

"And Alessandro?"

"He didn't say. Alessandro was still a teenager at the time. The family that took them in sponsored his career. They spotted that he had a voice, and paid for his musical education. I'm told that he still stays in touch with them."

Mark nodded. "I heard a similar story in London, from another journalist. It certainly gives Alessandro a colourful background."

"I would have thought it was the sort of thing he'd want to keep quiet about."

"It doesn't seem to have affected his career. I understand he had engagements in Poland between the Verdi *Requiem* and the London run of *Tosca*."

"Why not? He has Italian citizenship and travels with an Italian passport. Anyway, he's very famous. I shouldn't imagine that the authorities in Eastern Europe would want unfavourable publicity. Otherwise, they wouldn't invite him to appear. They probably prefer to close their eyes to his background if they are aware of it. It's amazing how absentminded they can be when it suits them."

"You're probably right. Did you get the impression that these facts are common knowledge?"

"No, it was just idle gossip. He knew we weren't directly involved with Alessandro, and I think he talked about him in the hope that it might persuade me to buy the Cavalcanti story. When I said I wasn't interested in any of it, he complained that I had been wasting his time." Rudi looked at his watch impatiently. "Do you think it would be possible to move Wiesman out of my office? I have someone coming to see me in a few minutes, and I need my room back."

"I'll see what I can do. Otherwise, you can use mine."

"I don't wish to inconvenience you."

"I'll tell you if you do."

"Very well. Incidentally, Konstantin Steigel telephoned. He said he would call back later. It wasn't important."

Mark smiled. The old conductor called almost daily, but he rarely had very much business to discuss. Mark had become his contact with the outside world, as much a friend and a listener as a business adviser. It was a role he enjoyed. "I'll try to reach him. Did he say where he was?"

"Amsterdam, at the Okura Hotel. He has rehearsals with the Concertgebouw from tomorrow."

The door to Rudi's office was open. Wiesman was deep in conversation on the telephone, his chair swivelled so that he faced the window. The film producer's voice was subdued.

"I understand what you're saying, but a percentage as substantial as that cuts into any profit that my company could make. How do you expect me to operate under those conditions?" He listened for a moment. "But that's unreasonable! I know we agreed that you would underwrite half the production, but what you are suggesting now is unacceptable. I can't work with conditions like that!" He was silent for a long time, his head lowered. At length, he spoke again. "Very well. I'll call you back within a few hours. By all means prepare a contract, but I should warn you that I expect to come up with an alternative solution. Your terms simply don't work." He hung up, and Mark was about to speak, but Wiesman immediately dialled a new number on the instrument, which he held in his lap.

"*Allo? Monsieur Alessandro, s'il vous plaît. . . . Oui, j'attends.*" He waited, his head still bowed. After a moment, his call was connected. "Antonio? It's Wolfgang Wiesman." His voice was further reduced, and only just audible. "Listen, I've considered your proposal. . . . Yes. . . ." His voice barely suppressed his anger. "Of course I'm not happy with the arrangement, but I don't seem to have much choice, do I? My New York partners have let me down."

Mark hesitated, wondering whether he should withdraw or at least make Wiesman aware of his presence. He did not like the idea of listening in to the film producer's conversation.

Wiesman spoke again. "Are you prepared to guarantee immediate payment? . . . Yes. . . . Is that why you need to go out of town? . . . I see." He hesitated, then seemed to make up his mind. "Very well. I'll agree to your proposal, but only on this one occasion. I'm not happy about it, and I have no intention of making this a permanent arrangement between us. I hope we understand one another?" He listened again. "All right, I accept that. You can give me the details later today when we meet. As for the risks involved, I don't share your opinion, but I can't see any alternative. We'll talk again." Wiesman hung up and remained immobile, apparently staring out of the window.

Mark tapped on the door, and the producer swung round in his chair, as though startled by the sound. His appearance was surprising. His shirt was crumpled, and the impeccably placed tie was lost under one upturned collar. Wiesman's face looked strained, and there were dark patches under his eyes. The skin on his face was blotchy.

Wiesman smiled with an effort. His voice was calm. "Good morning, Mark. I hope you will forgive me for commandeering this office, but I needed to make a couple of urgent phone calls."

"Of course. I hope everything's going according to schedule?"

His normal self-assurance seemed to be returning. "Yes, yes. I was just sorting out a minor problem with Frankfurt. You know how it is: nobody wants to make decisions in my absence. Everything's going well. I must say I'm looking forward to the recording sessions very much."

"I understand Alessandro's already here."

Wiesman hesitated fractionally, but his expression was bland. "Is he? I must give him a call." He stood. "In the meantime, I'd better go back to the hotel. I'm expecting several telexes, and there are a number of details I need to discuss with Simon Vincent. I ought to call Madame Morini."

"She's arriving around noon. Abe Sincoff's meeting her."

"Good." Wiesman seemed distracted, gathering papers from the desk and putting them into a rather gaudy Florentine leather briefcase. "Please thank Rudi for the use of his room. I'm most grateful to him."

He walked briskly through the main office, nodding to Frau Emmi and pausing momentarily to speak to Agnes. Mark did not hear what he said, but she smiled brilliantly, and her hand again strayed to her hair. Perhaps Agnes was hoping to be discovered by the film world.

Mark lit a cigarette, inhaling deeply. If Wiesman had production problems, he was not prepared to discuss them. How did they involve Alessandro, and why pretend he had not spoken to him? He had talked about risks and an unhappy arrangement. What the hell had he agreed to? For a moment, he considered Rudi's new information. Did Alessandro have some shadowy Sicilian connections? He had laughed at Katya's suggestion in London, but now it did not seem as farfetched. As soon as Abe returned from the airport with Bianca, they would talk, but he would leave out the possible connection with Rossiter. If there was a connection. He had heard nothing from London.

"I can give you back your office." Rudi was hovering at his side, anxious to return to his desk.

"Thank you." Mark stood aside to let him pass. A new thought occurred. "Is Madame Cavalcanti in Geneva?"

"I think so. I arranged for a double room at the hotel and sent flowers addressed to her. Would you like me to check?"

"She'll show up if she's here. I must call Emilio later."

"Was he at the hall?"

"Yes. We persuaded him not to have all those extra rehearsals."

"I heard about them. Mr. Levin was very upset."

"Actually, it didn't take much persuasion, once he understood the situation. Everyone's bound to be slightly on edge until the recording begins."

"I suppose so." Rudi looked superior. "They take themselves very seriously, don't they?"

"Yes. That's what makes them good."

"Of course." The young man looked embarrassed. "I did not mean to suggest . . . Shall I call the hotel, to ask if Madame Cavalcanti is staying?"

"Perhaps you should. Emilio said he was going back there."

Except that the taxi had been heading in the wrong direction. He wondered whether Diana had noticed. She was very bright, and Mark had the feeling that she did not always say what she was thinking. Maybe that was one of the reasons why he found her intriguing.

SEVEN

MARK COULD HEAR the telephone ringing as he entered his apartment. For a moment, he wondered whether to let the answering machine take the call, then decided against it. There were too many crises brewing.

"Mark? It's Katya. I hope I'm not disturbing you?"

"No, I just walked in. Welcome to Geneva."

"Thank you." She sounded slightly breathless. "I've been looking forward to it . . . and to seeing you again. I came in a couple of hours ago, and did a little exploring, but I hope you're going to keep that promise to give me the official tour. Is everyone here?"

"Just about. The recording people have been in for some time, setting up the hall."

"Including the delicious Miss Nightingale?" There was an edge to her voice.

"Yes." He wondered why he felt slightly self-conscious. "She'll be Levin's assistant during the sessions, moving the singers round the stage."

"What fun! How about Bianca Morini?"

"I left her a few minutes ago, but I'll see her again this evening. She's holding a sort of open house at her hotel, and everyone will stop by to pay their respects. It's a little like having visiting royalty."

"Oh. I don't suppose you'd like to have a partner for your visit, would you? It would be a marvellous opportunity for me to meet her unofficially. I promise to behave myself."

Mark smiled. If Katya did not behave, Bianca would soon rectify the situation. "That's a good idea."

"Wonderful! What time, and where?" She was suddenly very business-like. Maybe that was why she was such a successful journalist.

"About eight o'clock."

"Good. When does one eat? I can have something sent up to my room before I leave."

"Don't bother. When Bianca is entertaining, Room Service is kept on the trot all evening. You'll probably run into everyone. My partner Abe Sincoff and his wife will be there, and I'm sure Cavalcanti and his wife will look in. Apart from them, and possibly Alessandro, Wiesman and the film people are sure to make their presence felt."

"And the recording crew?"

"Not unless they're specifically invited. Record people are more inclined to keep to themselves. You'll also see half of Geneva's upper crust. Don't forget that Ettore's a banker."

She laughed. "I should have made a deal with *The Tatler* to cover the event. We working journalists aren't proud. Where should we meet?"

"They're at the Hôtel des Bergues, but I can collect you, if you like."

"Don't worry, I'll find my own way. Do people dress up for this sort of thing?"

"Well, it's all very informal, but people are ultra-conscious of the fact. Pierre Boulez used to joke about *l'air casuel du premier arrondissement.*"

"I'm not exactly sure what that means, but I get the general drift. I think my little black dress is going to come in very handy. What would we all do without one? Heavens, look at the time! I'd better go and bathe my sticky body if I'm going to look suitably presentable on your arm. I'll see you at eight."

Mark replaced the receiver. Katya was certainly determined to get what she wanted. For a moment, he wondered whether he should invite the people from Magnum to join the party. Perhaps not. Bianca liked to hold her own court and did not necessarily welcome too many attractive younger women at her gatherings. He was disappointed that Diana would not be there.

The opera singer's suite occupied several large rooms of the hotel, with a main reception room big enough to accommodate a small sales convention. A buffet, complete with chef and waiters, had been arranged in one corner, and Mark smiled wryly at the memory of his negotiations with Larry Austerklein for the soprano's per diem allowance during the period of the recording. It would barely cover the cost of the flowers that seemed to decorate every available table space.

The room was already filled with guests. Mark recognized several journalists and a local composer whose music, although much discussed in the press, was rarely performed. Ettore was standing with a group of elderly men who, by their sober appearance and sombre dress, obviously came from the banking world. They were deep in conversation, and Mark assumed that the subject of their discussion had little to do with music. There were a number of other men and women whom he did not immediately recognize but whose faces were familiar from concerts and other local functions. He wondered where they all came from, except that when Bianca was entertaining, the word seemed to spread like wildfire. Everybody who was anybody assumed the right to be there.

In a corner, Abe Sincoff and Myra, plates of food on their laps, were talking to Wiesman and Layton. Wiesman, looking preoccupied, concentrated on his food, while Layton smiled winningly at Myra. Abe caught Mark's eye and winked.

At his side, Mark felt Katya hesitate slightly, with a quick intake of breath.

"My God! Her photographs really don't do her justice." Katya's comment was awe-filled.

Draped across an ornate chaise longue, Bianca Morini dominated the room. She was so theatrically placed at the centre of attention that Mark would not have been surprised to see a discreet spotlight trained on her. She was dressed in a simple ivory-coloured silk sheath, high at the neck, that seemed to cling to her hourglass figure and emphasize her dark hair, piled high on her head. Her only jewellery was a thick band of gold around her throat, and she seemed to be wearing little makeup: perhaps a hint of eye shadow and a touch of lipstick. She had the sort of classic features that did not need adornment, and the creamy texture of her skin was unblemished. Mark could understand Katya's admiration. At forty, admitting to thirty-nine, Bianca was a beautiful, sensuous woman, serenely self-assured and accustomed to being the centre of attention. From time to time, every man in the room glanced longingly in her direction.

Perched on the edge of a chair facing her, Simon Vincent, resplendent in a white shirt with billowing sleeves and tight black trousers, was talking animatedly. He looked as though he had just stepped off the stage from a performance of *Giselle*. Mark noted with relief that Cliff was not present. Presumably, Simon had left him behind to sulk in their hotel room. As they approached, the director's voice became audible over the murmur of conversation.

"You see, love, I've had this theory for quite a long time that Tosca is basically attracted to Scarpia, but doesn't want to admit it, even to herself."

Bianca stared at Simon with wide-eyed attention, a polite smile on her face. Her stillness should have warned the director that he was getting into deep water. "Really?"

"Yes. After all, look at the plot. She doesn't really trust Cavaradossi, does she? We know that in the first act, when she has that ding-dong with him over the face of the woman in the portrait."

The smile had not left Bianca's face, but her voice was dangerously calm. "I don't think that changes the way she feels about him. She would hardly sing *'Arde a Tosca nel sangue il folle amor!'* if she didn't love him. Do you speak Italian, Mr. Vincent? It means 'A mad love is burning in Tosca's heart.' "

Simon was not to be dissuaded. "Oh, I know that, but it's the sort of thing you'd expect an actress to say, isn't it? I mean, she's likely to go in for the grand gesture. As soon as Scarpia creeps in with the woman's fan, she's suspicious again."

"The purpose of the scene with the fan is to show how passionately Tosca loves Cavaradossi, so that she is instantly jealous at the thought that he might be interested in somebody else. Her love for him is an *ossessione.*" For a moment, Mark was suddenly reminded of Tony Rossiter in London. What was it he had said about the agonizing nights he had spent, convinced that Danuta had tired of him or, worse still, had found somebody else? Perhaps the opera was not such a blood-and-thunder melodrama after all.

Simon pressed on, apparently unaware of Bianca's growing coolness. "What I have in mind is a whole new slant on the story. Tosca's attracted to Scarpia because he's powerful. She doesn't admit to it, even to herself, but an actress like you can put that across to the audience. I think I can show you how."

"Really?" Bianca's eyes took on a hooded expression.

"Yes. For me, the critical moment in Act Two comes when she reveals where Angelotti is hiding. When Cavaradossi learns that she's betrayed him, he curses her before they take him out to be executed. That's the justification she's been looking for, subconsciously."

Bianca looked at Simon. "Subconsciously?"

"Right, love!" He did not notice her flinch at the endearment. "All the time, she's been attracted to the evil of the man. By rejecting her, Cavaradossi provides the excuse for her to give herself to him. Scarpia *thinks* he's blackmailing her, of course, but he hasn't realized that she's a willing victim."

There was a look of utter disbelief on Bianca's face and, for a moment, it seemed that she was about to explode with anger. Mark flinched inwardly. Then, quite unexpectedly, she smiled sweetly. "Tell me, Mr. Vincent, why does she kill Scarpia?"

"Ah, that's the whole point!" He leaned forward and, almost unconsciously, Bianca moved back. "Once Cavaradossi rejects her, Tosca realizes with remorse that she has betrayed him and his cause, allowing herself to be attracted to Scarpia for baser reasons. That's why *'Vissi d'arte'* is full of all those soppy religious references about going to church every day. She only kills Scarpia because Cavaradossi's accusation stings her conscience, making her want to redeem herself in his eyes. In my opinion, she's a complicated woman and a typical actress, more concerned with what people think of her than with what she really feels—if she feels anything at all very deeply." Like a barrister who had just summed up, Simon sat back, awaiting Bianca's reaction.

For a moment, the soprano was silent, eyeing the director with distaste. Mark could sense the tension, and the moment lasted long enough for him to wonder whom Wiesman would have to find as a substitute director for the film. Simon Vincent would never survive. Then Bianca caught Mark's eye and smiled brilliantly.

"Marco, *caro*, how lovely to see you!" She raised a cheek for him to kiss. "Mr. Vincent has been giving me such an *interesting* personal view of *Tosca*. It is quite different from that of Puccini, Giacosa or Illica, and certainly very different from poor old Sardou." She smiled charmingly at Simon. "Have you ever read the play, Mr. Vincent?"

Simon became uneasy. "Well, I've skipped through it briefly. I just thought—"

"I'm sure you would find it *very* revealing. Perhaps you should have another quick look at it"—her voice hardened but her smile remained—"and at the libretto of the opera that I am going to sing. I cannot find a single word in either that will back up your fascinating theory." She looked suitably contrite. "Besides, I am really not a good enough actress to convey all those subconscious emotions you have been telling me about. I will be much too busy with the words and the music. So will the rest of the cast and, quite possibly, the public."

"I see." Simon was suddenly very subdued.

"But what a vivid imagination you have, reading all those conflicting theories into the story! You must be sure to tell me about any others you have. It will make working together a really memorable experience." Her attention shifted to Mark, totally dismissing the director.

Simon made a final try. "Then you won't consider my interpretation?" There was a hint of pleading in his voice.

Bianca smiled kindly. "No, Mr. Vincent. I am going to sing Puccini's *Tosca*—not yours." Her gaze moved to Katya. "You have not introduced your friend, Marco."

"This is Katya Philips from London. I believe you're supposed to give her an interview."

"Oh yes, the lady who writes." She extended her hand to Katya, who held it nervously. "Your dress is charming." She gazed pointedly at Simon, then back to the journalist. "We must find you somewhere to sit." The director departed hastily, his complexion ruddier than usual, and Bianca motioned Katya into the empty chair.

Katya's voice was unsteady. "Do you think you'll be able to spare me some time?"

Watching Simon's departing figure, Bianca sighed. "I may have more time than we all expect." She looked towards Mark with an expression of pure innocence. "Who would have suspected that Tosca secretly wanted to screw Scarpia?" Katya jumped.

"It's a new slant."

"A little too new, *caro*." She returned to Katya. "Are you going to ask me all those boring questions about my different lovers? People question me so often that I make up new stories to please them, but I am beginning to run out of plots."

"Oh." Katya looked trapped.

"Never mind. It is expected of me. I am a woman of passionate tastes. What about you, my dear? Do you have a lover at the moment? Is he good in bed?"

Katya blushed, and laughed nervously. "I'm not sure what I'm supposed to say to that."

"Really? You have a good body, which is something to be proud of. Don't you like to use it?"

"Yes, I suppose so."

"Is he here with you? What do you like to do with him?"

"No. I . . ." Katya was at a loss for words.

The soprano patted her hand. "I am only teasing you. You see, people— almost total strangers—ask me questions like that all the time, and expect me to tell them. It is sometimes very tiresome."

Katya was silent for a moment. "Yes, I suppose it is."

"I think we will be able to make a good interview." She smiled. "If you like, I will even tell you *my* interpretation of Tosca, but it should not really be necessary. Marco, *caro*, please make sure that Miss Philips and I have a long talk." Her eyes twinkled, and she took in Katya's slim figure. "But you must have something to eat, my dear. We will talk later." Katya was sent away to the white-capped chef, and Bianca patted the empty chair, motioning to Mark to sit. "She is quite charming, *caro*, but painfully thin. Too many bones! Is she good? I am told that English girls can be very—what is the word?—inhibited. A real woman gives herself completely."

"I wouldn't know, Bianca, but I imagine she'll think twice before she asks any impertinent questions. Some of the time, she's considered to be a serious writer."

"Good. I am a serious artist all the time. Maybe, if she behaves herself nicely, I'll give her one naughty story." Bianca's eyes narrowed slightly. "Ettore will be leaving in a few days. Perhaps you will help me to prepare something for her? We can have one of those business discussions in your bedroom, like London."

He laughed. "One of these days, I'll take you seriously."

"You should, Marco. Don't you remember New York?"

"That was a long time ago."

"I know. That is why we should do something about it. We have both had quite a lot of practice since then." She glanced across the room. "Ah, here is our maestro. He looks nervous."

Emilio Cavalcanti walked quickly towards Bianca, then bowed low over her extended hand. *"Buona sera, signora."*

She acknowledged his greeting gracefully. "But you must speak English, Emilio, or our friends will not understand us." Her eyes met his for a moment. "I will only speak Italian if we find ourselves alone together." She glanced at Mark and smiled kindly. "Is your charming wife here with you?"

"Yes, but she is not feeling very well. She has a headache."

"I am so sorry. Please send her my kind regards. I hope she recovers quickly. Tell me, how is the orchestra?"

Mark left them talking about the opera, and wandered over to Abe and Myra. The American moved a chair into the group.

"How're you doing, kid? You should try the food. It's good. At least they learned what rare roast beef should be like. Who's the skinny broad with the nice tuchis?" Myra glared at him.

"An English journalist who's covering the recording and hoping for an interview with Bianca. Her name's Katya Philips."

"I remember. We had an official request a couple of weeks back." He winked. "At least it spared Bianca any more crap from that schmuck Vincent." He turned to Wiesman. "Is that guy really as good as you say?"

"Yes, he's outstanding." Wiesman concentrated on the food on his plate. He seemed preoccupied.

"What was all the bullshit he was handing her about the opera? I only caught the odd word here and there."

"He has a theory that Tosca secretly wants Scarpia. It's all very subliminal."

"Subliminal my ass! What is it with these arty movie guys? You know, Joe Losey once tried to persuade me that Mozart was a closet queen, and that Don Giovanni secretly hated women and had the hots for Leporello. Christ, I told him none of those guys ever heard of Freud; they just liked getting laid. He wasn't convinced. Did Bianca let him have it?"

"No, she just smiled sweetly and told him where to stuff his theories. She behaved very well."

"Good for her." Abe slapped Wiesman on the shoulder, startling the film producer. "Wolfgang, my friend, you'd better have a chat with your fairy queen if he wants to last the course. Bianca's not always as friendly, and if she blows her stack, your movie goes down the toilet, contract or no contract."

Wiesman nodded. "I'd better talk to him." He stood, bowing to Myra. "Please excuse me."

Watching him depart, Abe shook his head. "He looks like a man with problems."

"More than you think, Abe. I overheard a strange conversation between him and Alessandro. Perhaps we can talk about it later."

"Let's meet tomorrow. I've got more than a few doubts of my own about this whole goddamn setup. Tonight, I'm just quietly kibitzing."

Myra looked at Mark. "So where's this nice girl you met?"

"She's not here. The record people weren't invited. They're sometimes excluded from the social gatherings. I think they're considered too parasitic, and only interested in profits."

Abe grinned. "And we're not?"

Myra ignored him. "You're not eating. The food isn't good enough for you?"

"I'll find something in a minute. Wiesman's not his normal self, is he? Whenever we've met in the past, he's exuded charm and self-confidence. I wonder if Alessandro's going to make an appearance."

Abe shrugged. "Maybe. This is Bianca's solo spot. Whoever heard of a tenor allowing himself to be upstaged?"

An hour later, when many of the guests had departed, Alessandro had still not made an appearance. Mark divided his time between the Sincoffs and Ettore, occasionally finding himself trapped by a local *genevois* dignitary eager to take part in the event. Katya joined him briefly.

"I think I'm going to disappear. It's been a long day, and I'm beginning to feel the effects."

"I'll run you home if you like."

"Don't bother. There are plenty of taxis." She seemed anxious to depart. "Thank you for everything. Can I call you in the morning?"

"Yes. The first session is tomorrow afternoon. Do you have the schedule?" She nodded. "What do you think of Bianca?"

"She's amazing, and much nicer than I anticipated. I'm not sure I'd want to be in Simon Vincent's shoes."

"He'll manage. Bianca's very cooperative. You simply end up doing things her way."

"I'll remember that." She smiled. "In fact, I may quote you." She kissed Mark briefly on the cheek. "I'll see you tomorrow."

Abe looked up when Mark returned. "What was her hurry?"

"She was tired."

Myra looked knowing. "She seems like a nice girl. It's time we left, too. Everybody's going."

There was a steady exodus of visitors, and Mark guessed that Ettore had discreetly encouraged their departure. It was still quite early, but Bianca was recording the following afternoon and needed her rest.

He found himself in the elevator with Cavalcanti.

"Did you have a good talk with Bianca?"

"Yes." He smiled briefly. "We agreed to ignore Vincent's ideas!"

"I don't blame you. Bianca's handled much more difficult directors in the past. If he survives, he'll end up adoring her and telling the world how brilliantly he handled her." They reached the foyer. "I'll walk you back to the Hilton. It's on my route."

Cavalcanti hesitated. "No. If you don't mind, I would prefer to take a little night air on my own." He looked embarrassed. "I would also like to apologize for my behaviour this morning. I did not intend to be so abrupt with you." He spoke stiffly.

"I wasn't offended. Things will settle down once the sessions begin."

"I am sure you are right. Nevertheless, I apologize." He held out his hand.

Mark shook hands, and there was an uneasy silence. "I hope your wife will be feeling better."

The conductor shrugged irritably. "That was just an excuse. She didn't want to come."

"I see. I'm sorry."

"I have already explained the situation. Hopefully, she will become bored with Geneva and go home. I will be too busy to look after her."

"You'll have quite a lot of time between the sessions."

"Perhaps, but not for her." He turned away. "I will see you at the hall tomorrow afternoon."

"If there's anything you need, call my office." The conductor was already walking briskly away.

Mark lit a cigarette and strolled in the direction of his apartment. The Quai du Mont-Blanc, along which he was walking, passed the Hilton, and he was tempted to stop there and invite Diana for a drink. It was still early.

Some distance ahead, Mark saw Cavalcanti turn right to cross the Pont du Mont-Blanc into the city. As he idly watched the departing figure, a movement caught his attention. A man emerged from a car parked along the road and walked in the same direction as the conductor, keeping some distance between them. There was nothing particularly unusual about it, until Cavalcanti paused halfway across the bridge, leaning over the wall and apparently staring down into the dark water of the lake. The man behind him immediately paused, moving slightly back so that he was in a shadowy area between the streetlamps. He waited until the conductor moved off again before stepping forward, and continued at the same pace, so that the distance between them did not change. Cavalcanti paused again momentarily, and the man behind him halted in mid-pace. On the bridge, his presence was exposed, but the conductor did not look round, and continued walking, followed by the other man. Almost unconsciously, Mark had been walking behind them, watching their movements. It was apparent that Cavalcanti did not realize that he was being shadowed.

The conductor passed from the bridge into the Place du Port, walking quite briskly, and the man behind increased his pace, drawing closer. Mark followed suit. Cavalcanti headed up the hill towards the old town. As his follower reached the Place, he turned and looked back. Mark was only thirty yards behind him, and continued to walk, but he sensed that the man realized that he was being watched. Under the streetlamps, the man's face was not familiar. He was thickset and broad-shouldered, with dark curly hair, and his clothes were covered by a military-style raincoat. In the poor light, he was too distant for his features to be clearly discernible.

The man hesitated, as though undecided what to do. Then he turned and quickened his pace to catch up with Cavalcanti, who had slowed down slightly as he climbed the hill. Mark walked faster, steadily closing the gap between himself and the stranger.

Halfway up the hill, Cavalcanti turned to his right, moving into one of the smaller streets that crisscross the old town. His shadow followed suit, and Mark hurried forward. The town was already quiet, with only a minimum of traffic. It would remain apparently deserted until the evening cinema and theatre audiences emerged. By the time Mark reached the corner, he could see the conductor's retreating figure at the end of the street, turning left to move deeper into the old town. The man following him had disappeared.

For a moment, Mark hesitated, wondering whether he should warn the conductor. Perhaps he had imagined that the man had been following him. It was a quiet evening. The man may have halted on the bridge behind Cavalcanti because it was deserted. In recent years, people had developed a sort of natural caution when walking at night. No, that was ridiculous. The man had been shadowing the conductor. Why, and who the hell was he? Anyway, where was Emilio going? He had said he wanted an evening stroll, but he seemed to know exactly where he was heading. Mark moved forward again, his eyes fixed on the distant corner round which the conductor had just passed. If he did not catch up quickly, Cavalcanti would soon be lost amid a maze of tiny streets and alleys.

He did not even hear the swish of sound as the blackjack hit him. He was conscious of a movement behind him, and then a flash of sudden pain at the base of his skull. For a moment, white light seemed to blaze in his eyes, followed by darkness. He could feel his senses slipping away as his legs buckled. Instinctively, his hands reached out to protect his body as he fell, and he was vaguely aware of a second blow before he became unconscious. As though in the distance, a low rumble of sound slowly receded, followed by total blackness.

For a moment, Mark felt totally at peace. Then someone was shaking him and, distorted out of focus, he was aware of a voice. It sounded familiar, but he could not place it. The pain in his head was suddenly searing.

"Mark! What is it? Are you ill?"

He longed for the voice to go away and for the peace to return, dulling the pain, but the shaking persisted.

"Please, Mark! Shall I get a doctor? Can you hear me?"

He opened his eyes slowly, and the light from the streetlamp hurt them. His head throbbed.

"Mark!" The voice was urgent.

He tried his eyes again, cautiously, to control the stabbing needles that afflicted them. A shadowy figure blocked out some of the light.

"Can you hear me?"

Slowly, consciousness returned, and he recognized the voice. It was Diana's.

"Can you speak? What happened?"

He tried to sit up, fighting back waves of nausea as he moved his body. Her hands were on his shoulder blades, helping him to a sitting position. There was a strange smell in his nostrils. After a struggle, he sat forward, his head bowed.

"My God! What's happened to you?"

"Give me a moment. I'm just coming round." His voice was harsh. Speaking made his head throb more.

"Can you sit up?"

He nodded, levering himself into position, one hand supporting the weight of his body. With his free hand, he felt the back of his neck, and his fingers came away dry. At least he was not bleeding.

"Can you talk?" Her voice was anxious.

Mark paused, breathing deeply, fighting back the nausea. "Somebody hit me."

"Oh God! Shall I find a doctor?"

"No, I'll be all right." He turned his head gingerly. Sharp spasms accompanied each movement. Then he recognized the unfamiliar odour. It was whisky. Someone had poured it on his face, and he could taste it on his lips.

Diana's face was very close to his. "How did it happen?"

"Someone came up behind me and hit me on the back of the neck. When did you find me?"

"A moment ago."

"What time is it?"

"I don't know." She looked at her watch. "A little before ten. Why?"

"I'm trying to work out how long I've been out cold. It can't have been more than a few minutes." He tried to stand, but his legs were still weak. After an effort, he leaned back against the wall. Diana kneeled at his side. "How did you find me?"

"I just saw you lying there. At first, I didn't realize it was you. I was going to run and get help. Nobody seems to be around. Then, when I realized . . . Who did this?"

"I don't know. He came up behind me." He saw the expression on her face. "He also poured whisky over me."

She watched his face suspiciously. "Are you sure?"

"Certain. I don't drink the stuff, although I could probably do with some right now." He smiled weakly, and she seemed to relax. Mark felt the back of his head again. The pain was beginning to recede. "I suppose I'm lucky he didn't break my neck." Incongruously, a thought occurred. Why did he say "he"? With a heavy enough weapon, a woman could have inflicted the same blow. "How did you come to be here?"

"I was taking a walk. Josh and the engineers went to the bar after dinner, and I didn't feel like watching them drink all evening, so I came out." She shivered slightly. "I walked up into the old town to look at some of the antique shops, and then I lost my way coming back down. When I saw you, I . . ." She left the sentence unfinished. A new thought struck her. "Have you been robbed?"

Mark reached into his pocket. "No."

"Then why . . . ?"

"I'll explain in a minute." He tried to stand again, this time remaining on his feet. A wave of dizziness overtook him, and he leaned against the wall until it passed. Diana stood close, holding him against the brickwork. "I don't think I can hold you up."

"You don't need to. I'm back among the living."

"God, you gave me a scare! Should we try and find a policeman?"

"It won't help very much. I didn't see my attacker. Besides, I have other reasons."

"I don't understand."

"I'll explain in a while. Let's walk back down the hill."

"Can you manage? You could rest a little longer."

"The movement will help."

They walked slowly back to the Place du Port. Mark could feel his strength returning. Diana stayed close, her arm about his waist. She was too small to offer much support, but he enjoyed her closeness. The warmth of her body gave her perfume added strength.

She looked round. "We should be able to find a taxi somewhere here. Can you see one?"

"I'd rather keep walking. I'm feeling much better."

They crossed the bridge in silence. Occasional cars passed, including an empty taxi. As it approached, Diana looked up at Mark's face, but he shook his head.

"Do you want to come to the hotel?"

"No. I live just beyond. Let's go directly there." She nodded, and said nothing.

Inside the apartment, Mark smiled wryly. "I'm going to have a hell of a headache in the morning."

She looked at him. "You're sure it won't just be a hangover?"

"Quite sure. I told you: I never drink whisky."

"If you say so." She looked embarrassed. "While we were walking, I realized that I don't really know anything about you."

"And wondered whether you'd stumbled on a secret alcoholic?"

She blushed. "Something like that."

"I promised I'd explain. Why don't you help yourself to a cold drink." He smiled. "It's all right. There's Perrier in the fridge. I'll get out of these things and take a quick shower. That should revive me."

For the first time, she smiled. "I wish you would. You smell horrible."

"Gross?"

Her smiled widened. "You picked up my favourite word? It seems to be the flavour of the month."

"I'll be back in a few minutes. Make yourself at home."

When he returned, she was curled up on the sofa, nursing a glass of mineral water with both hands.

"You're looking better." She shivered slightly.

"The shower did the trick. How about you?" Diana was shaking, and he moved quickly to her side.

"Just reaction, I'm afraid. Finding you was a bit of a shock."

"Are you sure you wouldn't like something a little stronger to drink?" She shook her head and, with an effort, stopped shivering. "In that case, I'll have a sip of your Perrier."

She watched him. "It's strange, but you seem to be taking this more calmly than I am. It's almost as though you're . . . used to this sort of thing."

Mark paused. "I suppose I'm still coming round. The shock of it will probably hit me later."

"You were going to tell me what happened."

"Yes. I have to ask you something first."

"What?" She was wary.

"Will you keep what I tell you to yourself, for the moment?"

"Why?"

"Because I want to try and find out a little more. Something's going on, and I'd like to keep it quiet until I've learned what's happening. Will you trust me?"

"I don't know. We've only just met. I don't know anything about you."

"Will you at least trust me for a couple of days? You found me unconscious, after all. I'd have to be a contortionist to knock myself out with a blow to the back of my own neck."

She smiled, relaxing slightly. "That's true."

"The recording's about to start. The last thing we want is any additional problem. Please say you'll help."

She was silent again. "All right, but I want to know what happened this evening."

"Someone was following Emilio Cavalcanti when he left the party."

Her eyes widened. "Cavalcanti? Who?"

"I don't know. I don't think he realized he was being followed. It was only by chance that I saw what was going on, and followed the man who was tailing Emilio. I didn't know he was on to me until it was too late." Mark described the events, and she listened in silence.

Diana did not speak until long after he had finished. "What does it mean?"

"I'm not sure, but I have my suspicions."

"Which are . . . ?"

"Cavalcanti's wife. She thinks he's having an affair. He told me about it when he was in London. I think she may have hired someone to watch him."

Diana's eyes widened again. She was more beautiful than he realized. "Do you think that's who he was?"

Mark nodded. "The part that doesn't make much sense is that he'd go to such lengths to remove me. Divorce detectives are usually scared little men who stay out of everyone's way." He rubbed the back of his neck. "This one certainly didn't. He was built like a tank!"

She seemed to be regaining her composure, and suddenly giggled. "Perhaps he's new to the job, and doesn't know he's not supposed to do that sort of thing."

"Perhaps. I wonder whether he caught up with Emilio after fixing me."

"It's strange that this should involve Cavalcanti. I thought I passed him in the street before I found you. He was walking very quickly, and didn't seem to notice me. I'm not completely sure that it was him. It was rather dark, and he was on the other side of the road. Finding you rather put it out of my mind."

"Did you see anyone else?"

"No, I don't think so. It was just after seeing Emilio that I started to lose my way, and took the first street going downhill, assuming that it would take me back to the lakefront. You know what happened after that."

"Yes. Now do you understand why I'd rather keep quiet about all this?"

She nodded. "With any luck, it will all sort itself out. Besides, once the sessions start, Emilio's not going to have much time for evening strolls." Mark spoke softly. "I haven't thanked you. I'm glad you found me when you did."

"I think I'm rather glad, too, but you scared the life out of me."

"I'll try not to make a habit of it."

She seemed embarrassed. "I think I'd better let you go to bed and sleep. It's a big day tomorrow, and Josh will probably start calling me from seven in the morning. I didn't realize he'd be so nervous, considering all his experience." She laughed. "I must admit I'm on edge myself. After all, it's only a record. When you go into one of those big shops, and see thousands of albums in all those racks, you wonder what all the fuss is about."

"Not if you're involved."

"Oh, I'm involved all right. I like your flat, by the way. Is that a real Chagall?"

"It's a real lithograph, but it is signed by him."

"I'm suitably impressed." She walked to the door. "I hope you don't feel too terrible in the morning. I'll give you a call, in case . . ."

"In case he comes back and hits me again?"

She laughed. "No. Just to see how you're feeling." She hesitated, uncertain. "Well, good night."

Mark's arms enfolded her, and she pressed her cheek close to his. For a moment, his mouth brushed against hers, and he felt her lips part. Her arms tightened around his waist, bringing her body closer. Her breasts pushed gently against him.

"I'd better go." She was slightly breathless. "I hope you feel better."

Long after Diana had gone, Mark found himself still standing by the door, her perfume lingering with him and with the memory of her body against his, as though it had left an impression on his skin. How fortunate it had been that she had found him in the old town, and yet it was a strange coincidence that she should have been there at the right moment. Had it been a coincidence, or was she somehow involved? He shook his head. She couldn't have known he would follow Cavalcanti's shadow.

In the morning, he would talk to Abe about the Wiesman call. What was the producer cooking up with Alessandro? He'd been a changed man since he'd arrived in Geneva. And what was Mr. Alessandro—correction, Mr. Abashili, from Georgia—up to? Wiesman's call seemed to suggest that he had other reasons for leaving town than a Hungarian record award. It might be of interest to Quentin in London. Which brought him back to Emilio Cavalcanti. Was he really taking an evening walk? He appeared more like a man hurrying to keep an appointment. That could interest Quentin, too.

Mark frowned. The hell with Quentin! There was a *Tosca* to be recorded, Bianca to be looked after, Simon Vincent to be silenced, and God knew how many other problems to be solved along the way. That was what being involved was about!

EIGHT

"I WISH HE'D MOVE the bloody thing along." Joshua Levin drummed his fingers anxiously on the table next to the recording console. "If he rehearses them at this pace, we'll never get through the score. He's probably doing it to teach me a lesson for arguing with him!" He looked at Diana. "How are the singers doing?"

"Warming up nicely. The last time I looked in on the rehearsal room, Alessandro was trumpeting like an elephant. Bianca sounded marvellous. Should I go and fetch them?"

"There's no point until Cavalcanti's ready. I promised him enough time to prepare the orchestra."

She glanced at her watch. "It's only just after two-fifteen, so he's only had a quarter of an hour's run-through."

Joshua sighed. "It feels as though he's run through the first act of *Parsifal.*" He stared at the black-and-white television screen between the loudspeakers, which revealed the empty space which would be occupied by the singers, and concentrated again on his score. At his side, Graham Budd turned knobs and moved sliders on the large console, isolating the sounds that were feeding into the microphones outside. Jack stood next to him, awaiting instructions to adjust any equipment in the hall.

Diana joined Mark at the back of the room, sitting close enough for her shoulder to press against his. "How are you feeling?" She kept her voice low, to avoid disturbing Levin, and he had the feeling that she did not want the record producer to hear what she said.

"Better than I expected." He smiled. "Hardly any hangover!"

"Don't joke about it. You scared the living daylights out of me last night. I called you this morning, but only got your answering machine."

"I had an early meeting with Abe Sincoff."

"You must be made of iron. Abe's nice. Does he make wisecracks all the time?"

"It's part of being a New Yorker, but don't let it fool you. Under that amiable exterior, there's a mind like a steel trap. We had to catch up on a lot of other business." He decided not to discuss Wiesman's conversation with Alessandro. "How are you?"

Diana was pale and slightly tense. There were brown shadows under her eyes. "I've felt better in my time. What with today's session and last night's drama, I didn't sleep very well. I thought Geneva was going to be a holiday!"

Graham Budd spoke briefly to Levin, then sent Jack to the hall to reposition two of the microphones. To Mark's ears, the sound of the orchestra was already rich and luxuriant, but the engineer was apparently not yet satisfied. He sat at the console stretching his clasped fingers like a concert pianist preparing to attack a keyboard, then made a minor adjustment to one of the knobs. If there was a difference, Mark could not detect it.

Levin looked round irritably at Diana, as though resenting her conversation with Mark. "You'd better stand by to go and fetch Bianca and Antonio in a minute. Cavalcanti's almost reached the end of the sequence we'll be doing. Is the awful Katya Philips going to be here?"

"No." Diana walked to the door. "I suggested that she give the first session a miss, while we settle in."

"Thank God for that. You're learning fast." He managed a smile.

"She didn't seem to mind. Now that Bianca's definitely promised an interview, she's not so concerned with the sessions. She was rather friendly on the phone."

"Good. What about the film people?"

"Wiesman's wandering round somewhere. He's probably looking for a phone to use. Simon and Cliff are already out in the hall, watching. He's set himself up with a little makeshift desk halfway down the stalls, complete with stopwatch and an enormous great pile of coloured pens and paper." She grinned. "Pink paper!"

"Let's hope he knows how to write quietly." Levin relaxed slightly, and turned towards Mark. "This is the worst part of all, before anything begins."

"What are you recording today?"

"The big first-act scene between Tosca and Cavaradossi. It's only about ten minutes."

"I'm surprised you're going for that on the first day."

"Well, originally, I scheduled the scene with Angelotti, but Alessandro's doing his famous disappearing act later this week, and Bianca suggested we try and get it out of the way. She's been very helpful."

"I told you she would be."

Levin smiled. "It has to be recorded sooner or later. Besides, I think she probably figured that it would give her time to do it again later if she's not satisfied with today."

"That makes sense. Have you left room for emergencies?"

"There's always some space. It's a short opera, and if one of the later sessions goes quickly, we can always slot in the extra aria."

Diana returned, accompanied by Wiesman. The film producer seemed to have regained his normal self-assurance, and smiled genially. In contrast with everyone else's casual attire, he was impeccably dressed in a three-piece navy-blue suit, with a carnation in his buttonhole. If anything, he looked as though he was on his way to a wedding.

"Do forgive me for disturbing you. I know how busy you must be at the moment, but Simon would like to know when you'll be starting. Shouldn't you be recording by now?"

Levin was irritable. "Not yet. Cavalcanti's putting the orchestra through its paces. He doesn't want to waste the singers' voices. They should be ready quite soon. Diana, why don't you go and fetch them." She nodded, and departed again.

Wiesman paced in front of the loudspeakers. "I'm accustomed to all those horrendous delays on a film set. I thought it would be different on a recording. You've lost nearly half an hour."

"We're putting the time to good use. There's no point in starting until everyone's ready." Graham whispered in Levin's ear. The engineer seldom spoke above a mutter. Levin nodded. "Would you mind sitting behind us, Wolfgang? If you walk in front of the speakers, it changes our balance."

The film producer sat next to Mark at the back of the room. "Thank God recording sessions don't cost the same as shooting. It's extraordinarily calm, isn't it? I'm accustomed to film sets, surrounded by hundreds of technicians."

"Haven't you been to a recording before? I thought you made several opera films."

Wiesman shook his head. "In the past, we worked from existing tapes, which was never entirely satisfactory. This time, we'll have our own multiple track to play with, which will give Simon much greater freedom." He looked at his watch again. "He's getting very fidgety out there. Perhaps I should take him over the road for a coffee."

Diana returned with Bianca and Alessandro. The soprano, looking serenely calm, was wearing an outsized white sweatshirt and beige slacks. On most women, the garments would have been a shapeless mass, but on Bianca they seemed to emphasize her sensuous figure. Her hair hung loosely to her shoulders. Looming over her, Alessandro was squeezed into a multicoloured silk shirt, with a towel swathed round his throat. His stomach hung precariously over tight black trousers. He was already sweating.

Joshua rose from his chair in greeting, then lifted a portable telephone from the console and pressed a button. Over the loudspeakers, a bell could be heard ringing, and the orchestra stopped playing. Levin's voice had a hard edge.

"Maestro, we're ready to begin." He listened for a moment. "I'm sure it will sort itself out. Madame Morini is waiting."

The tenor slapped his chest. "So is Antonio Alessandro."

Cavalcanti joined them a few moments later. He did not look happy. "I hoped to work a little longer. There are still a number of points I have not covered."

Bianca took his hand. "Don't worry, Emilio. It sounds wonderful. I was very impressed." She turned to the tenor. "Didn't you think so, Antonio?"

"*Sì, sì.*" He puffed out his chest. "Anyway, I am ready. I do not like to be kept waiting once I have warmed up."

Before Cavalcanti could argue further, Joshua took over. "I think we should be able to record the whole scene, from Tosca's entrance." He smiled at Bianca. "Diana here will show you where you walk in from. Your first 'Mario's' should be off-mike." She nodded. "After that, it shouldn't be necessary to move either of you. I don't think recordings should have the singers moving around too much unless the action calls for it. It confuses the listener. Shall we try?"

Alessandro held up his hand. "We will not sing the whole scene. I will make a break after '*Ah, quegli occhi!*' "

"But that's in the middle of the scene."

"No, it is a natural place to make a pause. I do not sing beyond there." He spoke with finality.

Cavalcanti frowned. "I would prefer to make the whole scene."

"No." Alessandro folded his arms.

There was an uneasy silence. Then Bianca smiled sweetly. "That is a good suggestion, Antonio. I'm sure you need a little rest before '*Quale occhio al mondo.*' It must be *very* tiring for your voice."

Alessandro's complexion darkened, but he shrugged. "It does not matter to me, but it makes no sense to sing this entire *scena* without a break. This is a recording. Why should we tire ourselves unnecessarily?" He glared at Cavalcanti.

The conductor looked stubborn. "Musically, it would be better to continue. If it goes well, we will not have to record it again."

"No!" Alessandro stared at Wiesman, but the film producer avoided his eyes. "Who is in charge?"

Joshua spoke quietly. "I am."

"Then you hear what I say. I stop when I stop."

Joshua pretended to study the score. At length, he looked up. "Since this is the first take of the day, I think we should do it your way. We have to make a couple of voice tests first, so why don't you just mark most of it? That gives us a chance to balance you with the orchestra." He turned to Cavalcanti. "It will let you make sure the orchestra's with you all the way."

Cavalcanti's face was expressionless. "Very well."

"Then we're all agreed." Alessandro still stood with his arms folded, an obstinate expression on his face, and Bianca thumbed through pages on her score. Levin continued quickly. "Diana, why don't you show everyone where to stand."

The singers trooped out behind the girl in silence. For a moment, Cavalcanti was about to speak, but he changed his mind and walked briskly after them. Wiesman, looking embarrassed, said, "I think I'll watch outside with Simon," and departed.

The control room was silent for a moment. Then Graham turned a switch and the sounds from the hall returned. Levin spoke softly. "Christ, that man's a shit!" The engineer nodded complacently. In explanation, the record producer turned to Mark. "His next entry's a little taxing, so he wants to make sure his voice is rested. Bianca spotted it immediately."

"I suppose it's natural enough."

"The real point is that he's going to try to run the sessions his way. That little display was just to test us. Do you think Morini will put up with it?"

"As long as he doesn't go too far. She's a professional, but she's also got a temper like a wildcat if you push her."

Levin nodded. "Why does he have to be so bloody difficult from the first moment on?"

"Nerves, mostly, together with the onset of time. You can see it in his eyes. His voice has lost some of the bloom it used to have, and he knows it."

Levin sighed. "He could have proposed a break instead of spoiling for a fight. Why be so bloody aggressive?"

Mark smiled. "He's a tenor!"

Alessandro appeared on the television screen facing a microphone. Standing next to him, Jack pointed to a piece of masking tape on the floor, indicating where the tenor's feet should be in relation to the microphone.

Budd spoke quietly. "You watch. He'll move in another six inches." Jack was already motioning Alessandro back, but the tenor ignored him, refusing to budge.

Levin watched. "Shit! He'll be too present. Can you manage him if he stands there?"

The engineer smiled contentedly. "I took it into account when I taped the floor. He's exactly where I want him to be!"

Jack returned and positioned himself in the small anteroom to work the tape machines. Outside, the cacophony of the orchestra tuning slowly receded. When near silence was achieved, Levin pressed a button on the console.

"Stand by, please. This is Take One."

Immediately, Alessandro raised his hand. "No! This is a test."

Joshua grimaced and pushed the button again. "Very well, this is a test, but I'll call it Take One to identify it." He took his finger off the announce button and called to Jack, "It's still Take One, so log it that way!" Then he pushed another button on the console and a red light shone on the wall between the loudspeakers. On the television screen, a light bulb on a metal stand also blinked into life.

Almost under his breath, Budd added, "And may the Lord bless all who sail in her!"

It seemed to Mark that the "rehearsal" went very well. Bianca's calls floated over the orchestra while Alessandro fiddled with his music, riffling the pages. Anticipating his actions, Graham had carefully switched off the tenor's microphone.

Levin made a note. "I can use that entrance if I need it. Trust that bastard to try and spoil it!"

A moment later, Bianca, led by Diana wearing headphones, appeared on the television screen standing before her own microphone. Joshua pressed another button on the console.

"That's fine. You can leave her there." On the screen, Diana seemed to acknowledge his comment and backed away.

Bianca was the ideal Tosca, combining the passionate concentration of her love with moments of fierce jealousy. Listening to her, Mark was once again struck by the intelligence of her singing. She explored each syllable of the libretto with the flexibility of a great actress and yet never lost the musical line. Her voice was a mixture of honey and cream, with an underlying dramatic intensity, and she seemed to soar through Puccini's endearing melodies effortlessly. It was easy enough simply to enjoy the glorious sound, but the powerful characterization she brought to the role was extraordinarily moving. So few singers combined all those qualities. What was it Joshua had said at Covent Garden? It was a role so demanding that nobody could sing it, until someone came along to disprove him. Mark watched for the record producer's reaction.

Bianca had just embarked on her little aria, *"Lo dici male,"* in which she tells her lover that, after her concert, they can go to his villa in the country to be alone together. It was a difficult aria, filled with tenderness and calling for great vocal control. As she sang, Levin leaned back in his chair, ignoring the score that he had been following.

"My God, I never thought I'd hear it sung like that!" He shook his head as if in disbelief. At his side, Graham Budd lifted his hands from the console, his eyes on the television screen. The voice was perfectly focussed, and there was no need to adjust the controls. It was one of those rare "moments" that the record producer had spoken of.

The passage ended, and both men seemed to sigh in response. Antonio Alessandro chose the next moment to revert to his "rehearsal" half voice, almost inaudible.

Levin brought his fist down on the desk. "Bastard! How could he do that to her?" He looked at the engineer. "Can we save her part?" Budd nodded silently. The producer turned to Mark. "I'm sorry. She shouldn't have to put up with that sort of shit."

The scene continued, with Alessandro alternating between full and half voice, making the tape unusable. He ended abruptly at the point he had indicated, and placed his score on the music stand.

"Okay. Now we will see what they have done to our voices. A playback, please." The last was called imperiously.

Cavalcanti spoke to him. The words were not clear in the general hubbub, but Alessandro's face darkened. "No! I sing nothing more until I hear the playback. If my voice is not right, I do not sing at all. Playback!"

Waiting for their return to the control room, Budd placed three chairs behind the console, so that the artists would listen from the best vantage point. He stood nearby, in case any adjustments were required.

Alessandro appeared first. He glared at Joshua. "Did you pick up my voice right?"

Joshua stared back at him, but kept his tone pleasant. "I'll let you judge that for yourself." When Bianca entered, he walked to greet her, taking her hands. "That was wonderful! I've never heard it sung so well!"

"Thank you. It had some good places, but I think it could be better, and more dramatic."

"That's hard to imagine, but I'll take your word for it." He glanced at Alessandro, who had helped himself to the centre seat behind the console. "We can use the entire *'Lo dici male,'* if you like it."

The tenor frowned. "This was only a rehearsal."

"We recorded it, nevertheless."

Alessandro was about to reply, but was interrupted by Cavalcanti, who entered briskly, walking up to the soprano. "Please forgive me. The clarinets were behind you at one point. I should have rehearsed them more. Your singing was . . ." He waved his arms, at a loss for words.

Bianca smiled graciously. "I am happy, Maestro." Her eyes held his. "You were very sympathetic. It went well, but we will do it again—her smile sweetened—"for Antonio. He is a perfectionist!"

The tenor assumed she was making a compliment. *"Sì.* I do not record until I am satisfied."

Diana hovered by the door, and Mark joined her. "Do you want to listen?" She shook her head. "In that case, I'm going to smoke while they have their playback. I'm dying for a cigarette, but that's one thing Bianca doesn't allow. Is Wolfgang coming to hear them?"

"No. I think he decided it would be more discreet to lie low until Alessandro decides to cooperate. Can I have one of those?"

"Of course. I didn't know you smoked."

"I don't, most of the time, but today's an exception. What's wrong with old Fatso?"

"Alessandro?" She nodded. "According to Josh, he's trying to run the session his way. There's a sort of battle of wits going on between them."

"Oh Lord! You'd think they'd have enough on their plates trying to get it right."

"Levin seems to know what he's doing."

"Oh, he'll fix our Antonio all right. There's more to Josh than meets the eye. He's much tougher than you think." She was silent for a moment, then clasped Mark's arm, hugging him. "Bianca's incredible, isn't she? What an experience, witnessing a living legend in the flesh!"

They stood close together, listening to the music filtering through the door. When it ended, Diana closed her eyes. "It really is gorgeous stuff. I nearly cried. I was ashamed of myself."

"For crying?"

She nodded. "For not being in control. I don't like that." Her hand tightened on his arm. "You must think I'm a terrible amateur, behaving like this."

Mark looked at her. "No. If you want the truth, I think you're—"

The door of the control room was flung open before he could complete the sentence, and Diana quickly released his arm. Alessandro strode out.

"Now we will record. Maestro, a little slower, please, before *'Lo nego a t'amo!'* "

Joshua called after him, "Are you happy with the pickup on your voice?"

The tenor kept walking. *"Sì, sì,* it is all right. I will tell you if it is not. *Andiamo."*

Cavalcanti and Bianca emerged. The soprano glanced at Diana, then looked at Mark. There was a quizzical smile on her face. "It goes well, I think." Her fingers glided against Mark's cheek. *"Ciao, caro!"* Diana followed her down the corridor.

In the control room, Joshua Levin relaxed for the first time. "We're over the worst hurdle. Alessandro couldn't find anything wrong with his voice, what there was of it. God, I can remember some horrendous sessions with a baritone in Rome. Every time he listened to a playback, he announced, 'That's not my voice!' and walked out of the studio. I spent half the session running down the street behind him, pulling on his coattails!"

Cavalcanti rehearsed the orchestra for a few minutes, and Levin announced the new take. This time, Alessandro sang with his full voice. It was a glorious sound, rich and expressive, and the music suddenly blossomed with a new vibrancy. The tenor's heroic tone seemed to challenge Bianca's dramatic powers, giving the scene an even greater excitement. Tiny nuances of expression, which Mark had not noticed in the first take, added to the ebb and flow of the action, making Puccini's score come to life as he had never heard it. When they reached the previous stopping place, Alessandro continued to sing, his tactical games apparently forgotten. Tosca bade her lover farewell, and after a few more bars of music, Cavalcanti brought the orchestra to a halt. Over the speakers, Mark could hear the string players tapping their bows against their instruments in appreciation.

Levin pushed a button. "Bravo, everybody. That was wonderful! Shall we take the general pause?" He turned to Mark, his face glowing. "I'll say one thing for that son of a bitch. When he finally decides to sing, he's sensational! Jesus Christ, what a voice! It's almost worth putting up with all his nonsense."

Once again, Alessandro was the first to return. Sweat streamed down his face, and his shirt clung to him in dark wet patches. This time, he was beaming. "Was good, no?"

"It was magnificent!" Joshua shook his damp hand, and the tenor accepted the praise magnanimously.

"I think maybe I will improve a couple of places. I will show you where, but this is my basic performance." He decided to be generous. "Bianca sang well, too."

"You were both quite marvellous!"

Bianca and Diana returned, accompanied by Wiesman and several members of the orchestra, who lined the rear wall of the room. Diana said, "I'll go and find some coffee," and departed.

When Cavalcanti entered, his face was troubled. He walked rapidly to Bianca and Alessandro, congratulating them, and spoke quietly in Italian. Mark did not hear what he said, but watched the conductor's expression when Simon Vincent entered.

The director, dressed in a black roll-neck sweater and tight-fitting jeans, waved a sheaf of pink papers. "I've made a few notes." He turned to the singers. "It was gorgeous, loves, but I'd like to suggest a couple of teensy changes."

Joshua eyed him savagely. "I think we'll listen to the tape first." He raised his voice. "Quiet, please, everybody."

The take was replayed, and everyone in the room concentrated on the music. At one point, Cavalcanti pressed his hand on Alessandro's shoulder, expressing silent approval.

The tenor, basking in personal glory, pursed his lips and savoured himself like a connoisseur. "Is good. We keep it."

Mark was reminded of the American tenor Richard Tucker listening to himself at a recording session. As he scaled a particularly testing high passage, he had leaned over the producer and whispered, "Those are the money notes, kid. Those are the money notes!"

Diana returned carrying a large tray of coffee cups. She entered the room as the playback ended, and Mark wondered whether she had been waiting until the music ended. Their eyes met for a moment, but she looked away quickly.

The orchestra players filed out, and Levin turned to Cavalcanti and the two singers. Before he could speak, Simon Vincent stood before them, waving his notes. "That was all just super-duper, but I'd like to make a few little alterations."

Alessandro scowled at him. *"Que?"*

Assuming that this was his moment, Vincent addressed Bianca. "Your entry was fine, love, but would you like to pick up a bit on *'Lascia pria che la preghi, che l'infiori'*?" His Italian was dreadful. Turning to Cavalcanti, he added, "You'll have to help her a bit."

The conductor looked astounded. "What do you mean?"

"Well, I'd like to cut the bit where she prays and puts flowers round the altar. I think one quick genuflection will do the trick. I mean, it's really very out of character for an actress, isn't it?"

Bianca's voice was suddenly very cold. "Not this actress!"

Vincent flounced a little. "Oh, go on with you!" He bared his capped teeth. "After all, you're screwing the painter in your spare time, without the sanctity of marriage. The scene at the altar comes off a mite false." There was an ominous silence, and he continued. "We can go into that later, if you like. I don't want to spoil any nice little bits of business, if you have something special in mind." His eyes were turned to the ceiling. "It's a pretty static sort of scene, God knows! Maybe we can try a close-up of your face, seen from the crucifix. It might be fun. Actually, the part that worries me is the aria." He consulted his notes. " *'Lo dici'* what-you-call-it. You know where I mean?"

"Sì." Bianca's voice was icy.

"It all goes by too quickly, and I really need a little more time. What I have in mind is to get out of that dreary old church set and show the audience what you're singing about. It will liven the whole thing up no end. I thought a shot of the two of you running through the woods in slo-mo, with a couple of shots of moonlight on dew-covered ferns." He giggled. "I know it sounds very Ken Russell, but it would work beautifully, if you give me long enough to establish it."

Bianca turned to Mark. "This is a madman—*pazzo!*"

The director looked hurt. "No. Really, love, it would add just the right feeling of movement to the scene, instead of the two of you just standing there. If you're worried about the nudity angle, we can always cover it with long shots and a couple of stand-ins."

"Nudity?" Bianca stood.

"Yes." Simon was in full creative flow. "I visualize a sort of pastoral love scene, with the two of you running together through the woods down to a moonlit beach. It could be terribly sexy, and you sing it so beautifully. Then, with a slow fade back to—"

Bianca swore in Italian, a stream of words delivered in a low, hissing voice. If Simon Vincent did not follow them, he understood their meaning, and backed away. A shocked silence followed her outburst.

She walked to the door. "I will be in my room." Her voice was unsteady. "Please call me when the pause is over."

Alessandro now advanced on the director, his finger ready to jab into the other man's chest. "Listen, you. You don't say one word more, or I leave. You understand?" Vincent nodded, trembling. "This is a film of *Tosca*, starring Antonio Alessandro"—he thumped his chest—"and Bianca Morini! It is not some *pornografia!*" He turned towards a pale-faced Wiesman. "You! If you want to make this movie, you tell him!" For a moment, he looked as though he was about to say more, but checked himself. "I will be in my room also. Maestro, you talk to Mr. Levin. Make a plan for recording, and tell me what you want to do." His gaze returned to Vincent. "You, stay away from me! I don't tell you again!" He slammed the door behind him.

The control room was silent. Simon Vincent looked from Wiesman to Cavalcanti. Then, mustering what dignity he could, he straightened his papers.

"I don't know what all the fuss is about. I was only throwing out a few creative ideas." His voice was petulant. "This is supposed to be a feature film for general release, for God's sake, not a bloody museum piece!"

Wiesman joined him. The producer had regained some of his composure, but he looked uneasy. "I think you and I had better have a quiet talk, Simon. There may be some aspects of this production that I haven't fully explained to you." He placed a hand on the director's shoulder, steering him out of the room.

Levin and Budd remained silent, and Diana put her tray down. There was a ghost of a smile on her face. "Coffee, anyone?"

If the director remained in the hall for the second part of the session, the control room was not aware of his presence, and Wiesman was noticeably absent from further playbacks. The rest of the afternoon was taken up with rerecording small sections of the scene, to improve upon minor lapses of ensemble and small vocal faults. It seemed to Mark that little improvement was made. Cavalcanti was more accurate, Bianca and Alessandro more vocally perfect, but the performance lacked the magic of the earlier take. The tedious repetition of sections destroyed any feeling of spontaneity. Simon Vincent's "creative" suggestions had made the singers nervous and irritable, disturbing their concentration. At one point, Wiesman had tried to reassure them, but Alessandro had raised his hand.

"Don't tell me about it. If you want to make a movie, tell him to shut his mouth!"

At the end of the session, Bianca stood for only a moment in the doorway of the control room. "I am tired, *caro,* and so is Antonio. Miss Nightingale has offered to drive us back to our hotels."

Diana appeared at her side, and Joshua reached into a pocket for his car keys. "The scene is wonderful, and you've covered everything—twice over!"

"Thank you." She blew a kiss in Mark's direction. *"Ciao,* Marco. We will talk later?"

"I'll call." He was disappointed to see Diana leave.

Cavalcanti seated himself behind the console. "May we listen? I would like to be sure of everything."

"Certainly." Levin was not entirely pleased, but he disguised his impatience.

"I am sorry to be a nuisance, but it is good to hear what we have done while it is still fresh in our minds." He smiled at Mark. "I am hoping you will help me convince La Morini that she does not have to rerecord anything."

They listened for nearly an hour. Levin and the conductor marked the score, noting where the best takes should be edited into the master tape.

At length, the conductor stretched. "Thank you for your patience. I am very pleased." He shook the engineer's hand. "Bravo! The sound is magnificent. I have never heard such clarity and detail. You are an artist!" Budd looked vaguely embarrassed.

At the stage door, Cavalcanti put his arm round Levin's shoulder. "We must celebrate. Will you take a drink with me?"

"Delighted to."

"Mark?"

"I'd love to, but I ought to look in on my office. Can I run you home?"

"No." The conductor was still keyed up, exhilarated by the recording. "After such nerve-wracking concentration, I will enjoy the walk to the hotel."

"You seem to enjoy exercise. Did you walk far last night?"

Cavalcanti looked up sharply. "No. I took a stroll by the lake and went to bed. Why do you ask?"

"No reason. I just wondered why you weren't tired. Conducting's a very physical occupation." He watched the man's face, but it was expressionless.

"I am accustomed to it. It is very healthy exercise. That is why conductors live such long lives."

"All those calisthenics? You're probably right."

Cavalcanti smiled. "Thank you for staying behind to listen with me.

Your moral support was appreciated. You know, I was worried before we began, but I found it tremendously exciting!"

"It's going to be an outstanding performance. The rest will seem easy after this. While you're in Geneva, I hope you and Maria will have time to come to dinner one evening."

"I would like that, once we have settled into the routine of the recording. For the moment, I must study the score. *Ciao!*"

Mark watched the two men set off in the direction of the Hilton. A solitary figure was standing across the street, reading a newspaper. As they passed him, he folded the paper and put it in a pocket of his raincoat. Mark caught a glimpse of his face. He was almost certain that it was the man who had been following Cavalcanti the night before. The stranger ignored the conductor and Levin, and remained by the corner, apparently lost in thought. Mark crossed the road, walking towards him. The man looked up and for a moment their eyes met. Then he turned and walked briskly in the opposite direction. He moved surprisingly quickly.

Mark followed, lengthening his stride. He was forced to wait at the next corner when a light changed to allow the busy afternoon traffic to pass. Staring over cars and vans, Mark could see the other man heading towards the centre of the town. He dodged between two vehicles, ignoring the drivers' horns, and broke into a trot. The man was nearly a hundred yards away and walking quickly. For a moment, Mark lost sight of him, and ran forward. On the corner of the Place de la Synagogue, he spotted the stranger again. He had reached the Rue du Stand and had slowed his pace. Mark hurried, closing the gap between them.

When he reached the Rue du Rhône, the man paused for a moment, apparently looking at a window display. His movement was slightly too casual, and he glanced over his shoulder. Mark ducked into a shop doorway, but the man saw him and moved off again. The street was crowded, hindering his progress, but he moved quite swiftly. Avoiding oncoming vehicles, Mark stepped into the road and quickened his pace. He was gaining rapidly on the man.

Halfway down the street, the stranger turned suddenly to his right and entered one of the arcades that served several large shops. Mark cursed under his breath. The shops were busy, and it would be hard to find him in the crowd. Even as he reached the entrance to the arcade, he realized that he could not tell which direction the other man had chosen. He opted for the left, which gave access to a department store. If he had been the quarry, it was the way he would have selected. At the entrance to the shop, he stood for a moment scanning the crowded display counters. Someone in a military raincoat, several aisles away, was walking quickly through the store. Moments later, he lost sight of him again.

"Hello. What brings you here?" Diana was standing in front of him.

"I'll tell you in a minute. Wait where you are." He brushed past her and headed quickly in the direction of his last sighting. There was a door leading to the next street, and he passed through it. Standing on the pavement, he looked in either direction. The road was crowded with rush-hour traffic and office workers going home. There was no sign of the man in the raincoat, and he reentered the shop.

Diana was watching him curiously. "Am I allowed to move yet?"

"I'm sorry if I was rude. Why are you here?"

"What a funny question." She held up a small box. "Toothpaste, and my favourite shower gel, which you can't buy in London. It's rather expensive, but I do love it." She smiled. "I hate to mention it, but you're looking at me rather oddly."

"I'm sorry. I was just surprised to find you here."

"I like looking at shops, especially in other countries. They all sell the same things really, but it seems more exotic in another language. I was going to invite Katya Philips to come with me—good PR and all that—but she wasn't in. She's staying in a little hotel somewhere up the hill. What were you doing just now?"

"I think I saw the man from last night. In fact, I'm sure I did."

"Oh." Her eyes widened. "Where?"

"He was hanging around the hall when I came out with Cavalcanti and Joshua. I went after him, but he saw me and got out of the way. I lost him in the crowd. He probably walked past you a few moments before I arrived. I should have moved faster."

"I think I'm glad you didn't."

"Why do you say that?"

"Well, if it was the same man, he's pretty dangerous. Look what happened last night. Shouldn't you call the police, Mark?" She looked worried.

"Not for the moment. There's nothing to tell them. I can't prove he was the one who hit me. I'm not even sure he was the one who did."

"How do you mean?"

"He could have had an accomplice to put me out of the way while he followed Cavalcanti."

Diana bit her lip. "What are you going to do?"

"Keep my eyes open and try not to get myself sapped again. It hurts!"

She put her hand over his. "Don't joke about it. We should get help."

"We've got nothing to go on. If this character is really shadowing Cavalcanti—God knows why—I'll stay close. If I need extra help, I'll send for it."

"Where's Emilio now?"

"With Joshua. They went to unwind over a few drinks."

"Oh Lord, I wish he wouldn't do that. Joshua drinks too much already."

"It's normal enough, after the nervous tension of a session. Has Levin got a drinking problem?"

"No, I don't think so. He's just under strain at the moment. New York gives him a hard time, and he seems to be burning up inside. It makes him very erratic. I wish he hadn't brought his car to Geneva. Perhaps I ought to go back to the hotel."

She turned to leave, but Mark held her arm. "I'd rather you stayed with me. If you like, I'll give you a quick tour of the old town. There are some beautiful shops. Do you like clocks?"

She hesitated. "Not particularly. I suppose there are bound to be lots of them in Switzerland, especially cuckoo clocks. Wasn't that the line in *The Third Man?*"

"Something like that. I was going to show you an antique shop that specializes in very rare timepieces. The last time I was there, they had one of a pair that were made in 1690. It was unique and very beautiful."

Diana smiled. "I'd like to see it." She leaned closer. "If I'm really honest with you, I have to confess to my secret passion. I love to look at jewellery, and I adore shoes. This town is a paradise of shoe shops. I never saw such a variety. I think I must be some sort of foot fetishist!"

"Maybe we can combine our passions: new shoes for you and antique clocks for me."

"That sounds like fun." Her hand tightened in his. "Just so long as we don't get the adjectives mixed!"

They walked slowly up the steep hill into the old town, scarcely noticing that the streets had become narrow and winding until they were a network of tiny alleys and cobbled paving stones. The modern town seemed to fall away below them, and the smart plate-glass displays were replaced by ancient houses with narrow windows offering antiques and objets d'art. Scarlet geraniums filled wooden window boxes.

Diana paused by an art gallery. "It's so different from down the hill, isn't it? We seem to have stepped back several centuries." She surveyed the street. "It's beautiful! How strange to live somewhere like this. I'd feel as though I were part of a fairy tale."

"There's much more to see, if you've got the energy." She nodded happily. "After which, I know an excellent restaurant tucked away at the top where you can have a genuine, original fondue."

"Then I'll keep going. I'm famished. I haven't eaten today."

"Not at all?"

She shook her head. "Breakfast is a cup of coffee, and I was too strung up at lunchtime. I didn't know how I'd manage the singers. I was terrified of Bianca, but she was lovely. We had quite a long chat in the car to her hotel." She glanced at Mark. "She thinks the world of you."

"We're old friends."

"Is that all? I mean, it's none of my business, but I had the impression that you and she . . ."

"Bianca likes to give that impression with everyone. It's part of her image."

"Oh." Diana walked in silence, but her hand remained in his.

They made their way slowly down the hill after dinner. The evening was warm, and they strolled contentedly, their bodies touching, without speaking. At the empty Rue du Rhône, Diana tugged at Mark's arm, pointing towards lighted shop windows.

"Can I look at shoes? I'm sure there are several shops I missed earlier." She seemed eager to prolong the evening.

Crossing the footbridge over the sluice gates that marked the end of the lake, she paused for a moment, looking down at the swirling water which glowed whitely in the dark.

"What are those for?" Her arm held his waist.

"To control the flow from the lake into the river. This is the start of the Rhône. It goes all the way to Avignon and Arles and on to the Mediterranean."

She stared down. "I'm tempted to jump in and float down."

Mark smiled. "Not from this side. At this time of the year, when all the mountain snow is melting, the pressure of that water runs into tons. If you fell in there, you would be crushed instantly."

Diana shivered at the thought. "In that case, I'll stay here."

"I'm glad."

When they reached the hotel, she did not pause. He looked at her for a moment, but she avoided his eyes and gave the tiniest shake of her head. Her hand clasped his.

Inside Mark's apartment, Diana turned towards him and raised her face. Her lips parted, and her tongue sought his. Then she moved back, her mouth close to his ear. Her voice was breathless. "I've wanted to do that all evening! Help unzip me."

Her dress fell from her shoulders, and she reached behind her back to manipulate hooks. Mark caressed her, and she gave a little sigh of pleasure, her fingers dragging at the buttons of his shirt. Her hands stroked his chest and shoulders, and she drew closer, tasting and probing with her tongue. She loosened his clothing.

"Now you're the one who's overdressed!" Mark knelt before her, slipping the rest of her clothes off and burying his face in warm flesh that seemed to envelop him. She brought his face to hers again, her mouth more urgently demanding. The tips of his fingers explored her body, and she shuddered, holding him closer. Mark stood, lifting her in his arms.

"I'm too heavy for you." Her arms tightened round him.

He kissed her cheeks and the delicate shells of her ears as he carried her to the bedroom. She felt weightless in his arms. On the bed, he lay by her side, gently caressing and touching her, savouring her earthy perfume. It was as though they had been lovers many times before and his hands and mouth knew instinctively how to elicit each sensuous reaction.

Her sighs became moans, increasing in intensity, and she suddenly arched her back with a loud cry that seemed to combine anguish with joy. His own response was lost in the sound.

NINE

MARK AWOKE EARLY when bright sunlight shone in his eyes. His body felt luxuriantly tired, and he allowed it to sink into the mattress. They had made love several times, deep into the night, talking almost in whispers, exchanging secrets until intimacy and passion had drawn their bodies together again. He did not remember falling asleep.

Diana was lying cushioned against him, her body turned away. She slept very quietly, like a child. A wave of tenderness filled him, and he drew her closer, fitting himself to the outline of her body, his hand cupping her breast. He gently clasped the nipple between his fingers and traced lines across the tiny folds of skin, as though memorizing each feature. She stirred in her sleep, then resettled herself, pressing her body against his. Diana did not appear to wake, but after a few minutes she drew his hand downwards. The bright sunlight on his back felt warm.

Later, when her heartbeat had slowed again and she breathed slowly, Diana sighed sleepily. "What a lovely way to wake up. It certainly beats an alarm clock!"

"I didn't intend to wake you."

"I wasn't asleep—just floating. What time is it?"

"Still very early. I forgot to draw the curtains, and the sun woke me."

She giggled softly. "You didn't forget. You were otherwise engaged! I'll make us some coffee." She turned to face him. "Good morning!"

He held her for a long time before she stepped out of bed and walked, naked, to the kitchen. Her narrow waist contrasted strongly with her voluptuous breasts and thighs. Watching her, Mark felt desire stir again.

In a few minutes, she returned with two mugs, handing one to him. "Black, with no sugar."

"You're very observant."

She shrugged. "I watched you at dinner last night. If you want to know the truth, I seem to have spent a lot of my time watching you."

"It was mutual."

"I suppose I was surprised to find you were unattached." She smiled. "Are you sure you haven't got somebody stowed away?"

"No. There was someone, for a long time. She died." He could not bring himself to say more, or to describe her betrayal and death. "How about you?"

"Oh, there have been others—quite a lot of them, I'm afraid. I suppose I was looking for the right one, without being very selective. It happens. Haven't you seen those plaques which say: 'Before she meets her Prince Charming, a girl has to kiss an awful lot of frogs'?" She looked at Mark. "Besides, men don't have a monopoly on sex these days. It's been a long time since women had to lie back and think of England."

Mark laughed. "I noticed!" Bianca had been wrong about the inhibitions of the British.

"Anyway, I'm not English. I'm Jewish. We're a passionate lot." She looked at the clock on the bedside table. "I'd better go back to the hotel. Joshua will start calling my room any minute."

"Is he married?"

"Joshua? No, he's too much of a loner. He likes women, but I don't think he'd be prepared to share his life with one."

"For a while, I wondered whether you and he were involved."

She shook her head. "He's not my type, too intense." Her hand stroked

Mark's chest. "I prefer strong, calm men with hidden possibilities. You're a very randy gentleman, Mr. Holland!" She watched his expression as he leaned forward to embrace her, and moved out of reach. "Just don't talk about love."

"Why not?"

"Because it's too soon. We've only spent one night together. Besides, I'm not sure that I can handle something like that." She grinned. "Let's stick to good, old-fashioned lust!"

"Speaking of which . . ."

She backed away. "Speaking of which, I'd better go. God knows what time Josh went to bed. He could be in a foul mood."

"Cavalcanti looked as though he was set for an evening of celebration. I wonder whether he invited Maria to join them. It was the first time I've seen him relax."

She frowned. "He's wound tighter than a spring. I find him hard to fathom, but I hardly know him."

"I'm surprised you didn't get to know him better during the Verdi *Requiem* performances."

"He was much too busy, and I was running circles round the great Alessandro. The world's greatest tenor was somewhat disappointed when I didn't fall prey to his charms."

"Did he try?"

"Lord, yes, but I was fast on my feet. Fortunately, he didn't really mind. He goes for the willowy type with long legs."

"Didn't you talk to Emilio backstage?"

She looked at Mark curiously. "No. I told you before when you asked me. I talked to Alessandro for a few minutes, and waited outside for Josh, who used his usual escape route."

"What's that?"

"The door at the far end of the greenroom leading into the back of the conductor's dressing room. You can get in and out before the crowds." She walked into the living room, and Mark lay back, closing his eyes. The warm sunlight was seductive. He was almost asleep when her lips brushed his.

"Will I see you later?" Diana was fully dressed again.

Mark nodded. "I want to talk to Abe, after which I'll be free. Will you be at the hotel?"

"Probably. Josh talked about taking a drive along the lake as far as Lausanne, but it will depend on how he's feeling after the night before." She kissed him briefly. "Call me later."

·   ·   ·

The telephone awoke him. "Mark? It's Katya. I'm sorry I haven't been in touch with you. How did yesterday's session go?"

"Very well. They finished the first-act love scene."

"I'm sorry I missed it. What time do they start again today?"

"Four o'clock. Bianca prefers late afternoons and evenings. I recommend you come to it if you want to hear Alessandro. He's disappearing for a couple of days after this to collect a prize in Budapest."

She was silent for a moment. "I'm surprised he gives something like that priority over *Tosca*, but you can never measure a tenor's ego. Bianca Morini is seeing me this morning at eleven. She's being terribly friendly. It's making me quite nervous."

"Would you like to meet afterwards?" Mark regretted the words as soon as they were spoken. If Katya agreed, he would not be able to see Diana.

She hesitated. "I don't think so. If the interview goes well, I'd like to put my notes together while they're still fresh in my mind. I'll probably go straight back to my hotel. However, I'll see you at the session. I just thought I'd check in."

"Do you plan to talk to any of the others? Cavalcanti could use the publicity."

"No, I don't think so." She answered rather abruptly. "My article is about La Morini, but I may do a bit of background work with the rest of the cast. I'll see how it fits together. Wish me luck for this morning."

"You won't need it. Bianca's happy, despite Simon Vincent."

"Is there a story in that?"

"Not really. He'll end up filming it her way and loving every minute."

She chuckled. "You've whetted my journalistic appetite, but I'll wait and see what happens. *Ciao*, baby, as they say!"

Mark replaced the receiver and, after a moment of self-indulgent relaxation, got out of bed. Standing under a hot shower, he thought again about Diana. She had been a passionate and generous lover for whom there seemed to be no boundaries of inhibition, and had shared her body with a mixture of tenderness and animal pleasure. Her perfume still clung to him, and he found himself longing to be with her again.

"I tell you, Mark, there's something about this whole lousy setup that doesn't smell good." Abe Sincoff looked uncharacteristically unhappy. "I talked to Wiesman this morning and asked him for the shooting schedule in Rome. He wouldn't give me a straight answer, and said that guy Vincent was still working on it, together with a whole lot of crap about hiring a new camera crew. On top of that, he tried to give me a hard time about

Bianca's fee, insisting that it was supposed to cover her living expenses for the period." He grunted. "I told him to take another look at the contract we signed, and hung up on him. I don't like the way that character's operating."

"He has budget problems. I told you about that strange conversation he had with Alessandro. When I spoke to him a minute later, he pretended he hadn't been in touch with the man."

"Yeah." Abe busied himself with lighting his first cigar of the day. Rudi, seated on the edge of a chair in Mark's office, put his notebook and pencil to one side and, with a disapproving glance in the American's direction, ostentatiously opened the window wider.

"What do you propose we do?"

Abe exhaled thick smoke. "For starters, we finish the recording. Magnum's covering us on that, but I want a few guarantees from Wolfgang before we tie Bianca down to six weeks in Rome. I don't want any last-minute cancellations. There was a telex from Sydney, Australia, offering a four-week tour during the same period, with some very fancy fees. If Wolfgang wants to pull out, I can make her available"—he grinned—"and collect the cancellation fee!" He turned irritably towards Rudi. "You don't need to write that last bit down, kid. I was just thinking aloud!"

Rudi put his writing equipment away. "Would you prefer me to leave?"

"No, there's no reason why you shouldn't know what's going on. Abe, have you discussed any of this with Bianca?"

"Sure. She's on her way over here with Ettore. I told that broad from the newspaper to find them here. Ettore sounded worried."

"What about?"

"He wouldn't say. It was something he heard on the grapevine. Listen, you know that little guy. He runs a service as well informed as the FBI. I'd sure as hell not want to cross him."

A noise in the outer office heralded the arrival of Bianca and her husband, and Agnes ushered them in. The soprano paused in the doorway, making her entrance.

"Dear friends, what would I do without you to help me?"

Abe grinned. "Save on twenty percent of your income. How're you doing, babe?" Rudi looked appalled.

Ettore's sober expression matched his elegantly tailored three-piece suit. "Thank you for arranging to see us at such short notice. You must be very busy at this time."

Bianca studied Mark's face. "*Caro*, you look tired." Her eyes glistened. "Did you not have enough sleep?"

"I'm fine, thank you. Would you like coffee?"

The banker did not bother to reply. "Since we are all busy, I may as well come to the point immediately. How difficult would it be for Bianca to withdraw from this film?"

Abe and Mark exchanged glances. The American spoke. "It can be handled. What's on your mind?"

"I think it would be better if she were not associated with the project. However, she signed a contract several months ago, involving a substantial sum of money, and I do not want her to be involved in a complicated legal dispute."

"No sweat. There's a clause covering script approval. As long as she doesn't film it for somebody else, we can go on turning down screenplays until Wiesman runs out of money or interest. How about the recording?"

"I would like to go on with that." Bianca smiled at her husband. "It has started so well, and it is the right moment for my voice."

"But not the movie?"

"No." Ettore's voice had a hard edge.

"If you're worried about that dopey director, he can be changed. I'm amazed that he's still around."

"It is a little more complicated than that." Ettore looked towards Rudi, who was hovering by the door. "This is a rather delicate matter, of a confidential nature."

Rudi almost came to attention. "I believe there are several calls requiring my attention. Would you excuse me?" He left the room quickly, closing the door behind him.

The banker seemed to relax. "I would prefer that we keep this information between the four of us. It concerns Herr Wiesman's financial arrangements."

Abe smiled. "You have your doubts, too?"

Ettore shook his head. "Unfortunately, no. I don't doubt his ability to raise sufficient capital for the production. I am more concerned with the source of the finance."

Mark looked up. "We were discussing that just before you arrived. We have the suspicion that Wiesman is having problems, and that he's looking for additional funds through associates of Antonio Alessandro."

The banker turned sharply. "You know about this?"

"Nothing definite. I happened to overhear a phone conversation."

The Italian nodded. "I have heard a similar story, but from a very reliable source. I would prefer not to say who the person is. It appears that

Signor Alessandro is planning to put up most of the financing, at a rate of interest that would best be described as usury."

"That's Wiesman's headache."

"Not entirely. You see, I am very unhappy about Alessandro's backers. I would not like to see Bianca involved in a project involving them."

Abe threw his cigar out of the window. "Are we talking about dirty money?"

The banker did not reply immediately. "I will only repeat that I do not think Bianca should be involved. The Italian press has been watching recent events very carefully. If the information that I have received became generally known, there could be a serious scandal. It would be unwise for Bianca's name to be linked with such people." He hesitated. "Mine also. The banking community is very conservative."

"Have you any proof?"

"Not yet, but my associates are looking into it. They will be very thorough." He looked thoughtful. "I understand that Alessandro is leaving Geneva tomorrow."

"Yes." Mark watched his face. "He's supposed to go to Budapest for an award."

"Indeed? He's chosen an unusual itinerary."

Bianca seemed to be enjoying the drama of the situation. "My dear, he is such a *bugiardo!* He is on a flight to Milano."

"How do you know?"

Ettore cleared his throat. "One of my colleagues happened to be nearby when he made the reservation."

Abe had been listening carefully. "Okay, we'll dump the movie but finish the record. One thing I don't understand. If Alessandro's such a shady character, how come you're singing with him?"

Bianca looked surprised. "Abraham, you do not understand? Antonio Alessandro is a wonderful singer and a great artist, even if he knows it. He is the finest Cavaradossi alive. There is nothing wrong with his voice."

"Just his funny friends?"

"Exactly. When Antonio sings, everybody admires him. I sometimes wonder whether those who know about his other associations do not forgive him for it."

Mark leaned forward. "Are you sure about his connections? I've heard the occasional rumour about his political affiliations."

Ettore looked puzzled. "I do not have definite proof, or I would never have permitted Bianca to agree to the film. What about his politics?"

"I learned quite recently that he was born in Georgia, and only moved to the West when he was a teenager. At the start of his career, he spent a lot of time in Eastern Europe."

Abe's eyes widened. "Are you trying to say the guy's a Commie?"

Mark smiled. Despite his New York worldliness, Abe was an American. "No, but it has been suggested that he might have some close connections on the other side." Quentin would have been proud of such discretion!

Ettore shook his head. "I know nothing about it."

"Rudi found it in his biography. He makes no great secret of it."

Abe look astonished. "Jesus H.!"

The banker stood. "I do not find it very significant."

"Then your colleagues haven't come across any stories suggesting that Alessandro may be maintaining unhealthy contacts in Eastern Europe?"

"They have not been looking into that aspect of his life. Do you think they should?"

"Perhaps."

"It's an interesting thought. You know, there has been very little to link Alessandro with the traffic that some of his . . . friends are associated with. As in all these matters, one studies the problems of supply and demand. I understand this has become a serious new problem in Eastern Europe, almost as much as in the West. Perhaps my researchers have been looking in the wrong direction."

Abe stared at Mark. "Have you been holding out on me, kid? You sound as though you know something I don't."

"No, Abe. Something happened recently in London which made me wonder whether Alessandro's Eastern European connections were stronger than I suspected."

"And were they?"

"I don't know. I haven't seen or heard anything to suggest it."

Ettore moved to the door. "I will make a few inquiries on your behalf, if you wish. If I learn anything, I will let you know."

"Thank you." Mark was aware that Abe was watching him curiously.

"In the meantime, I am late for my next appointment. Bianca said she would meet Miss Philips here." He smiled at his wife. "I will see you later at the hotel."

"*Sì, caro.*" She smiled tenderly. When the banker had departed, she sighed. "It is a shame. I had been looking forward to the film, even with that silly little man directing me. I will take a holiday instead. Maybe Ettore will find his information is incorrect." She looked at Abe hopefully. "Do you think so?"

"Perhaps. If you change your mind, there's a guy in Sydney, Australia,

who's begging for you. You never sang in that meshuga opera house, did
you?"

"No, *caro.*"

"Well, if Rome falls through, there's a bunch of beautiful rich Aus-
tralians who want you. Are you interested?"

"I don't know. It is a long way to travel. Would you keep me company,
Marco?" Her long lashes seemed to mask her eyes.

"It depends on how long the trip would last."

"I would be lonely, so far from home." She smiled wickedly. "I'm told
that Australian men are very big and handsome, like that crocodile man
with the long knife. Very masculine! Do you think I would like them?"

Abe patted her knee. "Sure you would, babe. Hell, I'll take you if Mark's
tied up."

"Then I will think about it." The idea seemed to cheer her. "I saw
Maria Cavalcanti this morning."

"Where?"

"At my hotel. She said she wanted a change of scenery from the Hilton,
but I think she was looking for Emilio. She's a very unhappy woman, you
know."

"I thought you didn't like her."

"I don't, but I feel a certain compassion. She is a wife, like me." For a
moment, Bianca tried to look virtuous.

"Did she say what was the matter?"

"No. I had the feeling she was going to, but Ettore joined us, and she
would not discuss it in front of him. I am sure she wanted to talk about
Emilio. She hinted that he was involved in something, but she would not
say anything more."

When Katya Philips arrived, she seemed slightly distressed to find Mark
and Abe. "I didn't realize this was your office. Madame Morini gave the
address, but I didn't make the association." The reporter looked tired.
There were dark shadows beneath her eyes, and her face was paler than
usual. It made her lipstick appear stark. "Are we going to hold the interview here?"

"No." Bianca was watching her speculatively. "It is a little too clinical
for me. I have Ettore's car, so we will go back to the hotel." She kissed Abe
goodbye and waved to Mark. "Will you be at the session, *caro?*"

"Of course."

"Then I will see you later. You must try to catch up on your sleep."

When she had gone, Abe looked puzzled. "Is it just me, or was Bianca needling you, kid?"

"Not that I noticed."

"All those cracks about not enough sleep—what were they about?"

"I wouldn't know. Do you believe Ettore's story about Alessandro and his financial friends?"

"Maybe. Ettore could have other reasons. Those Italian bankers can be very devious. What the Sam Hill was that other stuff about Alessandro? Is he a Red?"

Mark hesitated before speaking. "I don't know. If Ettore is right, our oversized tenor has some very unhealthy Sicilian playmates. Katya Philips suggested the same thing in London, but I didn't take it very seriously."

"And the Russian angle?"

"It's possible that his friends may be using his Eastern European contacts in some way to extend their empire, but I don't know how. For one thing, they're not going to be interested in money from that side of the border. It's useless in the West."

"Unless he's arranging payment in kind. Wasn't there a movie about a guy smuggling sables?"

"That was a movie, Abe."

"Then why all the sudden interest in Eastern Europe? Jesus, Wiesman's guy Layton was giving me some crap about Cavalcanti and the Italian Communist Party. I began to feel I'd walked in on a Commie plot. Is any of this for real?"

"I don't really know. It was just an idea. I think money is much more likely to be the motive than politics."

Abe lit a cigar. "There are times when I think this racket is getting too complicated for me. Whatever happened to the old-fashioned artists who worried about their music or which of their colleagues was getting the better reviews? Maybe these guys earn too much."

"You should know, Abe. You're the one collecting a percentage."

He grunted. "I'd trade most of it to go back to the old days. Musicians I understand; financiers I don't. Listen, I'll go through a few plans with you, then we'll pick up Myra for lunch at the hotel. She told me to invite your nice Jewish girlfriend to join us. Okay?"

"I'll call her. If we make it an early meal, she should be free. She's needed at this afternoon's session."

There was a quizzical smile on Abe's face. "This young lady wouldn't have anything to do with Bianca's cracks about your sleeping habits, would she?"

"No."

"Come on, kid, this is your Uncle Abe talking to you. Are you holding out on me?"

"Of course not."

"Then why are you looking so goddamn guilty?"

They did not finish lunch until two-thirty. Relaxing in the sunny restaurant overlooking the lake, it seemed to Mark that the problems and unresolved questions belonged to another place, and he allowed himself to be regaled by Abe's seemingly endless supply of jokes and anecdotes from the music world. He suspected that they were mainly for Diana's benefit. Abe entertained them like a professional raconteur, and Diana listened wide-eyed, reacting delightedly to each well-timed punch line. Myra, apparently concentrating on her food, inspected her through half-closed eyes. She was satisfied with what she saw, and caught Mark's eye, nodding approvingly and turning down the corners of her mouth, like a connoisseur giving approbation to a good wine.

Abe snatched the bill from beneath Mark's hand. "I've got to show Uncle Sam something for my travels. You do the next one."

"Will you come to the session?"

"Nah. We're six hours ahead of New York. I can only start making my calls to the real world around now. Besides, they don't need me for a recording. *Tosca* I heard already." Abe always affected a New York accent when there were spectators. In the quiet of his office, the Brooklyn-Jewish accent was scarcely audible.

Diana turned to Myra. "Won't you come? It's going terribly well."

"I'll be with Abe." She looked at Mark. "We'll be seeing Diana again?"

"I hope so."

"That's good. I'm looking forward to a nice, long talk."

As they walked across the footbridge towards Victoria Hall, Diana took Mark's arm. "They're lovely people. Abe's so funny! Did he really know all those musicians?"

"Abe knows everyone."

"He's amazing. Listening to him talk, I felt like such a beginner. I didn't notice how late it was getting." Her voice softened. "It would have been nice to have a quiet siesta before the session."

Mark smiled at her. "The way I'm feeling at the moment, I'm not sure it would have been that quiet! What happened to Josh?"

"After rushing back to my room, feeling guilty, I didn't hear a word from him. I finally called him, and he said he wanted some time to himself. He sounded a bit irritated to be disturbed."

"Maybe he called earlier."

"I don't think so. Josh can be very moody. Anyway, he was trying to rework the schedule for the tenth time."

"I thought you'd already done that."

"So did I, but he said he wasn't happy with it." She walked in silence. "Can I ask you something? You don't have to tell me if you don't want to."

"Anything you like."

"Is everything all right with this production? Every time I mentioned the film during lunch, Abe smiled and quickly changed the subject. I felt as though I was entering forbidden territory."

"You're very astute."

"Then something is wrong?"

"Perhaps. We're waiting to hear from Ettore."

"Poor Josh, New York will give him absolute hell! Will you tell me about it?"

"It's rather complicated, and it could yet be sorted out. Put in a nutshell, Ettore doesn't approve of Wolfgang Wiesman's financial associates, some of whom have rather shady connections. He's worried about any possible hint of scandal, so he's having them vetted by his banking friends."

"Oh Lord! What will happen?"

"If he doesn't like what he learns, he'll allow Bianca to finish the recording, but he'll pull her out of the film. You'll get your record either way."

"I see." She was thoughtful. "No wonder I kept feeling I'd put my foot in it. Do you think the man following Emilio had anything to do with this?"

"In what way?"

"Well, he might have been hired to check his movements, too. Something like that. If Ettore is worried, we could all be suspect."

"I doubt it. Ettore's only expressed concern with Wiesman's crowd." He decided not to mention Alessandro's involvement. "That doesn't include Cavalcanti."

"I suppose not, except that you keep showing a great deal of interest in him."

"That's not surprising. I'm his manager."

"But whenever his name comes up, you become . . . I don't know . . . different." For a moment, her face was serious. "Don't pretend with me Mark; not after last night. Is he tied in with this?"

"Not that I know of."

"Well, something's going on. I wish you'd tell me what it is."

"I will. I promise. Leave it for a while."

"When will you tell me?"

"As soon as I've found out. I'm as much in the dark as you are. Let's talk about it some more tonight."

"Are we seeing each other tonight?"

"I hope so." Something in his voice made her turn and look at him. "We'll talk again."

She suddenly smiled. "If we can find the time!"

At the corner of the Rue de Hesse, a small crowd had gathered. The spectators appeared to be surrounding several uniformed men. Nearby, a police car, its blue light flashing, blocked off the end of the road.

"What's going on?"

Mark shrugged, scarcely pausing. "Some sort of accident, I imagine. This is a bad corner."

An elderly woman carrying a shopping bag drew away from the others. She turned to Mark. "Someone was murdered!" She was enjoying the drama, and was pleased to find a newcomer to inform.

"Murdered?"

"Yes. Shot dead, in broad daylight." She shook her head. "I don't know what this town is coming to!"

"Did they catch the man who did it?"

"No. I heard someone say the assassin used a silenced revolver, and walked away from the scene as cool as a cucumber. Nobody realized until the poor fellow collapsed in the gutter. It's disgusting! There are too many foreigners living here. We don't want this place to turn into another Beirut!" She clicked her tongue and moved off, in search of a new audience.

Mark looked at Diana. "I'd better have a quick look."

"Why? What did she say?"

"Someone was shot." He did not mention the silenced revolver. Killing someone in broad daylight reminded him of Bruton Mews.

"Good God! Why do you want to look?"

"We're very close to the hall."

"You don't think . . . ?"

"I don't know. I'd just like to be sure it isn't anyone we know. Wait there."

He pushed his way past several bystanders. Guarded by two policemen, the body of a man lay on the pavement. Someone had draped a raincoat over the head and upper torso. A dark, sticky liquid stained the surrounding flagstones.

One of the policemen watched Mark approach. "Stand back, please. There's nothing to see."

"I was expecting to meet somebody on this corner. I was worried . . ."

"Who?" The policeman was cautiously polite.

"A friend."

"His name?"

"Jules Roche." It was the first name that came to mind.

"Wait." The policeman spoke to his colleague in a low voice, then returned. "You'd better take a quick look, in case it's your friend. This man doesn't seem to have any identification on him. Come over here."

Shielding the body from the crowd, the man leaned down and raised a part of the raincoat. "Is this your friend?"

Mark bent low. It was the man he had followed the day before. He stared at the ashen face, trying to recall whether he had ever seen it in the past.

"Well?" The policeman was watching his reaction.

Mark straightened up. "No, that's not my friend." As an afterthought, he added, "Thank God!"

The policeman eyed him severely. "Do you know him?"

"No. I've never seen him before."

The man remained suspicious. "Are you sure you were expecting to meet someone here?"

"Yes, I told you. Otherwise, why should I say so?"

"Because people can get twisted ideas. Maybe you just wanted to look at a corpse. I've had that happen before. Some people have ghoulish tastes. What is your name?"

"Mark Holland. My office is just round the corner."

"Oh? Why didn't you arrange to meet there?"

"We were going to have a coffee at that café."

The policeman hesitated, reasonably satisfied. "And you've never seen the deceased before?"

"Never. I'm sorry if I was a nuisance."

"That's all right. I can understand your concern. You'd better pass along."

Diana was waiting for him. "Who was it? You were a long time."

"The man who was following Cavalcanti."

"Oh." She looked frightened. "Did the policeman tell you anything?"

"No. He asked me if I knew who he was, but I decided not to say anything."

"Why?"

"Because it could lead to all sorts of complicated questioning. Anyway, I told the truth. I don't know him. He wasn't carrying any sort of identification."

"That's unusual. I mean, most people have credit cards or something these days."

"Yes." Mark was lost in thought.

"Then why didn't he?"

"Apparently he wanted to remain anonymous."

She took his arm. "Let's go away from here. I don't like what's happening."

In the control room, they found Joshua hunched over the console checking his opera score. He looked up, nodding his greeting.

Diana collected her file of papers. "Did you see the trouble outside?"

"No. What was it?"

"Someone was shot in the street. There was quite a crowd. It held us up for a few minutes."

"It must have happened after I arrived. Who was it?"

"We don't know. Some man." She glanced towards Mark.

Joshua put down his score. "Christ! That's not the sort of thing you expect in the heart of peaceful Switzerland. How did it happen?"

"We don't know. We saw people standing round, and someone told us about it."

"I imagine it will be on the news this evening. Have you heard from Cavalcanti?" She shook her head. "Damn! I've been trying to reach him all morning. I wanted to suggest a couple of changes in the schedule. If things keep going as quickly as yesterday, we should have some extra material up our sleeve. Where is that bloody man? I tried his room a couple of times, but he was never there."

"You should have asked him last night, when you went for a drink."

The record producer shrugged. "There wasn't that much time. He drank a glass of wine and disappeared. I don't know why he made such a point of inviting us to join him. He was desperate to leave as soon as we got there."

"That's strange. I had the impression that he was all set to celebrate."

"So did I. He was very edgy. He's a funny character, isn't he? One minute, he couldn't be friendlier, and the next, he's formally polite and cold as ice. I find him hard to read. It's as though he's trying to cover something up."

Cavalcanti entered the room, and Levin brightened immediately. "Hello, Maestro. Did you have a good rest?"

"Thank you, yes." He shook hands, nodding briefly towards Mark and Diana.

Mark stood. "You seem to have arrived at the right moment. We were about to start looking for you."

The comment seemed to disturb the conductor. "Why? I'm not late, am I?"

Levin smiled. "No, of course not. It's just that I've been trying to get in touch with you, to suggest some additional material for the session. Everything went so well yesterday that I thought we should plan an extra sequence today. We could find ourselves running ahead of schedule. I called your room a couple of times this morning, but I missed you."

Cavalcanti's mouth was set in a firm line. "We can discuss that now." He stared at Levin. "I do not have to discuss my movements with you." The record producer blinked, and was silent.

There was an uneasy pause. Mark exchanged a glance with Diana before speaking. "Did you see the trouble outside?"

"No." Cavalcanti was thumbing through Levin's score.

"A man was shot, on the corner of the Rue de Hesse. There was quite a crowd when we went past a few minutes ago."

"I didn't notice."

"Really?"

"Perhaps I came by a different route." He looked up. "Do you doubt me?"

Mark smiled. "Of course not."

"Then why are you and Mr. Levin so interested to know where I have been? I do not like people to pry into my private affairs."

"Josh wasn't prying, Emilio. He simply wanted to get in touch with you."

The conductor scowled. "I heard what he was saying as I came into the room." He looked from Mark to Joshua. "You seem to be taking an unhealthy interest in me."

"Not at all. We—"

"Understand this." The conductor's voice was raised. "What I do in my own time concerns me and me alone. It is none of your business!"

Mark could feel his temper rising. "Nobody's suggesting that it is."

"I do not like being interrogated in this way." He glared at Levin. "If you wish to speak to me, leave a message for me at the hotel, and I will call you as soon as I can." He crossed the room. "Otherwise, leave me alone and stay out of my private life. It has nothing to do with you." He strode out, slamming the door behind him.

TEN

"WHAT TIME IS IT?"

"Still very early. I'm sorry if I woke you."

"You didn't." Diana yawned and stretched lazily. "I was snoozing."

"I was watching you. You sleep very quietly." She was lying face down, her head turned towards him, and he stroked her back gently, his finger-nails making delicate pink lines on the surface of her skin. "Are you going to have to steal away with the dawn?"

She sighed sensuously. "No. I told Josh not to disturb me this morning, and said I wanted a long lie-in. After a late night, he'll probably sleep, too. I enjoyed the supper, even if everyone stayed longer than expected. They were all surprisingly friendly, for a change."

"It was a very good session. Bianca and Alessandro just about finished everything they have together."

She paused to kiss him. "They were marvellous. I never expected them to get the whole of that third-act scene completed, especially with Emilio throwing tantrums before we started. He certainly calmed down later. Do you think Alessandro will want to do 'E lucevan le stelle' again?"

"Probably, although he doesn't need to. It's his big war horse, and he'll keep doing it every time he gets the chance. Joshua handled him very well. When they'd finished the scene, I thought they would want to go home, but he played on Alessandro's ego."

"That's not so difficult." Her hands caressed Mark's chest and shoulders. "The man's a natural show-off. As soon as Josh suggested he was too tired to do the aria, it was like a challenge."

"Exactly. He knew what he was doing." Mark's fingertips traced patterns along the curves of her body, embracing and caressing, and she drew closer.

"So do you!" Her face rested against his cheek, and her mouth explored the line of his jaw. She giggled softly. "The earth moved several times last night! Do you think it registered on the Richter scale?"

"I hope so." They kissed again, and her arms tightened around his shoulders, her fingers pressing deeply. Mark's hands moved over her body, now familiar and yet still to be discovered, and he could feel her trembling response.

"I love it when you touch me." The words were whispered almost shyly, and her thigh moved against his leg, gently massaging it. She was breathing faster.

"You're so lovely!" His body covered hers, and her legs suddenly clasped him tightly.

Later, she lay nestled in his arms. "I didn't think this was going to happen."

"Nor I. I'm not usually so lucky."

She smiled. "Flattery gets you everywhere! If you want the honest truth, I thought you'd find yourself in the clutches of the beautiful Katya, although we've seen surprisingly little of her since she arrived."

"She interviewed Bianca yesterday, which was the main reason for her visit."

"I know. I've done my best to be friendly, but she stays very aloof. Magnum offered to put her up in the Hilton, but she insisted on choosing that funny little hotel in the old town, next to the restaurant where we had dinner. Do you know it?"

"I've seen it. I didn't know she was staying there."

"It's not very chic for a leading lady of the British press." Diana smiled. "Anyway, I thought she'd prefer to stay on this side of the lake. It would have been much handier for your apartment!"

"She's not my type."

"Maybe, but she was coming on very strong in London. I thought she'd already taken possession of you. I have to admit she's very good-looking."

"I hadn't really noticed."

"I don't believe you. Those lovely long legs! I would kill for them! When you've got short, thick stubs like mine, tall girls make you sick!"

"She's virtually anorexic, and flat-chested. It would be like going to bed with a boy." He reached down. "Nobody would ever mistake you for that!"

Diana sighed. "If you go on doing that, you know what will happen."

"Promise?" He smiled.

"I may never walk again!"

He was drifting, half asleep, when the telephone rang. At his side, Diana stirred, then buried her head in the pillow to escape the sound. Mark looked at the bedside clock. It was not yet eight o'clock. The telephone persisted, and he realized that he had forgotten to set the answering machine.

"Hello?"

"Mark? What the hell's going on?" It was Quentin. He recognized his voice immediately.

"Why are you calling? I said I'd be in touch if anything concrete developed." Diana looked up. "I'm not about to start reporting in. I told you that in London."

"I know, but quite a lot has been developing."

"What do you mean?" Diana was watching him, her eyebrows raised in a silent question.

After a pause, Quentin spoke again. "I took you at your word when you said you would do very little for us in Geneva."

"And?"

"I sent someone of my own from London."

"Good. That let's me off the hook. What has he learned?"

"Not much. He found some sort of connection with Budapest, but that's beside the point now."

"Why?"

"He's dead."

Mark sat forward. "When?"

"Someone shot him in the street yesterday afternoon. I thought you would have heard about it in a small town like Geneva. Did you?"

"Yes. I saw the body. It happened quite near the hall where the recording's taking place."

"Then why didn't you call me?"

"I didn't make the connection between you and him."

Diana whispered, "Who is it?" but he motioned to her to remain silent.

"I see." Quentin paused for a moment. "He was one of ours. I sent him over to keep an eye on your Signor Cavalcanti. Do you think he did it?"

"I don't know. He could have, but I have nothing to go on."

"Does that mean you think he did?"

"No. Don't jump to conclusions."

"Then why the doubt in your answer, or are you protecting your client?"

"No, it's just that he behaved rather . . . oddly yesterday afternoon. I asked him something, and he felt I was prying into his private life. I could be making all sorts of unfair assumptions. Cavalcanti's a very private man."

"Or a very guilty one. The whole incident seems rather too similar to what happened to Tony Rossiter, doesn't it?" Mark did not reply. "I've persuaded the Swiss police to help us, which is unusual for them, but I'm prepared to bet that the bullets taken from the body will match the ones that killed Rossiter." When Mark remained silent, he asked, "Are you still there?"

"Yes. I'm trying to think."

"The similarity is too coincidental, considering the circumstances."

"Perhaps. Are you holding anything back from me, Quentin?"

"What do you mean?"

"Is there additional information that you've conveniently forgotten to pass on?"

"No, I give you my word. I wish I had. All I know is that something involving Budapest came up. My man said he recognized a face, but he had nothing else to go on. Have you any idea who else, other than Cavalcanti, it might have been?"

"No, but it could have been any one of several people." Mark turned for a moment towards Diana, who was watching him with a troubled expression. He stroked the curve of her cheek. "I know one person who couldn't have done it."

"Who?"

"It doesn't matter. She was with me at the time it happened."

"She? I might have guessed! You haven't mentioned any women before. Was she a suspect?"

"Not really, but I left all possibilities open." Diana continued to look puzzled, and he leaned forward to kiss her lightly. She was about to speak, but he placed a finger on her lips.

"All right." Quentin sounded tired. "I'm waiting to confirm the matched bullets, after which I'll probably come over to Geneva. Keep your ears and eyes open."

"I intend to."

"Is there anything you can do to help?"

"Perhaps. I might even try to stir things up a little, to see what happens."

"In which case, for God's sake be careful."

Mark smiled. "Your sudden concern for my welfare is touching!"

"Don't get too sentimental, Mark. You're just about our last link. Without you, the whole trail goes cold."

"That's more like it! I haven't overlooked the fact that, until now, you neglected to mention the presence of a messenger boy in Geneva. Did he have a partner?"

"No. Why do you ask?"

"I wanted to be sure. I don't like surprises."

Quentin did not react. "I understand you ran into him."

"He certainly ran into me. Why the hell didn't you tell me he was going to be there?"

"I thought it would be safer if you worked independently of each other. You told me you didn't want to be involved."

"That's true."

"I hoped that if he operated separately, you wouldn't be drawn into it." Quentin did not sound very convinced by his own answer. "It seems you caught him following Cavalcanti."

"And got my head thumped for my troubles."

"I'm sorry about that. He was careless."

"So was I, or the situation might have been reversed."

"Quite. I should have warned you. He was a good man."

"They always are, in retrospect."

"I hope you didn't suffer too much discomfort."

Mark looked at Diana again. "There were compensations."

"I don't understand."

"You weren't supposed to. When do you expect to be here?"

"I don't know. I'm needed in London at the moment and I haven't anyone else I can spare. Will you hold the fort?"

"No. I told you I wouldn't, but I'll keep my eyes and ears open, as you suggest. Presumably, I'm more expendable than the rest of your valiant staff!"

"I've already conceded that you're our only link. Be cautious, and avoid taking on the world. You don't work for us."

"I'm glad you remembered!"

"What do you know about Antonio Alessandro? I've heard some strange stories."

"So have I, but they're all hearsay. It seems he's a Georgian by birth. His real name is Abashili, and he crossed the border illegally into Turkey when he was a teenager."

There was a pause before Quentin spoke again. "That could be very interesting. What else?"

"The family moved on to Italy, and there's more than a suggestion that they're involved in the drug trade." He glanced towards Diana, who was now kneeling on the bed, watching his face. "We think his associates are helping to finance the film involving Cavalcanti, Morini and Alessandro. That's why they're here, to record the soundtrack."

"I hadn't forgotten."

"Bianca's husband is investigating the situation through his Italian banking colleagues. He doesn't want her associated with a project financed with laundered money."

"I see." There was a long pause before he returned. "Sorry to keep you, but I was making a few notes. Anything more?"

"Yes, but it's vague. Alessandro also has strong associations with Budapest."

"It's funny how that city keeps coming up. How strong is his connection?"

"I'm not sure. He worked there a lot at the start of his career, and he still goes back quite frequently. He was supposed to fly to Hungary this week, to collect some sort of record award, but he booked himself to Milan instead. Bianca's husband thinks he's going there to raise extra funds for the film. He's making a few private inquiries before he decides whether she should stay in the film."

"Where does Budapest come in?"

"I'm not sure. It's been suggested that Alessandro could be providing a bridge between his Italian pals and Eastern Europe, but it's only a theory."

"I'll look into it. What you're saying could be true, but it doesn't really tie in with Rossiter and his girlfriend, does it?"

"No, unless the whole Italian operation disguises his real interests. For a man who officially defected years ago, he seems to move very freely in and out of Eastern Europe."

Quentin sounded testy. "You should have told me all this sooner. We've been wasting time. Where was Alessandro yesterday?"

"At the time of the murder? I don't know. Either at the hotel or on his way over to the hall." Diana was about to speak, but he placed his hand over hers to restrain her.

"And Cavalcanti?"

"Same thing. He made an odd comment when I mentioned the murder to him. The man was shot on a street corner lying directly between the hotel and the hall, but he claimed not to have noticed the police cars or the crowd that had gathered. He said he must have come there by a different route."

"Is that so odd?"

"Yes, if he was walking from the hotel. He wouldn't have missed it. It was just after that exchange that he lost his temper and said that I was taking too much interest in his private life."

"I see." Quentin sighed audibly. "So we're no farther forward than before."

"No."

"Except that I've lost one of my better men. I'll do some checking from this end."

"Do you have any news of the Polish girl?"

"No. We made some inquiries. She left the country around the same time that Rossiter went to Ireland. We traced her to a Lot flight from Heathrow to Warsaw. The Polish authorities refused to discuss her when we asked. At the first mention of her name, they became rather formal and very silent. They didn't hesitate to point out that we had requested them to pull her out of the country."

"Did you try your own people in Poland?"

"Yes, of course we did." Quentin sounded irritated. "We're not that inefficient! They didn't come up with anything. God knows where she is by now. We'll keep looking, but we don't have much hope. Why are you so interested?"

"For Rossiter's sake, I suppose. You didn't hear him talk about her. I'd like to think she was genuine."

Quentin laughed dryly. "You're becoming remarkably sentimental, aren't you? Why should you care?"

Mark looked for a moment at Diana. "No reason. I was just curious."

"If I learn anything, I'll let you know. Please call me if anything new comes up, no matter how insignificant. I'll be with you in Geneva as soon as I can get away. Meanwhile, for heaven's sake, stay in touch."

"You, too. I have an answering machine. Nobody else listens to it. If I'm not here, leave a message."

"Very well." The line was disconnected.

Mark replaced the receiver and lit a cigarette, turning his back to Diana. She had not moved, and when he turned towards her, she was still kneeling, her arms folded across her breasts, as though protecting them.

"You promised to tell me what this is about." She moved forward, suddenly holding him tightly. "Sweetheart, what's going on? Who were you talking to?" Her voice was edged with fear.

"A man in London."

"What man? You called him Quentin. Who is he?" When Mark did not reply, she continued. "Did Emilio or Alessandro kill that man yesterday? Who is the Polish girl, and what was the part about Rossiter? He was the man who spoke to you at Covent Garden, wasn't he? I thought you didn't remember his name. Please, tell me!"

Mark hesitated. "I'll tell you, if you really want to know. It would probably be better if you didn't."

"It's too late for that. Please, Mark! Who is Quentin, and why is he calling you?"

He stubbed out the cigarette before replying. "His name is Quentin Sharpe, and he works for British security."

"Like MI6?" Mark nodded. "Do you work for him?"

"No. Our paths have crossed in the past."

"But he's in MI6?"

"Something like that. They prefer to be less visible than the official security people."

"What does he want?"

"Quentin believes that either Emilio Cavalcanti or Antonio Alessandro is a courier."

"What does that mean? I don't understand." She leaned back on her haunches, her hands at her sides, looking beautiful and very vulnerable.

"He believes that one of them, or even both, is being used to transfer secret information from Britain to—"

"You mean they're spies?"

"Not exactly, if you want to split hairs. They're couriers, or they could be."

"But why?"

Mark shrugged. "Money, or politics—probably the latter. They both earn enough already, which could mean they're motivated by political belief. That makes them more dangerous. At least spies do what they do for a living. Cavalcanti was a member of the Italian Communist Party when he was younger, and Alessandro isn't even an Italian. He comes from Georgia. Maybe he feels closer to Mother Russia than we know. You heard what I said to Quentin."

"What about the Polish girl and Rossiter? I don't understand."

"I'll try to explain. It's rather complicated." For a moment, his hand caressed her body, and he smiled wryly. "Funnily enough, it's a sort of love story." He lay back on the bed, and she nestled against him, her head resting on his shoulder.

When he had described the transfer of the papers at the Festival Hall, Diana suddenly sat up. "Now I remember where I saw him!"

"Rossiter?"

She nodded excitedly. "He was standing next to me in the corridor, backstage, after the concert. I was waiting for Josh, and he was there in the crowd milling around the dressing rooms. I only noticed him because he was there after the second performance as well. I thought he must be an agent or someone involved with the performance because he was there both times. You know how it is. He didn't really register with me, but seeing him a couple of times left a vague impression. I'm still quite new to it all, so I don't know who everyone is. That's why I thought I recognized him when he spoke to you at Covent Garden."

"Can you remember anything about him? Was anyone with him at the time?"

"I don't think so. It's all just an impression. On the first evening, I'd been talking to Antonio, and came out into the corridor to look for Josh. Rossiter was standing there, but I didn't really think about it. Then Josh came out, and we left together."

"You don't remember anything else? Think back."

Diana closed her eyes, concentrating. "It's all too vague. I wasn't thinking about Rossiter at the time. I was probably trying to make Josh get a move on. He loves to stop and chat with all his friends backstage. It's like a club for him."

"What about the second performance?" Mark watched her. "It could be very important. Can you remember anything different?"

"I don't think so. I went to see Alessandro, but he was on his way out of his dressing room. I think he wanted to talk to Emilio, but I don't remember why. Then I waited in the corridor. I thought of introducing myself to Cavalcanti, but it was very crowded, so I decided to let Josh handle him. That must have been when I noticed Rossiter standing there again. I think I may have smiled at him, because I remembered him from before, but he just looked through me." She paused. "Oh, I know what happened. A moment later, Josh came out with Wolfgang Wiesman. He was at the concert that night. The three of us walked over to the Archduke for a drink. Wiesman was full of plans for the film."

"And Rossiter?"

She shook her head. "I can't think of anything else. I was too busy with Wolfgang." She looked at Mark helplessly. "I'm not much use at this, am I?"

"You didn't see a girl come out of the dressing room either time?"

"No."

"We'll talk about it again, at a later time. You never know, but you may be reminded of something." Mark frowned. "Something puzzles me about that evening, but I can't decide what it is."

"What do you mean?"

Mark smiled. "I wish I knew. I can picture it all in my mind's eye, with people going in and out of the greenroom. God knows, I've been there enough times. Something doesn't fit the picture. It will come to me, sooner or later."

"What happened to Rossiter?"

Mark continued the story up to the moment when Rossiter met him at Covent Garden, but she interrupted again. "Why did he want to talk to you?"

"Because I knew Quentin Sharpe. Rossiter was on the run, and wanted me to act as an intermediary. We talked the following morning. He wanted to warn somebody about Cavalcanti and Alessandro, but he wasn't ready to call Quentin himself. In his own way, he was still loyal, despite what he had done. He was desperate to keep the Polish girl in London."

Diana was thoughtful. "He must love her very much."

"Yes, I think he did."

"Did?"

Mark looked at her. "Someone killed him a few hours after he spoke to me." Her eyes widened but she remained silent. "He was killed in the street by someone with a silenced revolver, not far from the Westbury Hotel. The circumstances were very similar to what happened here yesterday."

Her face was pale. "Oh God! Did Emilio . . . ?"

"He could have. He was nearby at the time. So was Alessandro, but that's all I know."

"Then either of them could be the murderer." She shivered.

"Either of them, or somebody else. We could still be looking in the wrong direction."

"What about the man who was killed yesterday?"

"He was working for Quentin. That's why he was following Cavalcanti. I should have guessed."

"Why?"

Mark smiled ruefully. "Because he took me out of the picture very professionally. I never knew what hit me! It also explains why he was carrying no identification when the police found him. Those men are trained to be anonymous."

"You sound as though you know about it." She was watching him curiously, but he did not reply. "When you were talking to Quentin, you said something about knowing one person who couldn't have killed that man, and you looked at me. Does that mean that you suspected . . ." She left the words unspoken.

"No. It was a kind of joke."

"But was there a time, earlier, when the thought crossed your mind?"

Mark was silent for a moment. "Not really."

Her voice was soft. "Truly?"

"If I'm to be honest with you, I left all options open."

"Why? How could you think that I . . . ?"

His arms enfolded her, drawing her closer. "I didn't know anything about you, except that you had been in various places at the same time. For some reason, Budapest keeps coming up. It seems that Quentin's man recognized someone here in Geneva whom he'd seen in Hungary. You were in the Festival Hall for both Verdi *Requiem* concerts. The other night, you found me unconscious in the street. I even ran into you when I was chasing Quentin's man through the shop."

"So you wondered?" Her eyes were large.

"I didn't jump to any sudden conclusions."

She seemed to withdraw into herself. "I don't think I like what you're saying; not after what we've . . . shared together."

He held her, but she remained unresponsive. "Forgive me for even a shadow of doubt, but two men are dead, and someone we both know almost certainly killed them. Whoever did it has to be a pretty cool operator and a good actor."

"Or actress?"

"Or actress."

"And you wondered whether it could have been me." Her eyes avoided his.

"I didn't want to. When we walked over to the hall yesterday, and found Quentin's man dead, it proved that you couldn't have been involved, because you'd been with me the whole time."

"But until that moment . . ."

"Until then, I didn't know for certain. If you want a further confession, I'd reached the point where I didn't care. I only knew that I found you desperately attractive, and that I wanted to be with you." He smiled. "Ever since that first evening at Covent Garden, you've been occupying my thoughts more than I believed possible."

She relaxed slightly, and her voice softened. "What makes you think it was all one way?"

His mouth was very close to hers. "I didn't stop to think."

Her hands stroked his body. "Nor did I. I still don't want to think about it. Didn't you realize I wanted you just as much?"

In reply, he kissed her. Diana edged her body forward until she was lying on top of him, pressing closer. She buried her face in his neck. "I hate the idea that you ever suspected I could have . . ."

Mark's hands caressed her, and she responded with a quick intake of breath.

Afterwards, Mark could feel her heartbeat slowly returning to normal.

There was a thin film of moisture across her shoulders and back, and her perfume filled his nostrils.

"What are we going to do?" Her voice was almost sleepy.

"You're not going to do anything. I'm going to wait and watch. There's little else I can do. My greatest advantage is that whoever is the courier doesn't know that I met Rossiter and talked to him."

"You said something to Quentin about stirring things up. What did you mean by that?"

"I don't know yet. I'll play it by ear."

"I want to help."

"No. I don't want you involved. I would have been happier if you'd never known what was going on."

"But I do." She moved away, and knelt over him. "What shall I do?"

He kissed her breasts, and she held his head closer. "Watch and listen. Tell me about anything that happens. There's always the chance that he'll make a mistake."

"That's unlikely. He's managed to kill two people in the middle of the day, in full view of any passerby."

"That's what makes me think he could slip up. A professional would have been much more cautious."

Diana stared at him for a moment. "You talk like an expert. Mark, are you sure you're not working for that man Quentin?"

"Very sure."

"Then why do you—"

He reached up and kissed her. "There was a time, long ago. Don't ask me about it."

She spoke shyly. "Did it involve the woman who . . . died?"

"In a way."

"Will you tell me, one day?"

"Yes. One day. Not now."

She looked at the clock on the bedside table. "I ought to make a move. It's getting late."

"I suppose so. I'm needed at the office. Poor Rudi is probably desperate by now."

"He's very efficient, isn't he?"

"Ruthlessly. It's a part of being Swiss. There are times I wish he would be a little more human, but that's like asking a Swiss train to arrive thirty seconds late!"

She moved closer. "I'm glad you're English!"

. . .

He walked with Diana to the door of the Hilton. "I'll see you at the session this evening."

"Are you busy until then?"

"I think so. I'll be with Abe at the office for the rest of the day. We may hear from Ettore. Where will you be?"

"With Josh, I suppose. Giuseppe Belasco's coming in this morning, in case Alessandro doesn't show up."

"I thought he was definitely going away."

"No, he changed his mind. He said last night that he might change his plans. The recording is going so well that he doesn't want to spoil the 'rhythm' of it. When he gets down to work, he really is a great artist, isn't he?"

"Yes."

For a moment, her face clouded. "Oh, Mark, do you really think he or Emilio could—"

"I have no other choice at the moment."

"I don't know how I'll be able to face them."

"You'll manage."

"You will be there?"

"I promise." She turned and walked quickly into the hotel foyer.

Mark continued slowly along the street. The morning was cooler than usual, and high clouds masked the sun. The subdued light made the elegant façade of the hotel appear drab.

At the far end of the building, twenty yards down the street, there was another exit. As Mark approached it, Emilio Cavalcanti emerged through the door. The conductor turned to his right, and walked briskly along the pavement. For a moment, Mark considered catching up with him, but decided against it. The man was walking quite quickly, and Mark found that he had to increase his own pace to maintain the same distance between them.

Cavalcanti crossed into the main part of the town, using the wooden footbridge over the sluice gates. He moved like a man hurrying to keep an appointment. Following him, Mark smiled to himself. "Here we go again!" The conductor crossed the Rue du Rhône and started up the hill to the old town. Mark kept his distance. Cavalcanti seemed to be heading in the same direction as before, and Mark increased his pace slightly, for fear of losing the other man in the network of small streets above the town. As he walked, keeping his eyes fixed on the retreating figure, it suddenly occurred to him that he knew where the conductor was going.

Cavalcanti passed the restaurant where Mark had taken Diana. Just beyond, a small sign indicated a modest family hotel. The building looked more like a private house, and there were few of the placards and recommendations supplied by tourist agencies on its walls. A Diners Club sticker was discreetly placed in a lower corner of the glass front door. The conductor hesitated momentarily, then disappeared inside. Mark stopped, waiting on the corner of an alley, and lit a cigarette. Perhaps there was a simple explanation for Cavalcanti's irritation over his supposed intrusion into the man's private life.

He waited about ten minutes, then entered the hotel. A young man in shirt sleeves was leaning over the reception counter, reading the sports page of a newspaper. He looked up as Mark approached.

"Can I help, m'sieur?"

"Yes. I believe you have a Miss Philips—Katya Philips—staying here. He made his voice businesslike.

"Yes, m'sieur."

"She's expecting me for a meeting. I think my colleague has already arrived."

"Ah." The young man looked uncertain. "Would you like me to call her?" His hand hovered by the house phone.

"Don't bother. I'm late already. Which room?"

"Number sixteen, m'sieur, on the first floor. Perhaps I should tell her you're here."

"There's no need." Mark walked towards the staircase. "I'll probably be there before she picks up the phone. Our conference was supposed to begin ten minutes ago."

"As you wish." The young man returned to his newspaper with a Gallic shrug.

The corridor on the first floor was quiet. It was a short passage, with only eight doors. Number sixteen was at the far end, facing Mark.

As he approached, he hesitated, unsure what he should do next. He stopped in front of Katya's room, searching for an excuse to disturb her. At that moment, an unexpected sound came from within the room. It was a muffled cry, suggesting that she was in pain. He was about to knock on the door, when the sound increased in volume and intensity. Mark moved back a step, wondering whether to break the door down with his shoulder. The cries were redoubled, and bore a hint of desperation, breaking into short, sharp groans. They slowly diminished again, to be followed by a long sigh. Mark relaxed, smiling. Katya Philips had been enjoying a long and very loud orgasm.

The door to Mark's right was suddenly thrown open, and a young chambermaid emerged, dragging an old-fashioned vacuum cleaner behind her. She stood for a moment, looking at Mark suspiciously, then turned to lock the door of the room with a pass key.

He walked slowly past her towards the exit and, as he reached the head of the stairs, he heard the young woman clicking her tongue with disapproval. When he turned to look at her, there was the ghost of a smile on her face.

"*Bonjour, monsieur.*"

"*Bonjour.*"

"Were you expecting to see Madame?" There was a slight twinkle in her eye.

"Another time perhaps." He stared her out. "I believe she's in conference at the moment."

"Ah yes." She made her face solemn. "She has had several . . . conferences with the gentleman. He is a regular visitor here."

"Madame is a journalist from London. She's writing an article about him."

"Oh." She smiled openly. "I expect it will make very interesting reading!"

ELEVEN

WHEN HE OPENED THE DOOR of the control room, Mark was greeted by deafening waves of sound. Alessandro's *"E lucevan le stelle"* was blasting over the loudspeakers, and the tenor and Levin were huddled together by the console, following the score. In a corner behind them, Diana was sitting with Giuseppe Belasco. She greeted Mark with raised eyebrows, and her mouth pursed for a moment in a make-believe kiss. Alessandro and the record producer were too engrossed to notice his presence.

When the aria ended, the tape machine stopped, and the room seemed unnaturally quiet.

Alessandro shook his head slowly. "No, I don't think so. We will do it again later."

"But it was excellent!" Joshua looked surprised.

"Not yet good enough. I am not happy with it."

"Do you want to try again this evening? Perhaps, if there's time at the end of the session . . ."

"No. I will sing at the start, when my voice is fresh."

"Oh. I was hoping we could get rid of your Act Two scenes today. Signor Belasco is here."

"Sì, sì, that is what I planned. This evening, we will begin with my *'Vittoria!' "* It was a command rather than a request, and Mark saw the record producer stiffen.

"If you wish."

"I insist. It is the most important moment of the opera."

Joshua smiled. "There are one or two other high points."

"Not for tenors! Are the Sciarrone and Spoletta here?"

From the back, Diana said, "Yes. They should arrive any minute."

"Bene. I will rest." As Alessandro stood, towering over Levin, he nodded to Mark.

"I hadn't expected to see you this evening. I thought you were going to Budapest."

"I was, but this is more important, so I told them to send me the award." He shrugged. "I have several already."

Levin looked up. "I heard you were going to Milan."

The tenor scowled. "Who told you that?"

"I don't remember. Someone said . . ."

"Listen!" Alessandro jabbed with his finger. "I go where I wish. As long as I'm here for your sessions, it does not concern you. Understand?"

"Yes, of course, but I should point out . . ."

"You don't point out anything!" He gave an exasperated sigh. "Everyone wants to know what I am doing! La Morini invites me to dinner, and wants to know why I won't join her; Wiesman wants to know . . ." He hesitated in mid-sentence, then stared sulkily at Levin. "If you are so interested, I will tell you that I went to Milano last night, and returned to Geneva this morning. I had promised to visit some old friends. Are you satisfied?"

As Alessandro was speaking, Wolfgang Wiesman entered the room, accompanied by Katya Philips. The tenor glowered at them. "I will rest now. Tell Cavalcanti to rehearse the orchestra properly. I am not going to waste my voice because they are not ready for me."

Katya smiled sweetly. "Is the orchestra not to your taste, Maestro?"

He eyed her coolly. "They are Swiss. What do you expect? We should have recorded in Italy, where musicians play with blood in their veins. These ones play like watch repairers, and not very good ones!"

"I see. May I quote you on that?"

Joshua looked angry. "I'd rather you didn't, if you don't mind."

"Why not? Signor Alessandro said it in front of a number of witnesses."

"He was making a joke, and it wouldn't say much for our choice of orchestra if you printed it. We're talking about a film as well as a record." He glanced towards Wiesman for support.

Wolfgang smiled uncertainly. "I'm sure Miss Philips understands. We're always a little on edge before the session starts."

Before she could reply, Alessandro pushed past them. "Print what you like as far as I am concerned."

The film producer's reaction was smooth. "You know you don't mean that, my dear fellow. Everything's going so well! We want the public to anticipate the best possible results." He paused fractionally. "I'm sure our investors are relying on us."

Alessandro's eyes met his for a moment, and the tenor gave a casual shrug. "I suppose you are right." He smiled at Katya, but his eyes were cold. "I was making a joke. The orchestra is very good." At the doorway, he glanced back. "Call me when the orchestra is ready."

In the silence that followed, Katya took out a notepad and pencil. She was about to write, but Wiesman placed his hand on her arm. "You know, I heard two charming definitions today. Heaven is a place where the cooks are French, the mechanics are German, the lovers are Italian, the police are British, and everything is organized by the Swiss. On the other hand, hell is where the cooks are British, the mechanics are French, the lovers are Swiss, the police are German, and everything is organized by the Italians!"

She smiled. "I must remember that."

"Good." He looked relieved. "You have my express permission to quote me."

Katya gently released her arm from his grip. "In that case, I'd better write it down."

Wiesman retreated towards the door. "I think I'd better go and talk to Antonio. He seems a little . . . restless." He walked briskly out of the room.

Diana tapped Levin on the shoulder. "Why did you needle him about Milan?"

"I was pissed off with him for making me rewrite the schedule. I changed this evening's order twice to allow for his absence. Besides, he had no right to go anywhere. If he'd read his contract carefully, he'd have seen the clause which says he has to stay in the same town for the period of the recording. It's in every opera contract."

Katya looked interested. "Why is that?"

"Because opera singers are notorious for accepting other engagements the moment they have a free day. If you don't watch them, they'll sneak off for a quick *Traviata* in Munich, and whip back into town feeling off-colour and sounding tired."

"Doesn't that mean risking their reputations on the record?"

"It depends how important they are. Sometimes the result is that they insist on extra recording sessions at another time, when they're feeling better, and that can be hellishly expensive." As Katya began to write, he said, "Please don't print that. It was strictly off the record."

"My, you're being very diplomatic, aren't you, Mr. Levin?"

"Not really, but you must accept that if you attend a session, you're party to a lot of privileged information which isn't necessarily for public consumption. That's why some companies don't allow the press to attend. Anyway, when it comes to their idols, I see no reason to disenchant the punters."

"How very thoughtful of you! Is there anything I am permitted to write?"

Joshua settled back in his chair. "You'll hear for yourself. If what we've already got is anything to go by, you could say that this is likely to be one of the finest *Toscas* ever recorded, with Bianca Morini at her absolute peak, but I suppose that wouldn't make very interesting copy."

"No. Anyway, I'm not here as a music critic. I'll leave that to my colleagues when the records are released."

Joshua laughed dryly. "What makes you think they'd know?"

"You're not fond of the press?"

"They're all right, I suppose." He grinned. "Only when they give good reviews. A lot of the time, I have the feeling that they're more like a bunch of testy schoolmasters, correcting homework. Sometimes, I expect to read 'Fair, could do better. Seven out of ten'! You know the old saying: those that can, do; those that can't, write about it. An awful lot of blood, sweat and tears go into a recording, and it's seldom recognized. I can remember doing a recording, years ago, which had some of the finest performances of their time. One reviewer gave eighty percent of his column to complaining about the layout of the libretto!"

Katya smiled at Diana. "There speaks the bitter voice of experience, I suspect. This is going to be more fun than I expected. When does Simon Vincent get here? I'm dying to hear his opinion."

Diana looked past her to stare Levin into silence. "We haven't seen much of him. He likes to watch from the hall. I've hardly noticed him at the hotel."

"I expect he and Cliff are off exploring together." Katya turned to Mark. Her long, blood-red fingernails scraped the back of his hand. "Hello, stranger. I've been looking forward to seeing you. Why haven't you called?"

"I seem to have been rather tied up." He avoided Diana's eyes. "As a matter of fact, I was going to drop by this morning."

"Oh." Her expression did not change. "You would have missed me. I decided to make a little tour of inspection on my own, especially as I hadn't heard from you."

"Where did you go?"

"Here and there. I just wandered at random. I thought I'd let you be the official guide."

"I'll look forward to it."

Graham Budd had turned up the microphones on his console, and the room was filled with the general noise of musicians tuning their instruments. Above them, a familiar voice could be heard, calling, "Cliff sweetie, have you seen my notes?"

Diana smiled broadly. "I do believe that's Simon! Can I show you the way out to the hall?"

Katya eyed her disdainfully. "Don't worry. I'm sure I can find it." She turned back to Levin. "Are you sure it will be all right for me to sit out there while you're recording? I promise not to cough or sneeze or anything."

"Please make yourself at home." As a peace offering, he added, "Why don't you come here for the playbacks. It will give you the best view of both sides of the session."

Katya nodded and left. Joshua winked at Mark. "It also means she won't hear what we've got to say while they're singing. I don't like that woman. Is Bianca here yet?"

"Yes." Diana obediently started towards the door. "Do you want to talk to her?"

"Not really. She'll be here on the dot. She's the most punctual of them all. I just hope that twit Vincent leaves her alone. What about Emilio?"

"Not yet. I'll go and look."

Mark joined her. "I'll come with you. I want to talk to him."

In the empty corridor, Diana kissed him, then moved quickly away. "Did you really want to see Emilio?"

"No, but it was a good excuse to escape. How's everything?"

"A bit tense, as you can see. That Philips woman really is a bitch! She's dying to stir up something, including you, unless I'm mistaken." For a moment, she looked severe. "You didn't tell me you were going to see her this morning."

"Don't worry. Her come-on is a rather carefully contrived smoke screen. Either that, or she's a raving nymphomaniac."

"What do you mean?"

He told her about following Cavalcanti to Katya's hotel. When he described what he had heard in the corridor, Diana suddenly whooped with laughter, the sound echoing in the stone corridor. She put a hand over her mouth, feigning guilt. "Do you mean she makes even more noise than I do?"

"I doubt it, but it's hard for me to say. I'm too preoccupied to make accurate comparisons!"

She shook her head wonderingly. "So Emilio's bonking our Katya on the side! I suppose he tells Maria he's rehearsing!" For a moment, she was serious. "Does this mean he's in the clear?"

"Not necessarily, but it certainly explains a lot. No wonder he's so sensitive about his private life. If he was with her yesterday, it would explain why he didn't see Quentin's man. He would have been coming from the other side of town. I'm inclined to think that's what happened. He had nothing to gain by pretending not to know. On the other hand, I was with Katya when Rossiter died, and he could still have been around here when Quentin's man was killed. I suppose the only real difference is that we now know why he's been acting guiltily."

She nodded slowly. "And if it's not Emilio, it's probably Alessandro. I don't like him."

"Neither do I, but that doesn't make him a murderer. Incidentally, you mentioned that Wiesman was at the second Verdi *Requiem* concert. Was he at the first?"

"I didn't see him there, but he could have been. Do you think that he . . . ?"

"I don't know. I suppose I'm trying to work on a process of elimination."

Diana shivered slightly. "I don't like that expression! What are we going to do?"

For a moment, he held her. "You're not going to do anything."

"But I want to help."

"In that case, try to stay close to Katya. You can make it look like good public relations, and it will at least tell us where Emilio is—or isn't. Let me worry about the others. Quentin will be here shortly, and he can take over. Either way, I don't want you involved."

Diana was thoughtful. "If it is Emilio or Antonio, what will happen to the recording?"

"I haven't really thought about it."

"God! I don't know why I'm concerned either. We live in a very enclosed world, don't we? Two men have died, a third is some sort of spy, and I'm worrying about recording a Puccini opera! I seem to have everything out of perspective. Is it always like this?"

Mark nodded. "Musicians aren't accustomed to reality. I sometimes think that's the reason why I like them."

"But you didn't always work with them. Mark, is it too soon to ask about . . . ?"

Before he could reply, Joshua Levin appeared. "Is Bianca ready?" He glanced irritably at Mark. "Tell her Cavalcanti's rehearsing the orchestra."

"I'm just going." Diana hurried away.

"You'd better warn Antonio, too."

Mark looked suitably apologetic. "I'm sorry. I seem to be getting in your way."

The record producer glanced at his watch. "It doesn't matter. Sending Diana on errands gives me something to do. I hate the last few minutes of waiting."

"So you've said, but you've done it so often that I would have thought you'd become accustomed to it."

Levin smiled ruefully. "So would I!"

When the final playback was over, Joshua turned towards Bianca and Alessandro. "What do you think?"

Bianca replied first. "I am happy. Are you sure you can put it all together the way you have marked it in your score?"

"Certain."

Antonio frowned. "It is acceptable. I still need to cover some of my solos, but we will record them at a later time. Emilio, you are slowing down after *'Maledetta!'* Can you not keep things moving until my *'Vittoria!'*?"

The conductor nodded. "If you wish."

Bianca looked at her music. "Do you want to do it again before we leave?"

"No, it is not necessary. We will do a little insert with Scarpia and Sciarrone when I record the aria again."

The soprano checked the schedule. "We can do it tomorrow evening. I will be here to sing offstage with the chorus for your *scena* with Scarpia. If we finish that, you can do your *'Vittoria!'* again before I begin my scene with Giuseppe." She turned to Belasco, who was sitting in a corner, for his nod of approval.

Alessandro shook his head. "I must do it first, when my voice is fresh."

Bianca took a deep breath. She spoke quietly. "Very well, Antonio. You will do it first. I am sure the chorus will not mind waiting."

"Naturally." The tenor dismissed the chorus's problems with a shrug.

Wiesman, who had been listening quietly, moved in. "If that's settled, I hope you will all join me for a little supper at La Cave. I've sent Vincent and Cliff ahead to arrange a table."

Bianca hesitated, glancing towards Mark. "I am a little tired."

"Oh, please!" The film producer was at his most charming. "I'm sure you will enjoy it. Mr. Sincoff and his wife will be there, and it will give us a chance to celebrate."

Alessandro looked up. "What for?"

"The successful conclusion of your scenes together. They are quite magnificent! Besides, I don't think we need an excuse for a party, do we? It gives me the opportunity to thank you for your collaboration. You are all my guests."

The tenor laughed unpleasantly, and spoke to no one in particular. "When film producers are hospitable, it usually means they are spending someone else's money!"

Bianca stiffened slightly, then smiled at Wiesman. "I am delighted to come, Herr Wiesman, but you must forgive me if I only stay for a little while. It would be very ungracious not to accept such a charming invitation." She looked at Alessandro. "Don't you agree, Antonio?"

"If you say so. I am hungry. I must eat, anyway."

Wiesman turned to the conductor. "I took the liberty of inviting your wife to join us, Maestro."

Mark watched Katya's face. She looked vaguely amused.

Cavalcanti was expressionless. "Thank you. I am sure she will enjoy it." He spoke to Bianca. "She does not have much to do in Geneva."

"So she was telling me."

"Oh? When?"

"This morning. We had a coffee together at my hotel." For a moment, there was a glint in Bianca's eye. "You are very dedicated to your work, Emilio."

"It is important that the recording should be as good as possible. I find that no matter how well I think I know the score there is always something I seem to have overlooked. A recording is like a microscope. It reveals tiny details that I never suspected."

Katya eyed him innocently. "And have you discovered many interesting things since you have been in Geneva?"

"Yes." He did not look in her direction.

"I'd like to interview you about them."

Cavalcanti seemed abstracted. "I will try to find time."

Her voice had a slight edge. "I do hope so. I know what a busy schedule you must have."

Mark stole a glance at Diana, whose eyebrows were raised.

For a moment, Cavalcanti did not reply. Then he looked directly at Katya. "My work always comes first. I do not like it when people make too many demands of me."

"Yes, it must be very boring." She was watching his face.

He looked away. "I need time for myself."

As though sensing an underlying tension, Wiesman led the way to the door. "Shall we go, then? I hate to keep the others waiting. The owner of the restaurant is a wonderfully colourful character. He loves to create special desserts in honour of whatever is playing at the opera house. He promised me a special Coupe Tosca, and I'm dying to see what it will be."

"Fattening, almost certainly!" Katya was putting away her notepad.

"It's sure to be interesting. When *Lohengrin* was on, he presented an ice cream shaped like a swan."

"Goodness!" Katya's voice was brittle. "I wonder what he'd come up with for *The Rape of Lucretia!*"

Several of the musicians from the orchestra were in the restaurant, and Cavalcanti paused at a table to speak to them. Mark noticed that Katya hung back, waiting for the conductor to finish before they joined Wiesman and the other guests. Abe and Myra had already installed themselves in a corner and were sipping drinks. Vincent had ordered bottles of red and white wine for the table. The Americans created a space between them for Diana, and Mark sat on Abe's right.

"How'd it go, kid?" Mark sometimes wondered whether Abe didn't see himself as a latter-day Humphrey Bogart.

"Very well. Bianca and Alessandro have finished their scenes together, except for the offstage chorus in Act Two."

"Good. After that, she should take a rest." He lowered his voice. "I had a call from Ettore."

"And?"

"He's still digging. He doesn't like what he's heard." The smile never left Abe's face. "These guys are smart. They move money around the world and back, from one company to another, before it shows up again."

"If it's buried that deep, why worry? The film's a good project, and if Ettore and his friends can't trace the source of the backing, nobody else will."

The American nodded. "I'm with you, kid. We'll just have to hang in there a little longer."

Across the table, Simon Vincent, in a bulky Armani tropical suit, had placed himself next to Bianca. "Your performance is shattering, love. I was really very moved."

"Thank you, Mr. Vincent."

He waved at a sheaf of pink papers scattered before him. "Watching you has made me rethink the whole role."

"Oh?" Bianca looked interested but wary.

"You're quite right about her feelings for Cavaradossi. In fact, I think I overlooked the deeply religious aspect of her character. She's a very reverent woman. I'd like to build on that, especially in the early scenes, with backlighting that creates a halo around her as she enters the church. You know, by cutting between shots of the statues and Tosca's face, I think the audience will understand the allusions." He half closed his eyes. "I see you walking slowly up the aisle, with brilliant light behind you causing halation on the camera lens."

Bianca smiled. "I hope my face will still be visible."

"Ah." Vincent produced a Mont Blanc fountain pen and made a note on his papers. The ink looked like dried blood.

As soon as Cavalcanti and Katya were seated together, Wiesman joined Alessandro at the end of the table. The tenor spoke in a subdued voice, and the film producer bowed his head, turning away from his guests to reply. Left sitting together, Josh and Cliff stared at each other. The Australian drank some beer, and Levin filled a glass with wine, gulping most of it down. Looking across the table, Mark noted that Cavalcanti and Katya were not speaking. The conductor was staring moodily at the menu, and the journalist was listening to Vincent and Bianca, a polite smile frozen on her face.

The director was warming to his theme. "Don't worry about your face, sweetie." Bianca did not react, but there was a slight tightening of the muscles at the corners of her mouth. "I can use enough fill-in to catch those creamy features. I really love my religious angle. It's almost as though Tosca is virginal, enjoying her first encounter with passion. Until Cavaradossi, she was—how can I put it?—*intacta.*"

"I see." Bianca was pensive. "And are we still going to have that moonlit love scene in the forest?"

"We can tone it down a little if you feel it would be too much. If Tosca's doing the religious bit, we can't distort the image."

Alessandro had been following the last part of the conversation, and scowled at the director. "What's all this religious shit? Tosca is an actress. In the year 1800, that made her little more than a *puttana.*" His face was contemptuous. "You're trying to make her the Virgin Mary when all she wants is a good lay!"

Vincent looked trapped. "I didn't see it quite like that."

Alessandro glowered. "How else can you see it?" He had raised his voice slightly. "She's just an actress who fell under the spell of a famous painter. Forget the religion and the psychology." It occurred to Mark that only a tenor could see Tosca as a secondary role to his own.

The menace in Alessandro's voice, suggesting a new outburst, had caused a momentary silence to fall on the table, and the others looked up from their conversations.

Bianca smiled serenely. "I think, Antonio, that Tosca is just a woman in love. She is fiercely jealous of every other woman; she is prepared to betray his political cause if it will save his life, and . . ."

"No." Alessandro waved the argument aside. "She is a typical woman, caught up in a situation beyond her control. She takes the first action that comes into her mind. Women never think beyond the moment." His voice took on a bantering tone. "All they know about is *l'amore!* That's their excuse!"

Katya looked at him with distaste. "You seem to have a very low opinion of the opposite sex, Maestro."

He shrugged expansively. "On the contrary, I adore them. But I do not seek their company for intellectual stimulation. Women think with their bodies, not their heads."

The journalist coloured. "Charming! It's hard to imagine this conversation's taking place in the early 1990s." Cavalcanti placed a hand on her arm, but she shook it aside. "Are you really trying to suggest that we're still poor, ineffectual little creatures, unable to reason like our great big male counterparts?"

Alessandro regarded her icily. "It has usually been my experience. Men have minds. Women have bodies."

Katya was furious. "Well, really!"

There was an uneasy silence. When Mark spoke, his voice was slightly louder than he intended. "There are exceptions. Men can be equally infatuated."

The tenor looked at him irritably. "I find that hard to believe. Men are rationalists, able to reason in the abstract. Women are entirely subjective. You cannot deny that."

"As a matter of fact, I can give you an example. I came across an extraordinary situation in London last week."

Katya, her cheeks still flushed, turned her intense gaze on Mark. "What happened?"

"I met a man who was prepared to commit treason because he loved a woman."

"Treason?" It seemed to Mark that she was overreacting, but that might have been for Alessandro's benefit. "What do you mean?"

"It's a very complicated story. Perhaps I should leave it to another time."

"No. I'm a journalist. You can't say something like that without a follow-up. Are you serious when you say treason?"

The table remained silent, and Mark was conscious that he was the centre of attention. "Yes. He told me he'd stolen secret government documents and given them to a woman."

"Why?"

"Basically, because he loved her. She was working in the Polish Embassy, and he did it because he hoped it would let her stay in England. She was about to be sent back home."

"I don't understand."

Mark looked round the table. Wiesman and Alessandro were watching him. There was a puzzled expression on the film producer's face, but the tenor looked sceptical. Simon and Cliff exchanged private glances of amused interest. Abe and Myra listened attentively. Cavalcanti, his eyes still on the menu, was frowning, and Josh was pouring more wine into his glass. Diana was about to speak, but checked herself.

He lit a cigarette. "The man in question worked for a branch of the security services. He fell in love with this Polish girl, and when he learned that she was going to be sent home, he gave her the papers. His hope was that if she became a useful contact, her bosses would decide to keep her in London. He was prepared to keep supplying her with information in the hope that he could persuade her to defect. You see, he believed she loved him, too."

"Good grief!" Simon giggled. "D'you think I could get the television rights to his story?" Cliff sniggered.

Katya glared at them, then returned to Mark. "Are you making this up?"

"No."

"But you're talking about a traitor! Why did he tell you all this?"

Mark smiled. "I said it was complicated. He was on the run. His own people were on to him, and he was running for cover. Despite what he'd done, he wanted to tell someone about it."

"Why you? Why didn't he tell his own people if that was the way he felt?"

"He intends to, once he's safely out of the way." From the corner of his eye, Mark had the impression that Diana was going to speak, and he continued quickly. "I just happened to be there. We only spoke briefly, but he'd written all the details out: what he'd done and how he'd passed it on."

Wiesman leaned forward. "Do you have that information?"

"Not yet. He posted it to me care of an American Express office."

"Here in Geneva?"

"No. He chose another town. He was very cautious. I'm supposed to pick it up later this week. He wanted time to get out of England first."

Wiesman shook his head. "That's an amazing story. Are you saying . . . ?"

Katya cut across him. "Why did he tell you?"

"I just happened to be there. We'd met once or twice in the past, but it was pure accident." Mark looked past her to Alessandro. "He did it because he loved a woman. He didn't care about the consequences." The tenor did not reply.

Bianca was thoughtful. "I think I can understand that."

Katya was not prepared to be interrupted. "Who is this man? What's his name?"

"Rossiter. I knew him years ago, when I was living in London. Of course, I had no idea at the time that he was involved in security work."

Levin looked up. "Didn't you mention his name in my office last week?"

"Yes. He was the one who talked to me at the opera house. He came over to me at the bar."

"I didn't see him."

Diana spoke quietly. "I did."

Mark stubbed out his cigarette. "We met the following day and talked. I haven't seen him since."

Katya was watching him. "Have you told anyone?"

"Not yet. I'm waiting to pick up the letter he sent. Then I'll pass it on."

Abe looked concerned. "This sounds like dangerous stuff, Mark. Why didn't you tell the law?"

"Because I felt sorry for the man. I think he genuinely loves that girl. A few days' delay makes little difference either way."

"Jesus Christ, Mark! The guy's a spy! Where is he now?"

For a moment, Mark's eyes met Diana's. "I don't know. Presumably, he's holed up somewhere in Europe by now. He told me he'd worked out an escape route. As soon as I've picked up his letter, I'll take it into the British Embassy and let them handle it."

Wiesman shook his head. "You should have called the police immediately. Why let a man like that escape?"

"I told you: I felt sorry for him. He planned to confess to everything, once he was safely out of the way. According to him, the documents were not very important. They were to give his girl credibility."

Katya was making notes. "Where is she?"

"He didn't know. She disappeared. He was going to try to find her before he took off. That's all he would tell me."

"And you haven't heard from this . . . Rossiter since?"

"No. He said he would contact me again when he was safe."

"But that makes you a party to his crime."

"Not really. I'm just a post office."

She looked angry. "How can you be so calm about it? The man's a criminal, and you've allowed him to get away!"

"It wasn't like that. I gave him enough time to leave. As soon as I pick up his letter, it will go to the right authorities, and they can follow it up. He intends to call in once he's safe. Apart from anything else, his own life's ruined, and the best he can hope to do is live it out in obscurity. He's lost everything, including the woman he loves. I assume the police will catch up with the rest of his associates."

Katya was about to speak again, when Maria Cavalcanti arrived at the table. The conductor's wife looked pale.

"I am sorry I am late." She spoke hesitatingly. "I did not remember the name of the restaurant, so I went to the hall. The engineers told me I would find you here."

"Of course." Wiesman bent low over her hand. "Let me find you a chair. Where would you like to sit?"

She glanced round the table. "Next to Emilio."

Katya did not move, so Levin pushed his chair to one side, and an extra place was made. Maria sat next to her husband, speaking to him in Italian. He shrugged in response, but did not reply. A waiter hovered by the table, ready to take orders.

Katya returned to Mark. "I still don't understand your behaviour. How could you let the man get away?"

Before Mark could speak, Cavalcanti interrupted. "Please, Katya. Mark has explained." He looked irritated.

"That may be, but . . ."

The conductor's voice hardened. "I think we should leave the subject alone. It is too serious to discuss like this."

"But . . ."

"Mark has the situation under control. I am sure he will do what must be done." Cavalcanti's voice indicated that the subject was closed, and Katya bowed her head, angrily silent.

The meal proved to be an uneasy celebration. Simon Vincent occupied Bianca with small talk about opera, deferring to her with uncharacteristic grace. From time to time, he glanced towards Alessandro, fearful that he might incur another attack, but the tenor concentrated his attention on Wiesman, speaking in an undertone. Maria Cavalcanti spoke to her husband in Italian, and he replied mostly in monosyllables. At his side, Katya picked sulkily at her food. Myra chatted amiably to Diana. Cliff ate in silence, and Joshua washed food down with frequent glasses of wine. The Coupe Tosca, presented with great ceremony, was a passion fruit sorbet shaped like a fan. It melted rather quickly.

Abe grinned at Mark, and spoke under his breath. "This is some party. I've been to happier wakes! That was quite a story you were telling, kid."

"I had my reasons."

"That much I guessed. There's something screwy going on here. Are you going to let me in on it?"

Mark nodded. "In a while." He kept his voice low.

"Good." Abe raised his glass towards Wiesman and spoke in a loud voice. "Here's to a lovely party and a great recording, Wolfgang. Bianca, you're terrific! Antonio"—he paused—"you're the great Alessandro!" The tenor nodded, accepting the compliment as his due. Around the table, the guests joined in self-consciously, and Abe beamed amiably. "What happened to Belasco?"

Wiesman smiled indulgently. "Poor old Giuseppe said he needed an early night. He has his big scene tomorrow."

Bianca chose the moment to rise. "He is quite right. We should all be resting. If you will forgive me, my dear friends, I think I will do the same."

Wiesman looked distressed. "So soon?"

"Please do not allow me to disturb you, but I must go."

Vincent stood. "I'll drive you back. Cliff and I should be getting our beauty sleep, too."

Maria said, "I want to go, Emilio. I have a headache."

Cavalcanti helped her from her chair. "As you wish."

For a moment, Katya looked angry. "You're not leaving, are you? We were going to do an interview."

Maria waited for her husband. "I want to go now."

Katya was insistent. "I'm leaving tomorrow. If you don't give me the time, I won't be able to write the piece we discussed. We can use the lounge at my hotel. I left my tape recorder in my room." For a moment, she looked at Maria. "You can come, too, if you like."

Cavalcanti turned to his wife. "I did promise . . ."

Maria seemed close to tears. "I am leaving now, Emilio."

He eyed her coldly. "In that case, perhaps one of the others will take you to the hotel. I will join you later."

For a moment, Maria looked at her husband helplessly. Then Levin stood. "I'll take you, Mrs. Cavalcanti. Come on, Diana. It's time we left. You can drive. Diana followed him out of the restaurant. She did not pause to say goodbye.

By the time Wiesman returned to the table after seeing Bianca leave, only Abe, Myra and Mark were still seated. Cavalcanti and Katya, looking triumphant, met him on their way out, and Alessandro had already despatched a waiter to order a taxi.

"It looks as though my party has ended." The film producer glanced towards Alessandro, who was signing a photograph for the proprietor of the restaurant.

Mark smiled. "There's still a lot of recording to come. I'm sure we'll have another opportunity."

"In that case, I'll go back with Antonio. There are a couple of matters I need to discuss with him. Please stay and have some more coffee." He departed quickly, pausing to settle the bill with the proprietor.

Abe rested his elbows on the table. "Now maybe you can tell me what the hell's going on. Was that story about the guy in London for real?"

"Yes."

"Jesus! You said you had a special reason for telling it. Why?"

Mark spoke quietly. "Because it's reasonably certain that Rossiter's girl-friend passed the stolen documents to one of the people involved in this production."

"What?" Abe barked the question loudly enough to cause people at the next table to look round. "Are you serious?"

"I'm afraid so."

"Who are we talking about?"

"I don't know." Mark spoke slowly, telling them the details from the Festival Hall, and Abe listened without interrupting him. He deliberately excluded the death of Rossiter and the events surrounding Quentin's man in Geneva. There seemed no point in troubling Abe or Myra unnecessarily.

When Mark had finished, Abe sat in silence, digesting the information. At length, he said, "So you still don't know who was waiting in the dressing room?"

"Not yet. That's why I made up the part about a letter waiting for me at American Express."

"You mean he didn't send one? What the hell are you getting into, Mark?"

"I'm waiting to see who makes the first move." Seeing Abe's expression, he smiled. "Don't worry. Help is already on the way. The British security people will be here shortly."

"That's not good enough. You could get yourself hurt before they arrive. You must be out of your mind!" He turned to Myra, who had not spoken, but she remained silent. "What the heck are you hoping to achieve?"

"I want to see which of them makes a run for it. Now that the cat's out of the bag, and he believes there's a package of information waiting to be collected, our man is going to have to run."

"I hope you're right."

"He has no alternative. The security people will be standing by to pick him up."

"In Switzerland? That may not be so easy."

Mark's face was grim. "I doubt whether they'll worry too much about playing things by the book."

Abe was serious. "I don't like what you're doing. For Christ's sake, watch your step." He glanced at Myra. "We're kind of used to having you around."

"Don't worry. I can look after myself. I'll run you back to the hotel, or do you want to walk?"

They walked to the Hilton in silence. It was a mild evening, but overhead clouds made it seem darker than usual. At the door of the hotel, Myra took Mark's hands. "Have you called the police here?"

"No. They wouldn't help, anyway."

"I hope you know what you're doing."

"I'll be all right."

Myra was thoughtful. Inconsequentially, she added, "Diana's a very nice young woman. You owe it to her to take care."

As he watched them enter the foyer of the hotel, it struck Mark that Abe and Myra were growing older. They walked slowly, Myra's hand tucked comfortably in the crook of her husband's arm.

At the door of his apartment building, Mark paused, feeling in his pocket for the key. In the darkened street, it took a moment to insert it into the lock. He did not pay much attention to the sound of a car starting fifteen yards up the road. Then its headlights suddenly blazed, switched to full beam, and he was momentarily blinded by the light. The roar of the engine was unusually loud, and Mark turned towards the vehicle, puzzled that the driver should be accelerating quite so violently. As he did so, he realized that the car was heading directly towards him. Dazzled by the brilliance, he could only guess from the position of the headlights that the machine had mounted the pavement and was coming straight towards him, leaving no space to escape. His hand twisted the key in the lock, and as the door opened inwards, Mark threw himself forward with his full weight, falling heavily on the floor as the vehicle passed within inches of his body. He landed clumsily, feeling slightly winded. As he recovered, he could hear the squeal of brakes as the car reached the corner of the street. Mark scrambled to his feet and returned to the doorway, hoping to catch sight of the vehicle, but it had already gone. There had been no mistaking the driver's intention. Someone had made the first move.

When Diana arrived a few minutes later, her face was anxious. "Why did you tell them all about Rossiter tonight?"

"I promised Quentin Sharpe that I would stir things up. It's time to flush our friend out."

"But that story about a letter waiting for you at American Express isn't true, is it?" When Mark shook his head, she ran to him. "You deliberately set yourself up as bait. I'm frightened!"

"I'm not in any danger. If anything happens to me, he'll assume that American Express will open the letter. This country's small enough for a murder to make headlines. He won't risk going after me." He could feel her shiver, and decided not to mention what had just happened outside.

"Are you sure?" Her eyes searched his face.

"Certain. The American Express story was my insurance policy. It's going to force his hand one way or another. Anyway, Quentin should be here soon. Let's hope he gets here before our courier makes a break for it."

In bed, when he caressed her, Diana held his hands, restraining him, and burrowed her face against his chest. It was a long time before her breathing deepened and she fell asleep, still holding him tightly.

TWELVE

RUDI WAS ABOUT TO GO through a long and carefully prepared list of inquiries when Agnes rang from the outer office.

"I am sorry to disturb you, M'sieur Holland, but there is an English gentleman on the line who insists on speaking to you. He will not give me his name. He says he is an old friend who wants to surprise you."

"You'd better put him on." Across the desk, Rudi pursed his lips with disapproval.

It was Quentin Sharpe. "Sorry about the secrecy, but I don't want to advertise my presence in Geneva. I tried your flat, but got an answering machine. Can you talk?"

"In a moment." Mark cupped his hand over the instrument. "I'm sorry, Rudi, but this is a rather important personal matter. Would you excuse me?"

"Of course." The young man gathered his papers. "Will you set aside some time for me later? Maestro Steigel has telephoned three times from Vienna. He was quite irritated that you had not returned any of his calls."

"I'll be free again in a few minutes."

"Very well." It was apparent from Rudi's expression that he did not approve of personal calls in office hours, even when they were to his employer. He made an ostentatious point of closing the door quietly, and Mark returned to the telephone.

"Sorry. I was in the middle of a discussion. Do you want to meet?"

"Not for the moment. I think it would be better if we weren't seen together. What's been going on?"

"Quite a lot." Mark described the previous evening, concluding with the attempt to run him down.

When he had finished, Quentin gave a low chuckle. "That was a bloody stupid thing to do, if you'll forgive my saying so. Stirring things up is one matter, but setting yourself up as a target is going too far. You could have got yourself killed."

"Your concern is touching."

"Nothing of the sort. You're more useful to me alive. I thought I'd explained that."

"To be honest, I hadn't expected such an immediate reaction. Our friend seems to be operating at panic level."

"You're lucky he didn't go for his gun again. Ballistics came in with a report on those bullets, by the way. They were fired from the same weapon."

"So we now know that whoever killed Rossiter shot your man in Geneva. That was quick work."

"Our Swiss colleagues can be very efficient when they decide to be." For a moment, Mark thought of Rudi. "I suppose we should assume that it's all one person's handiwork, unless he has an accomplice."

"You think there are two?"

"It's possible, but unlikely. Couriers usually work alone. It helps their anonymity. Any idea who was driving that car?"

"No. It could have been anyone. Most of the people here have their own transport and, anyway, a professional would probably steal a car if he was going to use it to take me out. At the speed he was driving, I have the feeling I would have left a considerable dent in the paintwork."

"Quite. The only point about this whole affair is that everything seems to have an amateur ring to it. I can't see a professional risking identification by shooting two people in the middle of a crowded street."

"It worked both times. Have you managed to dig up anything on Cavalcanti or Alessandro?"

"A little. Cavalcanti's in the clear, as far as we're concerned. He was mixed up with the local Reds when he was younger, but that doesn't mean anything in Italy. Anyway, he was much too obvious about it. I worry about the ones who don't publicize it. The only other information I've come across is that he likes female companionship. Our files came up with a few old newspaper clippings linking him to a couple of jet-set dolly birds."

"He hasn't changed." Mark gave a brief résumé of the conductor's liaison with Katya Philips.

Quentin laughed. "That seems to cover him, as far as we know. I don't know where those conductors find the energy. They tell me Arturo Toscanini was still banging away when he was in his eighties."

"So was Monteux, and proud of it! It's a passionate occupation. What about Alessandro?"

"Ah, that's another story. Your Georgian friend has a nasty reputation in certain quarters. According to my sources, he's very definitely mixed up with the narcotics trade. Interpol has been watching him for months, but they haven't been able to catch him red-handed. He's a very smooth operator."

Mark was thoughtful. "Wouldn't that make it less likely to involve himself in espionage?"

"It depends on his motives, I suppose, coupled with the fact that he seems to lead a larger-than-life lifestyle. Maybe he thinks he can get away with it."

"I think I already told you that he's tied in with Wolfgang Wiesman. Bianca's husband hasn't come up with anything yet."

"I see. Herr Wiesman interests me. He moves around a great deal. We had a look at his background. A couple of his films were Eastern European co-productions."

"He was talking about the best hotel in Budapest the other day, if that's any help."

"It fits the picture. Mind you, people go in and out of Hungary all the time."

"I know. Diana met Alessandro there."

"Diana Nightingale from Magnum? What was she doing there?"

"Some sort of PR work. Her agency represented several Eastern European clients, and they gave her a free trip."

"That's interesting. Her name hasn't shown up anywhere else in our files."

"I can't imagine why it would. She's not involved." Mark replied more quickly than he had intended.

Quentin seemed slightly amused. "You sound as though you should know."

"Not really, but if it's of interest, she was having lunch with me at the time your man was killed."

"Well, that clears her, unless . . ."

"Unless what?"

"Unless, as I said earlier, we're looking for more than one person. You sound rather aggressive, Mark."

"I didn't intend to. All I meant was that she's an unlikely suspect."

"Was she at the Verdi concerts in London?"

"Yes. As a matter of fact, she saw Rossiter."

"Really?" Quentin was suddenly interested. "Tell me about that."

Mark explained, recounting Diana's recollections of the two evenings at the Festival Hall. When he had finished, Quentin remained silent for a while.

"How does she know so much about what's going on?"

"I told her."

"I see." There was another pause. "Why?"

Mark hesitated. "We've been seeing rather a lot of each other. I'll let you use your imagination if you're thinking of asking for details!" Quentin did not speak. "As a matter of fact, Diana found me in the street the night your man knocked me out. I'm prepared to guarantee she's not involved in any of this."

Quentin spoke softly. "If you say so. One's judgement can be clouded under the circumstances."

"She had every reason to be there. She went to the concerts with Joshua Levin, who's producing the record for Magnum and the soundtrack for Wiesman."

"Yes. We had a look at him, too, but his file was blank. He seems to spend his life in a recording studio. I'm told he likes a drink."

Quentin's research appeared to have been very thorough. "He drinks more than he should. It's probably the pressures of the job. Diana does her best to point him in the right direction and stay sober."

Quentin's voice was amused. "She sounds like a very compassionate young woman."

Mark was anxious to change the subject. "Will you come to the recording sessions? There's one this evening."

"I don't think so. For the moment, I'd prefer to stay out of sight."

"You could always show up on behalf of London Arts."

"I know, but I prefer not to advertise. Besides, I have one or two other people to see in Geneva."

"Where can I find you?"

"I'll be around. If you need me, call London. They'll put you through."

"That seems a rather roundabout way of doing it."

Quentin laughed. "Yes, doesn't it? I'll be in touch."

Mark replaced the receiver and sat staring at the telephone as though he expected it to ring again. A moment later, Rudi reentered the room. He must have been waiting outside the door until Agnes signalled that the call had ended.

"We may continue?" The file he was holding seemed to have grown larger.

Mark sighed inwardly. "Of course. Where were we?"

"Konstantin Steigel. He called again while you were on the telephone."

"Did he say what he wanted?"

"No. He never tells me." Rudi looked aggrieved. "He said only that he
wanted you to call, and that he hadn't spoken to you for a long time."

Mark smiled. "At least three days. All right. I'll call him in a few minutes."

Rudi nodded, and adjusted his rimless glasses. His list of questions,
neatly printed on his notepad, looked longer than ever.

Mark found Bianca pacing angrily in the corridor outside the control room.
She scarcely paused to greet him. "That *asino!* He has made me wait forty-
five minutes while he records his *'Vittoria!'* for the fifth time!" From behind the control room door, the strains of the aria could be heard. Judging
by the sound, it was being played at maximum volume. Bianca continued
to pace. "Not only that, he insists on using the session time to listen to
every take! The chorus has to wait, I have to wait, Giuseppe has to wait! I
have had enough!"

"I'll see what I can do."

"No. I have decided. If Antonio continues like this, I will go. If necessary, Mr. Levin can add my voice to the *coro* later. I will not be treated like
some twenty-year-old soubrette!"

"I'm sorry, Bianca. I should have been here earlier."

She relaxed. "It's not your fault, *caro.* Even an experienced producer like
poor Joshua will have trouble with that animal! For a little while, I considered walking out of this recording, but my performance is too good. I
would like to save it."

"Your performance is wonderful!"

"My voice is right for the part. In another year, it may not be so good."

"I find that hard to believe."

Her eyes narrowed. "I was not sure whether you had noticed, *caro.*"
Mark said nothing. "She is very pretty, that English girl; not like the skinny
one with the bad temper. But isn't she a little young for you?"

Mark shrugged. Little escaped Bianca. "I don't know her very well."

"Well enough, I think." Her voice softened. "Is she better than I am?"

It was the age-old question that men and women always asked, even
when they knew the answer would be appropriate. "No one is better than
you."

Bianca smiled at last. "Ah, Marco, you always say nice things to me. I'm
glad I no longer believe them!" She sighed. "There was a time when I
would have been very jealous, but I will not compete with someone as
young. It's strange, but I do not mind anymore."

"You're hardly old, Bianca."

"No, but I'm no longer young. There's a difference. That is why this recording is important to me. In a year or two, if we had to set it up again, my voice might not be so right. Maybe you would not notice. Maybe even my critics would not hear it, but I would know it. Tosca is the most demanding role I know."

"You'll sing it for years to come."

"Maybe, but I think not. I don't want to be one of those singers who go on long after they should stop. I would prefer to be remembered in my prime—not when I am doing five years of farewell performances!"

"I wouldn't worry about it."

"That's because you are not a singer." Her fingers caressed his cheek. "I'm glad we can talk to each other, *caro*. We always have. They say that old lovers make the best friends." She looked at him closely. "I have the feeling that this one is important to you. Yes?"

"I don't honestly know, if you want the truth. It's all much too soon. I do know that I like her very much."

"Then I am glad for you. You deserve someone good, like my Ettore."

"You're too many steps ahead of me, Bianca. It may just be the glamour of the recording, coupled with the exotic atmosphere of beautiful, sensual downtown Geneva!"

She laughed gently. "And would you steal secret documents for her?"

"Only if they contained details of the Swiss navy."

There was silence behind the control room door, and Alessandro suddenly emerged. "I am ready for the next sequence."

Bianca eyed him coolly. *"Bene.* We are *all* very pleased to hear it, Antonio."

Her sarcasm was lost on him. "My aria is difficult. You would not want me to make a fool of myself, would you?"

"No, *carissimo*. I would leave that to Mother Nature!"

They were joined by Cavalcanti and Simon Vincent. The director was dressed in a flowing white Indian cotton robe that reached over his jeans. The conductor looked strained. "Shall we continue?"

Alessandro nodded. He glared at Vincent. "You! No suggestions!"

Simon looked offended. "I haven't made any."

"Keep it that way!"

For a moment, the director plucked up courage. "There's no need to pick on me like that. I'm only trying to be helpful. You seem to forget that I have the responsibility of a big-budget film on my hands." He turned to Mark for support. "People keep getting at me. I don't know what I've done to upset them. Why do they take such an instant dislike to me?"

Alessandro grunted. "It saves time. Come. You are making us waste the session." He preceded them down the corridor, swaggering.

In the control room, Graham Budd was adjusting knobs on his console while Joshua was giving last-minute instructions to Diana. "I'll talk to you over the phones. If Bianca and the chorus sound too present, you'll have to push them back to the second position I showed you." She nodded. "See if you can get them there quickly, will you? We've lost nearly an hour." She hurried out of the room, pausing to give Mark's hands a squeeze.

"You look as though you'd like to be left alone."

Levin tried to smile. "It's been one of those days. That man is a king-sized Italian shit!"

"I'll stay out of your way." He went downstairs to the stage door and paused outside to light a cigarette. It was a sultry evening, with a hint of rain in the air, which accounted for the oppressive atmosphere inside the building. With Alessandro throwing his weight about, it was hardly surprising that tempers were becoming frayed.

He was about to return inside when he saw Abe approaching. The American waved. He was walking quickly, and the effort seemed to have made him breathless.

"I was looking for you at your office, but I guessed you'd be here. How's everything?"

"Tense. Alessandro's being difficult. Bianca's just about at the end of her patience."

"She should hang in there until the record's finished. After that, she's out. I'll see if she wants to take up the Australian offer. American Express wants to sponsor the trip with big bucks."

"Ettore called?" Abe nodded. "What did he say?"

"He dug up more dirt than a construction unit on the turnpike. The money started out in Palermo, shifted to Hong Kong, went from there to the Channel Islands, and finally showed up in an account in Zurich. According to him, there's a dirty trail wide enough to drive a Mack truck down. He wants Bianca out of it. Ettore says there's half a dozen financial specialists closing in, closely followed by Interpol. If Wolfgang isn't careful, he'll find himself pulled in with the rest of them."

"What about the recording?"

"The record's fine. Magnum is advancing the money, and Wiesman's supposed to repay them when he starts shooting. The deal is that he buys the finished soundtrack." For a moment, Abe grinned wickedly. "I'd love to see Greg Laufer's face when he learns there's no sale!"

"What will he do?"

"Who knows? Try to find another movie producer, I guess. He's still going to be the owner of a great recording and a ready-made soundtrack. Guys like Laufer always come up smelling like roses. He'll be okay."

"I feel sorry for Wiesman."

"Maybe." Abe shrugged. "My Russian grandfather used to say, 'If you lie down with dogs, you get up with fleas.' Wolfgang knew what he was at. He's been sitting in Alessandro's pocket ever since he got here. You heard him talking on the phone. Despite the fancy clothes and the smooth talk, he knew Alessandro's funding wasn't going to be strictly kosher."

"What should we do?"

"Nothing, for the moment. I plan to smile a lot, tell everyone what a great job they're doing, and beat it out of here before the proverbial hits the fan. Don't worry about Bianca. Ettore's got everything under control. If necessary, he's ready to fund a movie of his own, but I doubt that it would be with the team that Wolfgang's put together."

"You're remarkably cheerful, under the circumstances."

"Why not? Bianca's in great shape, Alessandro—for all that he's a pain in the ass—never sounded better, and Emilio's conducting like a dream."

"And if one of them turns out to be leading a double life?"

For a moment, Abe was serious. Then he smiled beatifically. "Then I guess we'll have a historic recording! Listen, has anything happened since your grand revelation last night?"

"No." He did not want Abe to know about the incident with the car.

"Then it could be your bad apple isn't involved with this production after all. From the way you told it, you had very little to go by. Backstage at a concert can be a madhouse, and that Polish broad could have delivered the papers to someone you didn't know about."

Mark frowned. "It's possible."

"Sure it is. More than that, everybody showed up today, didn't they?"

"Yes."

"Then you could still be wrong. Your story didn't throw a scare into any guilty parties, and nobody took a powder. The only one who quit was that Philips dame, but she said she was leaving anyway. She sent you her regards. She called to say goodbye and thank you for the interview with Bianca, and rode off on her broomstick. I guess Maria Cavalcanti will be relieved to hear the news."

Mark laughed. "You don't miss a trick, Abe! Are you coming in?"

"Nah, I'll wait for the record. Myra wants to try a restaurant she found. Why don't you join us."

"I'd better stay until the end of the session. Things are very uneasy in
there. Bianca was prepared to walk out a few minutes ago."

"You worry too much, kid. She'll finish the recording. It's going too well
for her to quit now." He shrugged expressively. "A little temperament
maybe—even an extra session, to show she carries some weight around here
—but she'll stay. I know my Bianca. Listen, call me later and let me know
how it went." He saw a passing taxi and gave a piercing whistle through his
teeth. The cab stopped suddenly, and the driver peered round to identify
the owner of such an earsplitting call. Abe walked sedately to the vehicle
and, with a final wave in Mark's direction, stepped inside.

When he returned upstairs, Mark found Diana in the corridor outside
the control room. She was pale.

"What's the matter?"

"I just had my head bitten off by Bianca. She's in a foul mood."

"What happened?"

"They recorded the offstage cantata sequence, and it went very well.
Bianca and the chorus were in the right place, thank God, and she did it
beautifully. That shit Alessandro claimed that he wasn't happy with his
onstage part with Scarpia, and said they must go through it again. I really
think he was doing it to get at Bianca. He sounded perfectly all right to me.
Anyway, they went through it a second time, and I could see her trying not
to lose her temper."

"Did they finish it?"

"No. We came in for a playback, and Alessandro said it still wasn't right.
Both Emilio and Josh were happy, but he insisted on doing it yet again.
They're about to do it now." As she spoke, music was audible through the
closed door of the control room. Diana paused to listen to it.

"What happened with Bianca?"

She sighed. "I went back into the hall with her, ready for the take. It's
my job to make sure they're all standing in the right places." Mark nodded.
"When she saw me there, Bianca suddenly exploded, and asked me
whether I thought she was such a fool that she couldn't remember where
she was supposed to stand. I started to explain, but she yelled at me to go
away and leave her alone. She threw in an extra crack about my sneaking
off in a corner to hold my boyfriend's hand. It made me feel horribly stupid
in front of the chorus." She seemed close to tears with the memory. "I
turned and fled. I don't know why she had to go for me like that. She made
me look like an incompetent idiot."

Mark hugged her for a moment. "Don't feel too bad. Bianca's upset
with Alessandro. She took it out on you because you were nearby. I doubt

whether she meant to be so unpleasant. He's been needling her all evening, and she was all set to have a tantrum earlier." It occurred to him that Bianca's feelings towards the younger woman were not quite as mellow as she had suggested earlier. The soprano did not like competition. "I think she just wanted to hit out at somebody, and you were the lucky one!"

"I suppose so. I know opera singers are supposed to be temperamental, but I didn't expect to be in the firing line."

"It's certainly not worth getting upset over. By the time she's finished, she'll probably have forgotten she said anything to you."

Diana relaxed. "Well, I won't! Being a great artist doesn't give anyone the right to be so bloody rude. God, the great Alessandro really is a horror!"

Mark smiled. "Gross?"

She finally relented. "Double gross! It wouldn't surprise me in the slightest if he turned out to be the man in the dressing room at the Festival Hall. He'd probably sell his own grandmother, let alone a few state secrets."

"More than likely." A thought occurred to him. "Did you see him actually go into Cavalcanti's dressing room after the second concert?"

"No, I don't think so. He was on his way out of his own room when I went to see him. Why?"

"Rossiter told me he saw Alessandro enter the conductor's room while he was waiting for Danuta."

"I don't really remember. It was very crowded both evenings, with people going in and out of the greenroom."

Mark paused. A mental image had formed, and he suddenly remembered the question that had been eluding him. "Would you repeat what you just said."

Diana looked puzzled. "What do you mean?"

"What did you say about the greenroom at the Festival Hall?"

"That it was very crowded."

"No. You said something else."

She thought for a moment. "I said it was very crowded, with people going in and out."

"In *and* out?"

"Yes. What's so unusual about that?"

Mark took a deep breath. "Let me put it together. After a concert, people go backstage to see the artists. Now, on some evenings, if there aren't many visitors backstage, they just go to the individual dressing rooms. Right?"

"Well, this wasn't one of those evenings. The place was a bloody mad-

house both times, what with the conductor, the four soloists, the chorus
and all their . . ."

"Exactly! On an evening like that, they always open up the greenroom so
that there's a proper reception area where the conductor and soloists can
meet their visitors. People go in there to wait until the artists have changed
and are ready to receive guests."

"Yes."

"You waited in the corridor outside on both evenings?" She nodded
again. "And on both occasions, you found yourself standing next to Rossiter. You thought you recognized him the second time because you'd seen
him standing there before. Right?"

"Yes, but I don't see . . ."

"Rossiter told me he was backstage for only a few minutes. On both
evenings, he waited outside while Danuta quickly went into the conductor's dressing room. Both times, she came out less than a minute later."
Mark closed his eyes. "On both occasions, he was standing next to you."

"Yes. I was waiting there for Josh."

"And Rossiter said that there was a crush by the dressing room door,
with half the people trying to get into the greenroom while the other half
tried to get out."

"That's right. There's always a jam. They should really work out another
system for . . ."

Mark looked at her. "But if people were already pushing their way *out* of
the greenroom, don't you see what that means?"

Diana frowned. "Not really."

"It means they had already seen or spoken to the conductor. Otherwise,
they would have waited in the greenroom for his arrival."

She spoke slowly. "Yes, that's right."

"But if they were already coming out again, it meant that the conductor
was there." He stared at her for a moment. "Cavalcanti wasn't in his
dressing room when Danuta went into it. He was in the greenroom, next
door."

"Of course! I never thought about it. Does that mean Emilio's in the
clear?"

"He must be. She wasn't gone long enough to have met him, and she
wouldn't have risked handing him an envelope of papers in the greenroom."

"But she wasn't in the greenroom. She was next door, in the dressing
room."

"I know, but she could have gone through the back door, using Josh's 'escape' route." A new thought suddenly struck Mark. "Did you go backstage immediately after the concerts ended?"

"More or less." She paused, remembering. "No, as a matter of fact, we didn't. We walked through to the backstage area, but we didn't go all the way to the soloists' dressing rooms. You see, there's a passage immediately behind the stage where you find the players from the orchestra. We stopped there both times so that Josh could say hello to Sandy Ross. He's one of the percussionists in the orchestra, and he and Josh are old friends. I think they went to school together. Sandy played the bass drum in the Verdi *Requiem*, which meant that he had his big moment in the *Dies Irae*. We stopped to talk to him on both evenings. Josh made his usual joke about the bass drum bit, saying it was the best thing in the piece. Why do you ask?"

"Because it means that by the time you reached the conductor's dressing room Cavalcanti had had enough time to change and go into the greenroom to meet his guests."

"Yes. When I think about it, you're probably right."

"And on both evenings, while you and Rossiter waited in the corridor for your respective partners to return, the conductor's room was empty and Emilio was next door."

"Yes." Diana seemed lost in thought.

"I take it that Joshua used his usual 'escape' route to see Cavalcanti?"

"He always goes that way, via the greenroom. It avoids the queues in the corridor." She looked puzzled. "Except that Emilio was already in the greenroom anyway."

Mark watched her face. "That's what I was thinking. Now, try to think back. Do you remember whether Rossiter left before you did?"

"We left first."

"Are you sure?"

"Positive. He was still waiting on the first evening, and I'm sure he was there on the second. I remember because I was going to say something to him—make some sort of joke about getting away first—when Josh came out, and we went for a drink with Wiesman."

Mark was silent for a moment. "We've established that you and Rossiter waited together, and we're pretty well sure that Cavalcanti wasn't in the dressing room. There's only one other thing I need to know. When Josh came back to you, where did he come from: the greenroom or the conductor's room?"

"The conductor's room."

"Both times?"

"Yes. The first evening, he came charging out and made some comment about the crowd. On the second, he walked over and took my arm to hurry me along because he'd just seen Wolfgang down the corridor."

"You mean he didn't come out with Wiesman? I thought you said earlier that they came out together."

"No. Wolfgang was farther down the corridor, talking to one of the singers."

"But on both occasions, Josh came out of Cavalcanti's dressing room?"

"Yes." Diana looked at Mark, and her eyes widened. "Oh, Mark! Are you trying to say that . . ."

At that moment, there was a disturbance at the end of the passage, and Bianca appeared, her eyes blazing. She strode towards Mark. "That's it! I have had enough! *Basta e finito!* I don't care if I never finish this recording! I will not work with him again—not ever!

"What's wrong?"

"Wrong? That animal! He just announced that he wants to record the scene again!" She gesticulated furiously. "Then he had the audacity to call out to me, in front of the chorus, that he thought I was singing sharp! Me! Who does that fat peasant think he is? I am going!" She turned to Diana. "Miss Nightingale, please forgive me. I was rude to you and behaved very badly. I am sorry. I was so distressed that I did not know what I was saying. Please say you forgive me." She held Diana's hands.

"Yes, of course. Don't worry about it." The younger woman looked embarrassed.

"You are very kind. I should never have spoken to you in that way, especially as you have been so helpful."

"It's quite all right. I do understand—really."

"Thank you. Now, would you be an angel and drive me home, please? I will not stay here another minute, and my car will not come for me for an hour. I wish to leave immediately."

For a moment, Diana looked helplessly towards Mark, unwilling to leave, but he nodded quickly, indicating that she should go.

Joshua appeared in the doorway of the control room, and Bianca turned to him. "I am leaving. I will do nothing else this evening." She seemed calmer. "Miss Nightingale will drive me to my hotel."

Levin was about to speak, but checked himself. He reached into a pocket for his car keys and handed them silently to Diana. "Perhaps we can talk in the morning?"

Bianca was already walking towards the exit. "If you wish. I will not discuss anything now."

There was a disturbance at the other end of the corridor and Alessandro appeared, accompanied by Cavalcanti. The tenor's face was troubled, and he made a gesture of contrition. *"Scusi, Bianca, ma . . ."*

"You!" Bianca glared at him with loathing. When she spoke again, her voice was low and guttural. The stream of invective was delivered in a tense half voice, barely audible. Although he understood Italian, Mark could not identify most of the words she spat at the tenor. Alessandro blinked, stepping back as though he had been physically struck, shocked by the language and the intensity with which it was spoken. He started to speak, but the flow of words increased, growing in volume and forbidding interruption. He bowed his head in silence, his hands clasped over his heaving belly, while her abuse enveloped him. It was a magnificent, dramatic display, projected with the timing of a great actress, and as the tirade ended, Bianca turned and swept out of sight.

Nobody spoke, and Mark could hear the click of the soprano's shoes as she descended the stone staircase to the stage door below. At length, Joshua said, "I'd better call a break."

Alessandro raised his head. "I will not sing again tonight. I am too tired, mentally and physically. Perhaps you did not understand the things that woman said to me."

"Not all of them." Levin smiled thinly. "I gathered that she was not very happy with you!"

"She was outrageously insulting." The tenor gathered himself. "I was only trying to be helpful." When nobody commented, he added, "I made suggestions because I want this recording to be perfect."

Levin nodded. "We all do, but I think you were going the wrong way about it." He looked to Cavalcanti for support, but the conductor said nothing.

Alessandro headed towards the staircase. "I repeat, I was only making a helpful observation. She had no right to speak to me like that. She should apologize."

"I wouldn't count on that."

"Very well. I accept that she was tired—we are all tired—but she was spoiling my *scena* with Giuseppe. I am not saying that she did it deliberately, because she is a serious artist and I respect her, but the result was the same." By the time he reached the head of the stairs, Alessandro had regained some of his former swagger. "I will go home now. Call me in the morning." His footsteps on the stairs were slow and heavy.

Cavalcanti looked at Levin. "What happens now?"

"There's not a lot we can record without either of them. Do you want to rehearse the chorus for the finale of Act One?"

"No, I don't think so. This whole session has been very distressing. I do not think I could concentrate."

Levin looked at his watch. "Well, if I exclude the break that's due, we've only lost a little over an hour. Why don't we leave it at that and give everyone an early night."

"Can we afford to lose the time?"

"We don't really have very much choice. It's not so bad. We're still just about on schedule all in all, and a good night's sleep will help settle everyone's nerves. I'll send the orchestra and chorus home."

Levin returned to the control room to make his announcement, and Cavalcanti turned to Mark. "I'm sorry. I am not being very professional, but this incident has completely unsettled me. I simply can't concentrate. Alessandro behaved badly."

"He usually does. I'm surprised Bianca held on for such a long time."

"Do you think she will return?"

"Probably." Mark remembered Abe's comments. "Once she's slept on it, and provided Alessandro makes the right noises, she'll be back."

"I'm glad." Cavalcanti smiled wryly. "There are times when I wish I did not love opera so much. Orchestras do not allow the same displays of temperament. I think I will go back to the hotel. Maria might be pleased to see me for a change. I think I have neglected her while . . . while we have been making the recording." He was pensive for a moment. "She may not have eaten yet. Would you like to join us?"

"Not this evening, if you don't mind, but I haven't forgotten your invitation. I know that Abe Sincoff would like to talk to you about some American plans he has been developing."

"Really?" The conductor brightened immediately.

"He's been talking to Houston and Santa Fe, and I know that Chicago's interested, too."

"And the Metropolitan?" The evening's drama seemed to have been forgotten.

"Not yet, but there's plenty of time. Abe has it all worked out."

"That's wonderful, Mark. I must tell you again how grateful I am. I am still a little ashamed that I was so abrupt with you the other day. Recordings seem to carry special pressures of their own. Besides, now that . . ." He hesitated. "Now that the project is so well established, I feel more in control."

"Despite this evening?"

Cavalcanti shrugged. "Opera singers are always having emotional crises. It is part of their character." He walked briskly to the staircase. "I ought to hurry if I am to find Maria before dinner. We'll talk in the morning?" He seemed eager to leave.

"I'll call."

"Very good. *Ciao!*"

Levin was seated behind the console in the empty control room marking his score. He nodded in Mark's direction.

"How serious is it?"

"Not too bad, all things considered. It's funny, but there always seems to be one session like this. I've allowed for make-up time in the schedule. We didn't lose that much."

"Has everyone left?"

"Just about. Wiesman and Vincent sneaked out as soon as the shit hit the fan. I think Simon was terrified that Alessandro would find some way to blame him for it! Otherwise, Graham and Jack are taking down a few microphones in the hall." He grinned mischievously. "I don't think even Alessandro would have the nerve to ask for another take of the offstage chorus! He's a right bastard, isn't he? I'm amazed that Bianca lasted this long. She's a real trouper."

"The recording means a lot to her."

"Will you talk to her tomorrow? She'll listen to you."

Mark nodded. "You might suggest a little tactful diplomacy to Alessandro."

Levin smiled. "I've already made a note to send her a huge bunch of flowers in his name. Greg Laufer will probably scream bloody murder when he sees the bill on my expense account, but he couldn't produce a rabbit out of a hat, let alone a recording."

"Good. I'll walk you home."

"All right, I'll tell the others." He pushed a button on the console and called a message to the engineers in the hall. As they left the control room, he said, "Do you want a bite at the restaurant opposite, or shall we try the bar at the Hilton?"

"The Hilton sounds better."

"Good. I could use a drink after this lot. Producers aren't supposed to have any nerves of their own. Or bowels, for that matter. We can't go to the lavatory during a take, and we're needed here for the playbacks. When's a fellow supposed to take a pee?"

There was a very fine drizzle of rain, little more than a mist, shrouding the street. The tyres of cars, moving slower than usual, hissed on the damp surface. "Do you want to take a cab?"

Levin shook his head, turning up the collar of his jacket. "Not unless you do. It's helping to clear the air. Doesn't a spot of rain make you homesick for London?"

"No, I'm happy living here."

The record producer hunched his shoulders. "I wish I could afford to."

"You might get bored. Switzerland's lovely, but very little happens."

"It seems to suit you."

"I was looking for a quiet life."

They walked in silence through empty streets towards the footbridge at the end of the lake. Overhead, the sky was dark and overcast, and the streetlamps cast pale shadows.

As they started to cross the bridge, Levin scowled. "Alessandro really is a pain. Everything was going so well, and he had to go and screw it all up!"

"He probably believes he's settling an old score with Bianca. I seem to remember that she won the last round, and that must have played hell with his ego."

"He's a schmuck! You'd think he'd be excited to be part of such a great recording. Any fool can tell this one's going to be spectacular."

"Not this particular fool."

Levin smiled. "You're right, I keep forgetting that I'm dealing with a tenor. Maybe creating all those heroic sounds damages the frontal lobes of his brain—something to do with air pressure!"

Mark nodded. "My guess is that he thrives on the adrenaline provided by a little offstage drama. It's hard to tell what makes people tick."

"Like your friend in London?"

"Which one?"

"Tony Rossiter." Levin walked in silence. "That's a tragic story, you know. I think I can understand why you gave him enough time to make his escape. Love does extraordinary things to people, doesn't it? I'm glad I never got myself that deeply involved."

They had reached the centre of the bridge. Below them, the rushing waters of the sluice gates sounded louder than usual. Levin paused to stare down at the white foam.

Mark stood at his side. He spoke quietly. "How did you know his name was Tony?"

Levin did not respond for a moment. "That's what you called him."

"No, I said he was called Rossiter. I didn't mention his first name."

"You must have. Otherwise, how would I know it?"

"How indeed? I think you've just answered some questions for me."
Levin was very still. "What sort of questions?"

Mark watched his face. "Who was waiting for Danuta in the conductor's room after the Verdi concerts, for example. According to Diana, you made a point of stopping to talk to a percussionist in the orchestra before going back to the artists' dressing rooms. That gave you a reasonable guarantee that Cavalcanti would no longer be changing and would already be next door, receiving guests. Even if he had been there, nobody would have questioned your presence in the dressing room."

Levin had not moved. "You're not making sense."

"No? You made a mistake by coming out of Cavalcanti's room rather than the greenroom. I wouldn't have thought much more about it, but I asked myself why you came from there when Cavalcanti was next door. Obviously, the answer was because you were in the dressing room to meet somebody else."

"You can't prove that." Levin had moved a few paces away.

"It's enough to work on. People can start digging. When Tony Rossiter left me in London, he said he was going to follow up one more lead. We can take it from there. Did he meet you in Bruton Mews and start asking embarrassing questions? And how about the man who died here? He had recognized a face from Budapest. Diana told me she first met you in Hungary at a recording session. The pieces are beginning to fit together."

"I don't know what you're talking about." Levin was uneasy, but made an effort to control himself.

Mark shook his head. "You know well enough. You were in the ideal occupation to act as a courier for one side or the other. Who would question a record producer, in and out of concert halls around the world, supposedly with his head full of music and recording schedules? What did Simon Vincent call you? The invisible man!" Levin did not reply, and Mark continued. "Your attempt to run me down last night wasn't very clever. Any number of people might have seen you. On the other hand, you were prepared to gamble with a gun in broad daylight. That was even riskier."

Levin moved slightly. In his hand, there was a small revolver with a silencer attached to it. "I didn't want to use this again."

"Why not?" Mark kept his eyes on the gun. Levin's hand was unsteady.

"Because a hit-and-run accident causes less attention." He tried to smile, without success. "I think you're bluffing about that letter from Rossiter. He didn't have time to send one."

"You're quite a gambler." Mark kept his voice even. "I'm surprised you managed to get a gun into Switzerland. Airport security's pretty good these days."

Levin seemed to relax slightly. "You seem to have forgotten that I came by car. They hardly give you a second glance at the border, especially during the holiday season. Which American Express office did Rossiter say he would use?" When Mark remained silent, he gripped the revolver tighter. "I still think you're bluffing."

Mark ignored the question. "What happened with Tony Rossiter?"

Levin shrugged. "He remembered my face from the Festival Hall. When he saw you at Covent Garden, talking to me, it rang a bell."

"And?"

"He called me at Magnum. After seeing you talk to me in the Crush Bar, he must have asked around to find out who I was. I'm quite well known in music circles." For a moment, Levin looked pleased with the thought, and it occurred to Mark that the record producer had an ego of his own that needed satisfying. "Anyway, he called me the next morning and asked if we could meet. I told him I was busy, but he made a remark about the Verdi concerts. After that, I didn't really have much choice, did I?"

"And the man here?" Mark was inching towards the producer, calculating the distance that separated them. He wanted to keep Levin talking.

"He confronted me in the street, told me he remembered seeing me in Budapest when I was . . ." He paused, realizing that he was further incriminating himself.

"So you killed him." Mark's voice was contemptuous.

"Look, I had to move quickly. I was bloody lucky that I had this"—he indicated the gun—"with me at the time." The confession seemed to have loosened Levin's tongue. "I just stepped close to him and pulled the trigger. Nobody noticed. Then I walked into the hall and went up to the control room. It was easy." His eyes narrowed. "Where did Rossiter post that letter?"

On the street behind Levin, the figure of a woman appeared, hurrying to cross the bridge. She was carrying an umbrella, which masked her face. In the pale light of the streetlamps, it was hard to identify her, but Mark recognized Diana.

"Someone's coming."

Levin glanced round quickly. The gun in his hand was steady. "In that case, stand very still where you are. You don't want to see an innocent bystander get hurt, do you?"

"It's Diana." Levin swung round. As he did so, Mark shouted, "Run, Diana! Get out of the way! He's got a gun!"

She paused uncertainly, lowering her umbrella, then moved forward again.

Caught between the two of them, Levin hesitated, glancing from one to the other. He moved towards Diana, increasing his distance from Mark, then turned towards him, the gun raised.

Diana was less than thirty feet away. She saw the gun in Levin's hand and ran forward, throwing the umbrella aside. "Josh! No!"

The producer spun back to her. "Stay away!" She ignored him and moved faster. There was panic in his voice. "Don't come any closer!"

Diana kept running. "Josh, don't do it! It's no use!"

Levin fired. The weapon made very little sound, and the rushing of the water beneath their feet masked it. The bullet struck Diana high on the shoulder, and she staggered backwards, a surprised expression on her face, before falling. Her cry was covered by the sound of the water.

Joshua watched her, and his gun hand dropped to his side. At that moment, Mark launched himself forward, crashing into the other man's side and throwing him down. The gun dropped from Levin's hand, clattering across the wet tarmac.

Levin moved surprisingly quickly, twisting his body and slipping out of Mark's reach. He was on his feet and moving backwards as Mark prepared to spring again. For a moment, his eyes darted in the direction of the gun, and he stumbled towards it. Anticipating the movement, Mark changed direction and ran for the revolver. Levin stooped to grasp it as Mark slid forward, kicking it out of reach. He lost his balance, but as he fell his left leg swept across the back of Levin's knees, and the producer toppled backwards, crashing against the metal barriers of the bridge. He staggered painfully, grasping the handrail to steady himself.

Mark rose to his feet, his eyes never leaving Joshua's face. The gun lay farther along the bridge, and to reach it Levin would have to pass him. He glanced in the direction of Diana and called to her, but she did not reply. His voice sounded hoarse in the misty darkness, and he was breathing hard.

Levin moved backwards, still holding the rail. He looked from Mark to the gun and, beyond, the immobile figure of the young woman. Mark thought he was about to turn and run, but the producer suddenly gripped the rail with both hands and lifted himself over, so that he was standing on the outside of the bridge. He looked down at the swiftly flowing torrent of water, then closed his eyes.

Mark moved slowly towards him. When he was a few feet away, Levin

said, "That's enough. Don't come any closer." He jerked his head towards
Diana. "You'd better go and look after her." There was the ghost of a smile
on his face. "I'm not going anywhere!"

Mark stepped closer, and Levin's tone hardened. "Stay where you are.
You'd never get to me in time. For Christ's sake, at least let me do this on
my own! I know what I'm doing." When Mark halted, Levin nodded his
thanks. "Tell Diana I'm sorry. I lost my nerve. She'll be all right, won't
she?"

Mark looked at the young woman. She had raised herself on her right
arm and was watching them. He thought that she said something, but her
voice was covered by the sound of the water. He turned back to Levin.
"Why don't you give yourself up. It's better than . . ."

Joshua shook his head. "I've never been much good at facing up to
things." He shut his eyes for a moment. "I'm just trying to pluck up
enough courage to get this over and done with. Don't come any nearer—
please!" After a moment, he said, "When did you realize?"

"Earlier this evening, during the session. Something Diana said triggered
a picture in my mind, and it all began to fit together." Joshua nodded
silently. "What happened to the Polish girl?"

"God knows. They never told me anything. Does it matter?"

"Not really. I'd like to think Rossiter didn't . . ."

For a moment, Levin looked contemptuous. "How very sentimental!"
He glanced towards the city. "I'm sorry I won't finish this recording. It's
going to be a great one. I would like to have seen my name in the booklet.
Oh well!" He sighed.

Mark looked at him. "Why? What made you do it?"

Levin paused, then smiled wryly. "I needed the money. Silly, isn't it?"
He took a deep breath, then closed his eyes and let go of the handrail,
leaning back lazily and allowing himself to fall.

Mark did not move forward to see the man hit the water. He knew what
would happen to him when the force of the current dragged his body into
the sluice gates, crushing him with its pressure. He turned and ran to
Diana.

Several hours later, when he had left her safely tucked into a hospital bed,
bandaged and mildly sedated, and had spoken briefly to Quentin, promis-
ing a detailed report the following day, Mark returned to his apartment.

The phone rang as he entered and, almost instinctively, he reached for
the receiver.

"Hello."

"Mark? Hi! This is Greg Laufer. I just got in this evening." Whenever he thought about it, the vice president of Magnum Records lowered his voice an octave, to swallow up the nasal New York tones that it usually possessed. "Listen, don't you guys ever return a call? I left three messages on your machine, and I've been sitting in this goddamn room in the Hilton waiting for someone to call back!"

"Sorry, but we've been rather busy."

His voice lightened. "I guess you have. So tell me, how's it all going?"

ABOUT THE AUTHOR

Paul Myers has had an illustrious career as a classical-record producer. A Londoner by birth, he spent eighteen years producing classical records for CBS Records, commuting between New York and London. His extensive travels have taken him to virtually every capital city in the world. Since 1980, he has been Manager of Classical Production for Decca International in London. He has made some five hundred classical recordings, many of which have won major international prizes, and he has worked with world-famous musicians, conductors and singers. In addition to his prolific record-producing career, Paul Myers presented a series of classical-music programs for New York's WQXR radio station which were syndicated to thirty American cities. London Films and Télé-Hachette have bought the Mark Holland character for a television series.